VORTEX

KIMBERLY PACKARD

abalos
publishing

Abalos Publishing
P.O. Box 333
Colleyville, TX 76034

Book cover designed by okay creations.
Edited by C.A. Szarek
The text in this book is set in Baskerville.
Library of Congress Cataloging-in-Publication Data
Available Upon Request

ISBN-13 Print: 978-0-9992015-6-5

ISBN-13 Ebook: 978-0-9992015-7-2

For Colby
The calm in my storm

ALSO BY KIMBERLY PACKARD

The Phoenix Series

Phoenix (Phoenix Series Book 1)

Pardon Falls (Phoenix Series Book 2)

Prospera Pass (Phoenix Series Book 3)

Standalone Titles

This Time Around

Dire's Club

The Crazy Yates | A Christmas Novella

1

E laina squinted into the midday sky, hoping the cottony
cumulus cloud wouldn't fade into the blue backdrop, like so
many of its brethren. A loose hair danced across her cheek
as a dry breeze blew down the prairie.

She lay back in the bed of her pickup truck, studying the cloud
as its edges teased out, like a child pulling at cotton candy. "The
front stalled." She cradled her head in her entwined hands.

"What's that, Dr. Adams?" her research partner, Heath Bryant,
asked. His long body lounged in the shade of the truck, a book
hiding his face.

In the field research part of their doctoral studies, they took to
calling each other "doctor." It felt at home in her ears, like a favorite
song she'd been humming to herself since childhood.

An early-season cicada chimed in, nothing in the atmosphere to
send it burrowing back into the ground. It was free to let its buzzing
call fill the air.

Elaina pushed herself to standing and hooked the edge of her
cowboy boot on the truck's toolbox, then climbed up to stand on the
cab. She hugged her over-sized University of Oklahoma sweatshirt,
as the northerly wind that'd been previously blocked hit her.

Like a boot-clad ballerina, she turned in a small circle, taking in the flat prairie land of the Oklahoma panhandle. Aside from a few trees and the errant farmhouse, the view was the same in every direction: flat with newly greening grasses fading into blue sky. The combination of the cool wind from Canada and the warm moist air drifting up from the Gulf should've stirred something up, but it was still early.

"Come on, Dr. Bryant," she said, hopping down from the truck over the side like a gymnast dismounting from the balance beam. "If we leave now, we can make it back to Norman before happy hour ends."

"You sure?" Heath leaned up and snapped his book shut, but he didn't bother standing.

"No, but there's a reason we're the only ones out here." She sighed as she knelt to pick up a piece of dried grass, crumbling it in her hands. "It was a long-shot day to begin with."

"It has nothing to do with it being spring break?"

Elaina couldn't tell if the comment was simply a question, or a dig at her for making him miss prime alone time in the lab while all the other students made the pilgrimage to South Padre.

Storm season in this part of the country was a year-round event. March was the official start of tornado season, but it was usually April and May that was the most active. The most congested. With storm chaser tours, amateur spotters, research teams, and adrenalin junkies with cameras clogging up the one-lane dusty roads, getting out early was the only way she could be sure they captured enough data to finish their dissertation.

A few good storms, a few good data points to finish their research, presenting and defending their dissertation — that was all she needed before she became the *real* Dr. Elaina Adams.

Ignoring Heath's question, Elaina stood, tossing the crushed grass in the air so she could free up her fingers for a whistle. "Come on, Nimbus, let's…" She watched the falling grass drift north, rather than fall straight down.

Her yellow Lab bounded out of the prairie grass, but screeched to a stop.

He felt it too.

"Wait up," she said, bending to pick up more grass, crushing it quickly before releasing it. The winds shifted from the south. She looked at her watch. It was a quarter to four, if something was going to heat up it had to do it fast. "Heath, get your laptop."

"What? Why?"

"There's a shift. It's slight, but enough for Nim to feel it."

"Are you sure he's not smelling the beef jerky in my bag?"

"He's the best meteorologist I know. No offense." She watched her dog look at the sky. A cluster of clouds pulled together like iron fillings to a magnet. "Chloe can wait," she teased, even though his fiancée was likely catching up on paperwork at her psychology practice.

Heath blushed and pulled his laptop from the backpack that'd doubled as a pillow.

The weather always spoke to her. Sometimes in dreams, sometimes like this, a flash of electricity tingling in her fingers, making the hair on her arms rise.

As her friend fired up his laptop, Elaina knelt beside her dog.

His nose worked the air, sniffing shallow gulps, his parted mouth making the smallest movement, as if he could actually taste the salt from the Gulf.

"What do you think, Nimbus?" She stroked his cornsilk fur.

The Lab's head whipped to the northwest, and she saw it. As if in fast-forward, thick cumulus clouds lifted high, forming gray towers stretching towards the heavens.

"Oh my God," Heath said, his jaw slack as he looked up from his computer. "How did you …? Unbelievable."

She let the compliment float by her. "Where?"

"Radar shows a hook forming about forty-five minutes northwest of here," he paused, and she imagined the screen refreshing. "Looks like this one is a sprinter. We could have touchdown before we get there."

Elaina jumped up and dusted her hands on the back of her jeans. "Let's go. Heath, you lead in the van with the radar. Come on, Nim, let's get you buckled in."

They worked in silence as her partner packed up the few bits of gear they'd gotten out of the van while she put her dog in his harness. She even took a minute to secure her old pink bicycle helmet under his chin, just in case the storm took a turn toward them.

She followed Heath down dirt roads, crisscrossing in a haphazard pattern that to the untrained eye looked like two cars playing chase.

Nim stuck his nose out the window, his big tail beating the back of the vinyl seat. As they approached the growing storm, the clouds shifted, flattening into a distinctive wall. At a crossroad, her partner slammed on his brakes and ran back to Elaina's window, cowering in the flashes of lightning.

"What's wrong?" she cranked down her window.

"I'm not sure where the best place to drop the pod is."

She closed her eyes and drummed her fingers on the steering wheel. Wet air flowed through the cab of the truck, tickling her nose and lifting the fine hairs that'd escaped her long braid. She always had a sixth sense with storms, even the less severe she just *knew* where they were going to turn, or when it would rain itself out. Elaina chalked it up to the fact that as a child, she'd pored over the science books her mom had bought her, memorizing the different types of clouds.

Nim shifted in the cab next to her.

West. They needed to go due west into the storm cloud for the drop, then high-tail it out of there.

"Go straight."

Heath looked over his shoulder.

The wall cloud was already lowering, like a baby crowning in childbirth. Only minutes before the tornado would be on the ground.

"We won't have time to get out of there." Panic gripped his eyes.

Like most of her fellow doctoral students, he'd grown up in some part of tornado alley. No matter how many storms they'd chased, there was always a healthy dose of fear when staring one down.

Elaina swallowed hard and looked at her dog. "Nimbus, take care of Heath," she nuzzled his fur. "I'll be right back." She grabbed her raincoat and popped open her truck door, nearly knocking Heath down in the process. "Let's switch. Take my truck, turn around and head back to the main highway with Nim. I'll do the drop," she shouted over the rising wind.

His eyes darted from her face to the sky and back to the truck. "Is it safe?"

"Safer than us standing out here discussing it. Go. And, take care of my dog."

She didn't bother with the seatbelt as she put the van into drive while closing the door. Dried leaves scurried across the road, first on the road, but gradually rising higher until she couldn't tell what was a bird or debris.

On a collision course with the pregnant storm cloud, Elaina allowed herself to glance up to the rearview mirror once, exhaling when red taillights stared back at her. Another quarter of a mile and she could drop the data pod and meet up with Heath and Nim.

The rain fell sideways and the old vehicle's windshield wipers could barely keep up with the deluge. Elaina leaned forward in her seat, peering through the rivulets of water coursing down the glass.

In the swipe of a blade, she saw it.

The tail of the tornado snaked down from the cloud, tentative at first, as if it wasn't sure it was ready to be born into a cruel world where people cursed its existence. But then, when the tornado touched down, it gained confidence and took its first wobbly step.

The tires skidded when she hit the brakes and turned the wheel. She'd miscalculated. The tornado would be on her in just minutes, if she continued.

The van rocked back into place, so she jumped out and pulled the pod from the back, letting it drop on the road with a heavy thud.

Heath's fear-filled voice crackled through the radio. "Elaina, are you there? Come in, please! Over."

Elaina pulled the door shut and grabbed for the mouthpiece. "I'm here. I got it in place. Heading back your way. You guys okay? Over."

The back tires spun in the mud as she floored the accelerator. The back end scooted to the right instead of forward.

She looked up in the rearview mirror. Her heart took a long, hard thump.

The funnel cloud skipped across the field, on track to cross over the pod.

The van too, if she didn't get it out of the way.

She took a short breath and lowered her right foot again, this time keeping her heel on the floorboard to lessen the pressure.

The van crawled forward. Once it got momentum, Elaina floored it, opening it up to a sprint.

Nearing the crossroad, she slowed and glanced into the rearview mirror, watching the funnel cloud devour the pod. It didn't matter if she never saw it again. The data it would send to her laptop would be instrumental in their research. Her eyes fluttered back to the road in front of her.

A felled tree blocked the road.

She stomped on the brake with both feet. "Shit!"

"Elaina, where are you? Over."

She looked up at the approaching tornado behind her. The tree in front of her was too big to move. The storm moved off the road, but danced dangerously close as it passed to her left.

Out of the car, Elaina. You have to get low, in the ditch.

"Elaina? Talk to me."

"Heath, listen to me. Stay where you are until it passes." It took every bit of self-control to not let her words tremble. If Nim heard any fear, he'd burst through the car window for her. "I'm taking cover."

Elaina dropped the radio and pushed against the car door, but it wouldn't budge. Ignoring Heath's frantic shouts, she scooted to the passenger seat, nearly falling face down when the door opened without protest. She scrambled to the ditch, lying on her stomach and covering her head.

The pressure of the storm made her ears pop, and her skin stung as pea-sized hail pummeled her.

When the shaking of the ground beneath her lessened slightly, she lifted her head to gaze at the funnel cloud moving away from her. Elaina pushed herself up to her knees to watch, not having been this close to a tornado since…

Debris shifted above her, forcing her deeper into the little cubby she'd made around herself. Dirty water poured down on her head as something was overturned. She buried her face into her hands, crying out as the water stung her eyes. The movement stopped, but it was only a brief respite, as shouts filled the air and metal on metal scraped above her. A burst of light blinded her before the shape of a head blocked it.

"It's okay, sweetheart. I found you. You're safe now," a soothing, yet unfamiliar male voice spoke to her.

"Elaina?"

She blinked at her name. The field in front of her was empty, a single beam of sunlight lit the spot where she'd last seen the twister. A yellow body flashed in front of her as Nim ran around the side of the van, barking first out of fear but then with the high-pitched happy yip of a dog just finding his owner.

"Elaina, are you okay?" Heath touched her shoulder, reminding her to breathe.

She hadn't been this close to a tornado since the day she'd been found.

2

The large tree was stubborn. It held onto its new resting spot with the ferocity of roots clinging to the ground before the tornado won the wrestling match and threw its opponent on the road between Elaina's truck and Heath's van.

Lucky for them, it had little fight left when they tied chains around it and heaved it out of the way.

Sweat poured down her neck, disappearing in the ribbed collar of her soggy sweatshirt.

"Did anything hit your head?" Heath tittered about like a mother hen. "Are you dizzy? Blurred vision?"

"I'm fine," she said, her jaw tight to keep her teeth from chattering as the last of the adrenalin faded from her blood. Elaina heaved the chains back into the bed of her truck, continuing to shrug off her partner's offers of assistance and pleas for her to rest. "Did we get anything good?"

He was hunkered over his computer, mindlessly tapping the keyboard as if his touch could make the data upload faster. "Yeah, but nothing we didn't already know." Heath snapped up the computer and shoved it into this backpack. "Wind speeds over a hundred, just a little EF1. This tree probably suffered the worst damage."

Elaina studied the field where just a little while ago, a deep gray twister had dropped to the ground. Tornados were rare, despite the annual spring outbreaks and the warnings, and the tired weathermen begging people to seek shelter.

While no continent on Earth, except for Antarctica, was immune to them, there were areas where cold air from Canada danced with warm, moist air from the Gulf of Mexico to create the most unwelcome of dinner guests. Lucky for her, Oklahoma was right in the middle of the dance floor.

The grassy field sat relatively untouched, except for a path clumsily shorn ahead. She followed the trail with her eyes, climbing up on the cab of her truck to get a better view. "Heath, did you get visual of how long it was on the ground? Where it went?"

"Tried, but your dog was fighting me to get to you."

Guilt clenched her heart in a grasp so tight fuzzy gray lines invaded her vision. She hopped down to the ground and nuzzled him closer, breathing in his warm, corn-chip scent.

It was degrading to call Nim her best friend. Since she'd found him cowering in a rainstorm as a puppy her junior year, he'd been the other half of her soul. So many times she'd get choked with fear of losing him, but she'd never contemplated him losing her.

"I'm sorry, Nimby," she cooed. "I worried you, but I'm okay."

Her dog answered with a deep sigh.

"What did you see?" Heath's question pulled her away from Nim. "You were really close. What was it like?"

Elaina wiped her face with the back of her hand before facing him. Her eyes darted to that place in the field where the tornado had dipped its tentative tail on the ground. A menacing greenish gray, it'd danced around before moving away, making room for the face of a man she'd never seen before, in a place she'd never been before.

Or, had she?

Growing up in central Oklahoma, she'd seen her fair share of tornado warnings and even spotted a few twisters in the distance.

This one was different. This one had felt like it was meant for her. Within it was a message.

She shook her head. *Nonsense. Tornados don't come with messages from beyond.*

"I felt like the air in my lungs was being sucked out," she said. "That the tornado wanted everything around it, including my breath. I kept my head down until it moved, then it just went away." Elaina busied herself with putting away the last of their gear.

Heath looked at the map on his phone and back to the open plain. "I think it followed Highway 33. Textbook northeast pattern. If it did..." he paused, his fingers moving across the screen. "If it did, then there's a little town right in its path."

Her heart dropped to her feet. This was the worst part of meteorology. The part where she'd see lives torn apart by Mother Nature's haphazard whim. It was the part she dreaded.

It was the part that made her face the worst weather warnings. To get in the path of a twister.

They finished packing their gear in silence. Nim lay down in the truck. His eyebrows quirked up, first right, then left, every time Elaina opened the door. He shared their unspoken concern.

Ahead of them they could find a town breathing a sigh of relief, or they could find a town ripped apart at the seams. With the finicky nature of tornados, they could even find one half of the town pristine, and the other half in shambles.

The sky behind them was clear, denying any trace of the earlier storm. The musky scent of upturned earth wafted through Elaina's open windows. Faint at first, the smell grew stronger until it was so intense her eyes watered.

"You know, we're really lucky. Over," Heath spoke over the radio. The slight quake in his words told her he was as nervous as she was about what they might find.

"Because we're alive?" She glanced up in the rearview mirror, trying to read her friend's face.

"Always that, but because this is our year. All signs pointing to one hell of a tornado season and it's all for us."

She laughed. "Us and all the other chasers, scientists, rubber-neckers and don't forget the tourists. It's going to get crowded—"

The shriek of a siren cut her off. Red lights danced across the windshield as the speeding patrol car flew past her.

"Look to the right," he commanded.

Elaina had noticed the withering barn earlier. Faded wood that'd once held someone's livelihood forgotten and left to fend for itself. Now it was a mess of broken boards that looked like a bomb went off inside. "It intensified," her throat closed around the words.

More police cars flew past her. When the town came into view, her stomach curled. The glass windows of the grocery store were shattered, some panes hung in sharp, snaggletoothed points, and a small sedan was parallel parked in front of the door.

A pickup truck had punched through the front door of a hardware store. The bricks on one side of the church were shorn off, and the roof of the school sat in the parking lot of city hall.

She pulled off to the side of the road. "Stay," she commanded Nim. "There's too much debris," she added against his whimpering back talk.

"We were out in the field taking storm data." Her partners's voice was steady against the pounding in her ears as he spoke with an officer. "What can we do to help?"

"How about a little warning next time," the officer snapped.

Elaina winced at the acid in his words.

The officer took a deep breath and closed his eyes. "Just help us find all the people," he said, softer but still edged with worry. "We need to figure out who has to go to the hospital and who can be treated here."

People streamed out of the various buildings. Some were crying, some shaking glass out of items strewn across the ground, and others had a vacant, confused look. It was Saturday afternoon, so the school was locked up tight. An older couple walked out of the church, the man helping his trembling wife climb down through the slippery bricks.

Elaina rushed to help them. "Is there anyone else inside?"

The man shook his head. "Another couple of hours, and the whole town would've been here for potluck."

"Are you hurt?" She tightened her grip on the woman.

"Just a little sur—surprised," the woman finally spoke. "I'll be fine."

She jogged to the grocery store; glass and branches crunched under her boots.

Heath and another man were knocking the shards of glass from one of the windows with an audience of people looking out from the darkened store.

The thick glass that'd crumbled against the tornado wouldn't budge and the muffled cries grew louder.

"Let me see if there's another way out from inside," Elaina said. A window broken from the bottom had a gap just wide enough for her petite frame to crawl through.

The inside was dark, but the fading daylight streaming in the windows lit up the chaotic scene of downed shelves and hanging fluorescent lights. Grocery carts were tossed upside down and water poured down from the back corner where the roof was peeled back.

She pulled her phone from her pocket, using its light to illuminate the darker corners. Finally she found it, the emergency exit. With a gentle push, the door opened, freeing the trapped shoppers.

A quiet sniffle caught her ear, drawing her back inside.

"Hello? Is anyone else here?"

A soft sob answered.

"Are you trapped? Can you tell me where you are?" Elaina paused, giving the person a chance to answer. "Are you bleeding? Hurt? Just make some noise and I'll find you."

She walked down the beverage aisle. Plastic soda bottles were flung about like downed bowling pins.

The dry goods aisle still had one shelf in pristine condition, but all the others had been raked clean. One large shelving unit in the cereal aisle fell forward, propped up against the shelf across from it, blocking her path.

She squatted down and flashed the light. Big blue eyes framed by dirty blonde hair stared back.

"Mr. Bear is stuck," the little girl said matter-of-factly. To prove her point, she tugged on the bear trapped beneath the shelf.

Elaina exhaled when it appeared that only the stuffed animal was imprisoned. "Is he now? What about you? Can you climb out?"

The girl nodded.

"Good, come with me, sweetie. I promise we'll find a nice fireman to rescue Mr. Bear."

She patted the bear's head. "Don't be scared, Mr. Bear, we'll save you."

She wrapped the child in her arms and carried her out the store. "I'm Elaina. You're safe now. Were you at the store with your mommy?"

The girl shook her head. "My meemaw," she turned in Elaina's arms as she looked out across the crowd. "There she is," she added, pointing to a woman with a red streak cutting across her white hair.

The grandmother sank into the ground sobbing when they approached. "Oh Amy, my angel, I couldn't find you, baby." Blood-shot eyes the same color as the little girl met Elaina's. "Thank you."

She smiled and backed away, suddenly feeling like a voyeur to this reunion. The once-chaotic scene eased into counting friends and family members, then patching up the wounded. Elaina raised to her toes, searching the crowd for her research partner's tall frame.

Heath leaned against his van, laptop in hand and head bent with a fireman over the computer screen.

Nimbus poked his head out her open window, beckoning her back to him.

She rested against the door, stroking her dog's head. The image of the little girl in the grocery store battled with what she'd seen in the storm. Was it a premonition?

No, the perspective was all wrong. She very clearly saw it as the little girl. Maybe it was a dream?

Elaina closed her eyes and played the image back, trying to freeze it to study the surroundings. It was dark. Very dark. She felt wet. The noises scared her. Metal crunching. Voices. So many voices. Shouting. Crying. Water. Even now, dirty water stung her eyes.

"Are you sure you didn't hit your head?"

She jumped at Heath's question. "What?"

"I've been talking to you for the past few minutes." He chuckled and wrung the back of his neck. "Everyone accounted for. Nothing more than a few minor injuries." He paused again, his brown eyes studying her through his glasses before looking back over the damaged town. "They're lucky, not much warning with this one. It's why we do it, isn't it?"

Elaina opened her mouth, but words wouldn't come out. She nodded and followed his gaze over the town. Just hours after the twister had gone through, people were already sweeping up the glass, patching up roofs and dragging tree branches away. Aside from a few scrapes and bruises, families were still intact.

That was why she did this. Not everything broken could be fixed, but she'd do her damnedest to stitch it back together.

3

Solitaire was made for monitoring weather radars on calm, clear nights. Seth Maddux stared at the empty United States map in the dark room of the studio. It was in that dead zone, between when the evening anchors of the Forecast Channel had gone home, and when the morning desk anchors were just rising to their ridiculously early alarms.

He wasn't made for the early shift. He wasn't made for the overnight shift either, but beggars couldn't be choosers. Neither could disgraced-nearly-fired-TV-personalities.

The screen refreshed and a green dot popped up in the middle of America.

"Topeka, Kansas, look at you having a party in the middle of the night."

Seth watched the little storm move east and fade into nothing. It felt oddly reminiscent of his career. *Appear out of nowhere. Look like you're going to be something and move up to bigger storm status and then, poof. You're nothing.*

Worse than nothing.

The overnight radar watcher.

He should ask to have that printed on his business card. Of course, that would assume they'd let him have a card to claim that he was on their payroll.

The newsroom started to stir. Seth's sign that it was time for him to disappear, like the phantom newscaster. If someone saw him, they might drop their coffee cup and stain their chinos. Then there'd be the murmurings all day, *"Did you see Seth Maddux?" "I heard it's bad luck to see him." "It's a clear sign you're going to experience career death."*

As much as his coworkers annoyed him, he wouldn't wish career death on anyone.

Well, most of them.

Okay, there was a handful he liked.

He loaded his thrice-read golf magazines into his messenger bag and logged off the terminal. Then hurried past the office of oppression, holding his breath. Seth didn't want to accidentally inhale any air Julia breathed.

"Hey, Seth," the station director called out.

The door leading to the garage, to his freedom, was just within reach.

"Got a minute?"

Seth plastered on his best TV-smile. Armando Wolfe was one of the good guys. Maybe the only one he didn't wish career death on. "Sure, Armando, just a minute. I got this thing…" he let his voice trail. He didn't have a thing. What thing could he possibly have this early in the morning? The gym. Then a shower. Then mindless daytime television until he fell asleep.

The boss waved him in and closed the door behind him. "It won't take long."

He eased into one of the chairs. The last time he'd been in there, there was no waving him in or sitting. There was no gentle click of the door.

Seth studied the stacks of paper spread haphazardly across Armando's desk. The last time he was in there, everything on that desk had gotten raked onto the floor.

He cut his glance to the corner. The putter was still there. The one he was pretty sure his boss would've used as a weapon during the fight that'd followed his on-screen meltdown.

"How you doin', Seth?" Armando perched on the edge of the desk and took a sip of coffee. "How's the overnight?"

He broke his stare with the putter and looked up at his boss, nodding. "It's great. I really feel like I'm in this unique role to connect the station. You know, I see some before they go to bed, and see the others as they start their day."

"I'm glad to see you're keeping your bullshit fresh, kid." Armando winked and took a seat behind the desk. "I'm in your corner, you know that, right?"

"Look, Armando, if this is about——"

The older man crinkled his nose and looked out the window. The rising sun glinted off his silver hair. "Nah, kid, we're not going back there. This is about moving forward. About getting you back in front of the camera."

Seth sat up straighter. He enjoyed being in front of the camera. Not because he needed to stroke his ego. Being in front of the camera talking about the weather served a deeper purpose. There, he could teach children what to look for in the sky. He could tell mothers how to dress their kids for school. He could warn grandparents to make their way to their safe rooms. "Did Julia quit? Get abducted by aliens? Sacrificed to angry gods?"

Armando grunted and shook his head. "No, and truthfully, this doesn't concern her."

He shivered. If his grandmother were sitting there with him, she'd say someone walked across his grave.

In Julia's case, she would've danced across it. With an open bottle of champagne. Hell, she'd probably even take her bra off and swing it over her head while gyrating her hips.

"Okay…"

"Don't give me that look, kid." His boss laughed into his coffee. "I swear, I'm not going to send you to the Arctic or into a bubbling volcano. It's a concept for a new show, one that I think is right up your alley."

Seth rubbed his palms on his thighs. He'd accepted his role beneath the bottom rung of the corporate ladder at the Forecast Channel. It was nice down there. No pressure. No expectations and no one watching. Could he handle moving up a rung? What if it happened again? What if he slipped? Could he survive another fall?

Could Grandma and Gramps handle me falling again?

He swallowed back the lump and looked Armando in the eye. "All right, tell me what you've got."

The man jumped up from his desk. "It's called *Riders in the Storm*. Get it? It's part weather forecast, part field reporting, and part reality show." Armando paced as he spoke, his words gaining momentum. "We will plop you right into the hotbed of seasonal weather, where once a week you'll file a packaged half-hour show, and then of course, be on call for live coverage." The station director drained his cup. "Advertisers are lining up, so we're feeling good about this. We want someone young, charismatic, energetic, and fearless."

Seth's neck ached from watching his boss move back and forth.

Armando stopped and gripped the sides of Seth's chair. "We want you, Seth." Sweat beaded on his forehead. This had to be more exercise than the man had gotten all week. "What do you say? *Riders in the Storm with Seth Maddux*. Sounds good, right?"

He inhaled coffee breath.

Field work. He'd done that briefly after college, but it was grueling, and he never felt like he could get the perfect shot or capture the essence of the story.

"Are you sure you want me?" Seth scooted his chair back. "I'm a desk jockey."

"Yes, we want you."

"I'm too picky in the field. I don't have enough control."

"You'll have a week to put a show together, and live shots are live shots. Get what you can get."

He shook his head and squeezed his eyes shut. *This was it.* A chance back. But…he couldn't do it. This had to be a joke. Julia was behind this.

Why would Armando play along?

"I need a teleprompter, computers. I can't just do all this with a cameraman and a live truck."

Armando reclined on his desk and crossed his arms, smiling down at Seth. "Kid, I get it. It's like riding a bike. Sure you may be a little wobbly at first, but you'll be fine. Did I mention the show is Thursday prime time?"

He pushed himself up and paced like his boss had. He ran his fingers over his face; the stubble on his cheeks scratched his palms. If he went back on-air, he'd have to shave daily. Seth made another pass across the office, rubbing the back of his neck. He'd need to get a haircut, too. "Okay, okay," he said as much to himself as to Armando. "So where's the set? Here in Atlanta?"

"No, for this we need you in the heart of it. For the spring, you'll be based out of Oklahoma City, then in the—"

"Wait, you're moving me?"

"It's just temporary. Tornado season is churning up. They already had a little EF1 this past weekend. You'll come home before hurricane season."

"Okla-frickin-homa?" Seth's voice rose as if it suddenly remembered that this was the shouting office. "She's behind this, isn't she?"

"No, Seth, it's *not* about you and Julia."

"She wants me gone. You couldn't fire me, so the next best thing is to send me into the field and pray that I get sucked up by a tornado." His line of pacing melded into dizzying circles. His breath was shallow and he saw stars on the outer edges of his vision. This was the same as before. The same as that night.

His body both fought for breath and against it.

"Calm down, kid." Armando stepped in front of him. "Breathe, okay, just breathe." His boss's fingers dug into his shoulders, fighting to hold him upright. "She doesn't know. And, I won't tell her if you don't want me to."

In the older man's eyes, Seth saw understanding, truth. A real second chance. He was never going to get out from under Julia's shadow.

Staying in Atlanta was guaranteed to keep him in the past.

"Where do I spend hurricane season?"

Armando smiled, his white teeth glowing against his tanned skin. "Pensacola. You'll be able to spend a lot of time back in Gulf Shores if you want."

Seth looked up at the ceiling tiles and nodded. "Good. I'm in."

4

The high-pitched whimpering invaded Elaina's sleep. One minute she was on stage, dancing like her tarnished ballerina charm to a faceless audience, and a second later, she opened one eye to her sun-drenched bedroom. "Five more minutes, Nim," she mumbled, burrowing her head deeper into the pillow.

Her dog's whining stopped and she felt the floating release of sleep drift up from her feet.

Just as her brain was turning out the light of consciousness, a heavy weight landed on her stomach and a deluge of dog slobber struck her face.

"*Oof*, okay, okay." Elaina tried to cover her eyes with her forearm, but Nimbus pushed it out of the way with his large muzzle and continued the wake-up bath. "I'm up, I'm up."

She picked up her phone, but an angry red battery stared back at her. The bright sunlight filtering through her blinds told her what Nim had said in his persistent dog-alarm clock way: she was going to be late.

Very late.

"Dammit." She sprang out of bed. She felt blindly under her bed for her power cord. A sock and empty coffee cup later, she had it plugged in and was typing a text to Heath. "Come on, Nim. We're on double time this morning. We have to be in Pierce's office in forty-five minutes."

With the coffee brewing and her dog eating, Elaina loaded up her toothbrush and hopped in the shower. Shampoo drained down her long hair as she scrubbed her teeth, spitting the extra toothpaste into the tub drain.

The two piles of clothes on her bedroom floor stared up at her. Which was the clean pile?

A sweatshirt worn two days ago sat atop one pile, but so did the T-shirt she'd worn yesterday. She sighed. This was one area of her life she couldn't get her arms around. Everything else had a process, a rhythm that followed a consistent beat. Laundry was a chaotic mess of lights, darks, cotton, and dry cleaning.

Elaina opted for the last shirt hanging in her closet, with *Cloudy with a Chance of No* emblazoned across the front. She'd picked it up years ago as a subtle way to ward off the advances of a classmate.

The guy had gotten the message, and soon began flirting with a bouncy blonde whose dinginess seemed to rise with the barometric pressure.

She cringed at wearing the innuendo-laced shirt at a meeting with her advisor but figured it would be less offensive than stinky, dirty laundry.

The traffic lights in Norman rallied against her. At every green light, she sped to the next red, using that moment to pull on a boot or work on braiding her wet hair.

Two minutes until her meeting with Dr. Pierce, she screeched to a halt in a parking spot reserved for faculty. Dealing with a parking ticket would be easier than tardiness.

Elaina raced across campus, her backpack bumping against her butt. The warm front had won against the invading cold front and sweat beaded her temple. Her phone dinged in her back pocket with a text from Heath.

Where R U?

In Dr. Pierce's world, on time was late. Judging by the time on her phone, she was already two minutes late, which meant she was screwed.

Here, she responded.

She hoped to beat the message to Pierce's office, but with three flights of stairs to climb and her lungs already burning from the sprint across campus, it was likely modern technology would win that race.

Elaina slowed to a fast walk three doors from her adviser's office. Her heart raged against her chest, as much from the exhaustion of the run as well as the anticipation of Dr. Pierce's anger.

It was already done. She was already late. Taking a second to inhale and get her breathing under control wouldn't change his mood, but it would make her better able to receive it.

With her eyes closed, she stretched her arms out, lifting them high over her head as she slowly filled her lungs with calming breath, bringing her palms together and down in front of her face as she exhaled.

She took another deep breath, holding it in this time, listening as her blood slowed in her ears.

"I'm so glad you're able to indulge in a moment of Zen, Ms. Adams, but let it be on someone else's schedule. Not mine."

Elaina's eyes flew open at Dr. Pierce's words. She glanced at his doorway just in time to see his wheelchair roll out of the frame.

Shit.

Dr. Pierce's sanctum was a dark cavern of glowing computer monitors illuminating bookshelves bulging under the weight of text-books. The consistent tinkling of an aquarium competed against the electrical hum of his equipment, and the occasional crackle of a weather radio.

"Sorry I'm late," she mumbled, taking her usual seat at the small conference table.

The professor wrinkled his nose at her apology. "Mr. Bryant was just filling me in on the data you secured this weekend."

Elaina met Heath's sideways glanced. One side of her mouth turned up in an apologetic smile. Ever since their first class with the man, Dr. Pierce had intimidated Heath. He didn't like meeting with their advisor alone, and let her do most of the talking.

"As you'll see from the information on wind velocity, we didn't capture anything new." She cleared her throat, hoping to deepen her voice to give it the authoritative edge she needed. "What we did capture is some interesting points on tornado genesis. This little guy sprang up fast on a day when the watch level was relatively low. I think as we dig into this some more we may be able to see why this particular tornado dropped."

Their advisor scratched the back of his head with his pen, nodding to himself as if considering each word. He pulled the pen from his wavy gray hair and clicked the end of it twice before making notes.

As one of the world's foremost experts on tornados, Dr. Tom Pierce was regarded as a rock star among rock stars. He was handsome, charismatic, intelligent and passionate about the science of weather. After the car accident that'd stolen the use of his legs, he was more revered in the weather community, even if it meant he could no longer make it into the field.

Elaina often thought of him as the Wizard behind the curtain.

"Very good," Dr. Pierce said to the notes. "Very good, indeed." He looked up at them, his gray eyes reflecting the white-blue lights of the computer screens. "It's going to be an active season. Actually…" He leaned over to the adjacent round table and plucked a sheet off a stack of papers. "I might have just the opportunity to help you further your research."

Her heart hammered against her ribcage with the ferocity of a hailstorm. Word on the street was a new round of funding was available to study various aspects of tornado genesis. Elaina was just a lowly doctoral candidate, but she wanted some of that funding so badly she could taste the ozone of a forming storm.

A light smile tugged at her professor's mouth. There was no doubt about it, Pierce enjoyed his hard-ass reputation, but he also thrived in seeing his students succeed. Especially the ones who worked the hardest. The ones who practiced equations until she could recite them in her sleep. The ones who memorized the maps of all of the back roads in the central U.S. so she wouldn't have to rely on cell signals. The ones who could look at all the radar models and tell exactly where a storm would drop.

"I'm sure you're aware that some new funding—"

"Did we get it?" Her excitement bubbled over, cutting off her professor's preamble.

The man chuckled. "Yes, Elaina, we secured funding for you and Heath to spend the spring out in the field."

Her legs twitched, eager to run out the door and get to work. She gripped the edge of the chair, holding herself in place.

Dr. Pierce leveled a steely look on them both. The proud professor look was now gone, replaced by narrowed eyes and a pinched brow. "I don't think I have to explain exactly how much is riding on this opportunity, for your futures and for the university." His voice turned hard, sharp. "You play by the book out there. Always professional, always following the rules, and always on time." The professor's gaze lingered on her for so long, Elaina had to swallow back the *'what?'* that crept up her throat.

"Mr. Bryant, thank you for being here on time. You may go. Ms. Adams, another minute if you will."

Elaina's heart somersaulted.

Heath gathered his papers and stood, pausing to look down at her, silently giving her a look that was equal parts apology and relief that it wasn't him.

Dr. Pierce waited until the squish of her partner's sneakers faded before speaking. "Elaina, do you want to tell me anything else about that tornado?"

This was the oldest trick in any parental handbook. A leading question with enough information to acknowledge that something happened, but open ended to allow the child to walk right into the web. Elaina had fallen into that trap numerous times with her mom. *"Elaina, do you want to tell me why my skirt's hanging from the basketball goal?" "Elaina, do you want to explain why my favorite vase is outside with hash marks up the side?" "Elaina, will you tell me what you've drawn all over the walls?"*

Luckily, her mom had realized that all of her childhood hijinks were centered around trying to understand the weather, so she'd redirected her daughter before it'd gotten out of hand. No matter, that leading question always caused the tingling sensation of impending trouble to travel down her spine.

"Well, it was a classic EF1, thin tail, dropped and headed northeast." She could feel her voice wobble like a spinning top losing its momentum.

Dr. Pierce rolled out from his spot across the table from her and wheeled himself beside her. "Look at my chair and now tell me about the tornado." His tone was warm, sad, and firm. It was more than just a run-of-the-mill car accident: it'd been a car accident during a chase.

Elaina didn't know Dr. Pierce before the accident, but the murmurings in the field alluded to the fact he blamed the tornado rather than the oncoming car that'd hydroplaned and slammed into him. Some even said his study of tornados morphed from understanding and predicting them to trying to control them. To put an end to them.

She stared at his wilted legs. They looked like they belonged on a frame much smaller than his barrel chest and strong arms.

Dr. Pierce never asked anyone for assistance. That was part of his demands on his students for timeliness to meetings and class. If he, someone who took extra time getting in and out of his car, across campus and up the narrow elevator to his office could make it with time to spare, then any able-bodied student should have no trouble.

"That'll show me for being late." She attempted to laugh, but her throat closed up. "Heath told you."

"He was worried about you."

Her face warmed. Just because Heath was secretly afraid of the very storms they chased didn't mean Elaina shared his fear. It was always there, this unspoken knowledge that she and tornados had a shared history.

As if the very formula that caused the air and moisture to roil around each other had created her. She'd always chalked it up to the same feelings of being unmoored that every adopted child felt. They'd just appeared out of nowhere, magically placed on earth.

"I took every precaution—"

"It doesn't matter. There will always be another tornado. Equipment can be replaced. But you, *you* can't be replaced." Her advisor cleared his throat. "And thank God, there is only one of you."

Elaina laughed and looked up from her hands into the eyes of her mentor. Dr. Pierce was the closest she'd come to having a father. As if sensing that need within her, he'd taken on that parental role outside of class.

Some of her peers gossiped, but there was nothing inappropriate between them. Even the father-figure moments had centered around her studies. It was just at a deeper level of friendship than with her other professors.

"Oh look at the time." Dr. Pierce broke the bond by rolling back behind his overburdened desk. "If you'll excuse me, I must scare some poor freshmen from making the unfortunate decision of declaring a meteorology major, and therefore causing me indigestion for the next three years."

"What? You don't want your ulcer to heal when I graduate, do you?"

She made it to the doorway before the professor called out. "Elaina, I can't protect you out there. You know that, right?" His eyes glistened in the light of the computers, like ripples in the water.

"I promise, I'll be careful."

5

H eath waited for her outside the science building. "How bad was it?"

Elaina shook her head. "He's the wrong person to confide a close call to."

Her partner exhaled and his shoulders relaxed. "Sorry. I didn't mean to go behind your back. I was just worried because you were late, and I was afraid you had a head injury or something."

"I'm fine, just forgot to plug in my phone. Thank goodness Nim knew I had to get up." She looked at her friend. The whoop that'd been building in her chest like a blossoming thunderhead was ready to erupt. "We're funded!" Elaina shouted.

Heath met her cheer with his hand raised high, forcing her to jump for the high five.

The deep blue sky stretched out overhead, unblemished by clouds. Squirrels chased each other and darted through the feet of students quickly making their way to class. It was midterm time and the whole campus buzzed with a collective tension.

"That's the shirt you got for Bobby Bumpus, isn't it?"

Elaina smiled. "Only had to wear it every day for two weeks before he finally got the message."

"Two weeks? It was either the shirt or the smell."

"My clean clothes pile and dirty clothes pile are starting to look alike. This was hanging in the closet, so figured it was safe." Her rental bungalow didn't come with a washer or dryer, and rather than spend an afternoon at the Laundromat, she always used the excuse to visit her mom.

That memory of being under the debris nagged at her since the storm. It grew. The more she played it through her mind, the more the memory felt real.

"Are you sure you're okay? You're never this distracted."

They stopped at her truck, and Heath plucked the parking ticket from her windshield, looking it over before handing it to her.

"Serves you right for sleeping in. Chloe wanted me to see if you want to come over for dinner soon. She seems to think there's a psychologist you need to meet."

"Great. I don't know what's worse, a guy trying to get into my pants or into my head."

"Wear a dress, then you only have to worry about your head." He jogged away from her, laughing at his joke.

When she slammed her truck door, her good luck charm, hanging from her rearview mirror, danced around the cab.

A child's necklace, tarnished to a grayish-brown. The little ballerina swayed to a standstill. She couldn't remember how long she'd had the necklace, or where it'd come from. The one time Elaina had asked her mom about it, she said she'd begged for it once at the store while going through the ballerina phase every little girl experienced.

The thing was, Elaina couldn't remember it.

She had plenty of childhood memories, some vibrant and others dull. She'd always counted herself lucky, because her mom, Connie, had a way of making her feel like her childhood had been special. That no matter how many times she'd made a windsock out of her mother's skirt, or used a vase to measure rainfall, it was okay to be a kid.

Her drive home was less hurried. She rolled down the window, saving the precious Freon in her air conditioner for the summer.

Many times she'd find herself slowing down by a car dealership, thinking that a new, or new to her, car would be worth the financial sacrifice. However, her line of work, buying something just to get beaten up by hail was a bad investment. Maybe one day, but until that time came, her faded brown truck would have to do.

Nim's snout poking through the wooden slats on the front blinds greeted her as she walked up.

"Hey buddy, let's call Mom and see if we can visit."

The dog answered with a two-footed happy dance, his tongue hanging loosely from one side of his mouth.

"Hi, honey." Connie answered on the second ring.

"Hey Mom, what's up?"

Elaina listened to her mom share the latest gossip about her small-town neighbors and the perils of gardening while she scurried about her house bundling up dirty clothes.

"I was thinking I may come up and see you, spend a couple of days there," she said during Connie's first pause. "This looks like an active storm season so between that, my dissertation, and work, I don't know when I'll get to come home."

"Of course, sweetheart. When are you thinking about coming?"

"I can head up there right now. You don't mind if I bring Nimbus with me, do you? And, maybe a few things to throw in the washer?"

A few seconds passed before her mom spoke again. "Elaina, you should know by now, I *am* aware there are two things you always come home with, your dog and dirty laundry. See you in a couple of hours."

The drive home was sacred. Sometimes she'd listen to the old radio until she'd run out of anything but farm reports and static. Then, she'd roll down the window and listen to the song of the wind.

Cornfields turned into towns, with names like Cotton and Wheat, named for the crop that drew people to the land. Others had sorrowful names like Dead Women Crossing, and Arapaho that made her recall childhood lessons on the pain of her state's history.

The air always seemed fresher when Elaina turned down the dirt road to her mom's land.

Nim stuck his head out the passenger window, barking a greeting at the small herd of longhorn cattle. They were kept more for pets than anything else. Ever since Connie had retired from nursing, she'd become more engrossed in ranching and farming, even though her mother's thumb was browner than dirt.

Connie was working in her vegetable garden when Elaina pulled up to the front of the old two-story house. Like a lot of other houses in the central plains, her childhood home had a grand wraparound porch, white clapboard with dark green shutters framing the windows.

Her eyes rested on the storm shelter just a few yards off the front door, a staunch reminder as to why she'd made the drive in the first place. Elaina opened her door and Nim bolted past her, greeting her mother with more wags and licks than *she* got during an entire week, which her mom reciprocated with an overabundance of kisses and scratches. She should've been jealous, but it was only fair. He didn't come home with dirty laundry.

Her adoption was never a secret. Connie's unmarried status was one reason, but another, was the fact that they could never pass for biological mother and daughter. At least not with looks. Connie's tall, sturdy frame towered over Elaina's barely five-foot-two petite size. Elaina's heart-shaped face with a dimpled chin showed no similarity to her mom's square jaw. She often wished for cornflower blue eyes like Connie, even though her mother told her that the forest green eye color suited her long brunette hair better.

What Elaina couldn't inherit physically, she made up for in personality. Raising a young child alone in small town Oklahoma while working as a nurse couldn't have been easy.

More than a few times Elaina would catch the sideways glances and behind-the-hand murmurings of some of the ladies, likely disapproving Connie's decision to raise a child on her own, a husband be damned. Rather than hide from the gossip, she'd met it head on, taking an active role in her daughter's school and extracurricular activities, doing more than families with two parents and several grandparents on-hand.

Once Connie freed herself from the excited yellow Lab, she wrapped Elaina in a tight hug. The smell of dried sweat, the rich scent of earth, and a hint of her mom's signature shampoo enveloped her in the embrace of a mother's love.

She released an involuntary sigh. It was worth a two-hour drive just to get one of these hugs.

"I missed you, Momma."

Connie held her at arm's length, lightly pushing back the curls that'd come loose around her face.

Water filled her tear ducts, but Elaina pushed them back. Any sign of moisture, and her mom would worry.

"I missed you, too, baby," her mom said, stroking the sides of her upper arms. She looked down at her T-shirt and frowned. "That must be your last clean shirt. Gracious, Elaina, go get some laundry started and come help me in the garden."

Glad to see Mom's inner hippie and southern belle are still duking it out.

After getting the washer working on her clothes, Elaina found her mom back in the garden, bent over a perfect little row of mounded dirt, her face half-hidden by a wide-brimmed hat.

Nimbus lay in the shade of the giant oak tree, happily chewing on a bone that Elaina would never have given him.

"What can I do?" she asked.

"Grab some packets of cucumbers and drop a few seeds in each hole, then gently cover them up."

"But you hate cucumbers."

"Yes, and if every farmer planted only what she liked, we'd all be eating the same thing. Get to work."

The early spring day was perfect for gardening. A cool breeze dried any sweat driven to the surface by the warm sun. When the wind did kick up, the sweet smell of tree pollen tickled her nose.

Elaina closed her eyes and turned her face up to the sun. A long-horn lowed, which was answered by two others.

This was her favorite part of her research. Being in the field, sitting in wide-open spaces and feeling the power of weather all around her. The heat of the sun, the flow of the wind, the moisture in the air.

It was like being home. Not like being *here*, in the house where she'd grown up. Like the definition of home was grander. Her home couldn't be confined by four walls and a roof. It was within her. All around her.

She went back to work, dropping more seeds into tiny holes. Elaina took a deep breath and dropped a few more seeds.

Now or never.

"Chased a tornado the other day. The one that struck Townsend."

"Elaina, you know the rules." Connie kept her head down as she spoke. "Please don't tell me all the gory details. I just want to make sure you're safe."

She scooted down the row, closer to her mom and the unfilled holes. "I was fine, don't worry. It was just a little EF1 anyway."

They worked in silent tandem. Connie dug holes and Elaina filled them with cucumber seeds. When a row was finished, Connie moved to the next, spacing these holes wider for growing lettuce.

The temperature rose as the late afternoon sun began its descent. A rivulet of sweat dislodged from her forehead and rolled down to her eye, the salt stinging. Elaina winced and the gesture reminded her of the vision, of dirty water pouring into her eyes and a man's soothing voice.

"Hey momma."

"Yes, baby?"

"Have we ever been in a tornado?" Elaina looked over at her mother.

Connie paused. The wide brim hat lifted slightly, but kept her mother's face hidden. Her long, gloved fingers trembled and lost their grip on the spade before clutching it tighter. "No, baby." Her words were as tight and firm as her hand on the spade. "Why would you ask such a thing?"

Elaina leaned back on her heels and hitched her hands on her hips. If she told her the truth, that she'd gotten too close to the storm, that would fall within the 'gory details' category.

Her mother was already well past motherhood age when she'd adopted her; Elaina didn't want to have the burden of her daughter's safety wreaking havoc on her health. Maybe Heath was right. Maybe something had hit her. Not hard enough to do damage, just enough to give her the daydream.

"Oh, nothing, just a strange dream I had the other day, that's all."

Her mother's hat bobbed once, as if nodding its approval. Connie stabbed the soil with the spade. There were never secrets between them, but Elaina couldn't help but feel instead of digging holes for lettuce, her mother was digging a hole to bury the past.

6

The grizzled old cocktail waitress had it in for Tuck the minute he'd walked into the casino. She might've had it in for anyone who dared to pull her away from the soap opera to order a drink early on a Wednesday afternoon in this middle-of-nowhere casino, but he'd just happened to be the only one there.

Not that he was keen on patronizing this shit-hole. He'd been banned from the ones in Oklahoma, New Mexico, Kansas and Nevada, so here he was, in far south Colorado. The last casino he could slink into. He had to mind his p's and q's because he was *not* driving to Louisiana the next time he felt lucky. It'd be damn-near impossible for his luck to hold all the way to Shreveport.

Tuck jingled the change in his pocket as he sipped on his watered-down whiskey. He'd asked for it straight up, so they must've watered it down in the bottle.

Can't even get a decent drink in this place.

The bright light filtering in from the parking lot made the inside even darker. Which might be for the best considering some of the stains he saw on the carpet.

Was that a chalk outline of a body?

A few rows of slot machines lined one side of the room. Like old soldiers, still ready for duty, but blind and toothless. Some of the machines were dark, having given up the ghost and now just stood as relics to a time when life was less crappy. Others flashed silently, a spark of life in there somewhere, but fading fast. A few roused long enough to play a torpid, distorted version of their mechanical tones.

He set the drink on the worn bar top and shoved his other hand in the pocket, cupping the roll of cash. Nine hundred bucks, in a mix of twenties and one hundreds. If he were a responsible man, he'd take that money and pay down the debt he owed his loan shark. He'd reinvest it in his business, Tuck's Tours, maybe add some horsepower to one of the vans. That way he could take his more daring clients closer to the heart of the storms and high-tail it out with adrenalin —and tips—flowing freely.

Or, maybe he'd finally get around to buying that headstone. One fit for a little princess.

Hell, a responsible man would've taken a respectable computer-screen-staring office job wearing short-sleeve shirts, neutral-colored pants and a high and tight hair cut instead of Hawaiian shirts, and cargo shorts. His last haircut had been at least three tornados ago.

Robert Tucker was many things, and a responsible man was toward the bottom of that list.

His attention turned back to the cashier's window. An old man reclined in his chair, eyes closed and arms crossed over his impressive belly. His face seemed to have collapsed in on itself like a mountain after a rock slide.

Tuck threw back the rest of the drink.

It takes money to make money.

Surely, Jimbo would understand, being an entrepreneur himself and all.

"Howdy." Tuck rapped his knuckles on the counter.

The man lifted one heavy eyelid. A lengthy sigh escaped his lungs. "How much you changin'?"

"What tables are hot today?"

He smacked his lips a couple of times before he managed to get his mouth to open. "I don't know about hot, but the Blackjack dealer and roulette croupier showed up today." Like a robotic fortune-teller, he closed his eyes at the end of his sentence.

Tuck tore his gaze off the old man and stared out over the casino floor.

An old woman, with her rolling oxygen tank, stared glassy-eyed at her slot machine. A heroin-thin man placed jerky bets on the roulette wheel, and a twenty-something kid sat hunched over at the Blackjack table, his features hidden behind dark glasses and a low baseball cap.

Roulette was like tequila. One good shot was all Tuck had the stomach for. If it was the good stuff, he'd come out for the better. The cheap stuff made him mean.

He was in too good of a mood to leave it to chance. Needed to be in control. To make decisions about his future. Like whether he was going to stay or hit. Stay or run. Stand up to authority or quietly walk away.

Tuck handed over the wad of cash. "Change it all." The chip-heavy pockets of his cargo shorts knocked against his legs as he walked over to the Blackjack table. "Mind if I join in?" He threw some chips on the table.

The player in the cap shrugged.

Without a word, the dealer tossed cards in his direction as he dealt a fresh hand. Turning over an ace on the house's hand.

His gaze darted to his cards. Two and a seven. Tuck swallowed his wince. Blackjack wasn't his game of choice. The only real strategy was being able to add quickly in his head, and at least try to keep track of which cards had been played.

Poker was his game. A game of cunning. A game of war. A game where his face remained the same, whether he was winning or losing.

Sometimes, just to mess with people he'd smile beatifically the whole time, especially when he'd royally lost a hand.

"Book says you need to hit that." The kid spoke beside him.

Tuck gave him a side-eye glance. "Ya think?" He knocked on the table and the dealer placed another card in front of him. A four.

Lucky thirteen. He could hold, and gamble on the dealer busting, or burst out of the gate with a bold bet. He stroked his goatee. Playing it safe was playing it boring. "Hit."

Ace.

Dammit.

"One or eleven," the gambler next to him mumbled. "Book says you should hit that. Or, you could hold if you can't handle the stress."

Tuck had been in enough casinos to know all the mind games people played. He rounded his shoulders and focused on the cards in front of him, gently tapping his finger on the table.

Seven.

His body deflated with a long sigh.

"Didn't think you'd make that one," the dealer said, flicking chips in Tuck's direction.

He didn't think so either.

"You should, like, give me a couple of chips," the kid said. "You know, consultation fee."

"How about this." He swiveled in his seat. "You shut that big mouth of yours and you can walk out of here."

The guy's face whitened around the dark glasses and under the bill of his baseball cap.

There were just some things a man couldn't hide, no matter how hard he tried. Fear of having his kneecaps busted was one of them.

They played several more hands. For the most part, Tuck climbed in the right direction. What started as nine hundred bucks turned into thirteen hundred, but only after dipping down to seven hundred for a short, bad run of luck.

After four good hands, he started fantasizing about what else he could do with his winnings.

Once he paid off Jimbo, of course.

The dealer stretched. "All right folks, time for my break." He started packing up his cards.

Dread slipped down Tuck's spine with the burning sensation of cheap whiskey. "What? No! Come on, man, we have a good thing going." It was playful begging, like when a dog wanted table scraps.

He'd survive if he came away empty-handed, but he'd be damn happy if he got his way.

The old dealer smiled with his rheumy eyes. "I'll be at the roulette table after my break. Come see me there."

He grumbled a half-assed agreement and tossed a couple of chips in the man's direction.

The dealer slid away.

"You!" Tuck said when his replacement took her seat.

The old waitress had changed from her ill-fitting, faded gold-lamé cocktail dress to an even more ill-fitting tuxedo. Her face was still heavily made up. The bright rouge of her blush settled into the cracks on her cheeks like grass growing through asphalt.

"This ain't no picnic for me, either," she growled in her two-packs-a-day voice.

As she took time getting settled into her seat, the guy next to him stood and stretched. Twisting his torso and reaching from side to side before throwing in a few jumping jacks and shadow boxing.

Was it possible that Tuck had found the most annoying person in the world at this waste-of-space casino in the middle-of-nowhere Colorado?

When she finally got settled, the new dealer tossed him two eights.

The kid hissed beside him. "Damn. Book says that's the worst hand you could be dealt. Book says you should split that."

Tuck cut his eyes in his direction. "What, did you read *Blackjack for Dummies* or something?" He split his cards and signaled for a hit. One hand made it to fifteen, the other nineteen. He held on both. There was no reason to get risky with this new dealer. He needed to feel how she'd affect the table.

She was like a cold front dipping down on the warm, pleasant air of the table. Her mojo would either stall before it hit him and nothing would happen, or it'd turn into a raging bitch of a tornado.

The kid busted.

The dealer flipped over her cards. "Twenty-one, dealer wins." She reached for Tuck's chips, pulling a piece of his soul back with it.

He shuffled his chips. Arranging them in even stacks of the

various amounts, moving them around each other like a shell game without the shells.

He was down to four hundred. The lowest he'd been since walking in. Jimbo'd expect nothing less than a thousand for his next payment. Maybe he could scrounge up another hundred if he could at least get back to even and call it quits. Cash in his chips and get the hell out of the casino. High tail it back to Colorado Springs.

The next round gave Tuck a five and a six.

The dealer slapped her own cards on the table, another five stared up. She challenged his manhood through her milky cataracts. Her sagging chin lifted in a dare.

Would he make the big play here? Go all in and at least come away with his investment?

Tuck reclined on the stool and crossed his arms over his belly, letting a serene smile creep across his face.

"Whatcha gonna do there, buddy?" she asked.

He pushed the rest of his chips onto the table. "Double down."

The kid's stool squeaked when he turned toward him. "Are you sure about that? The book says that's a risky bet."

"I've been listening to you go on and on about what's in that damn book. Look kid, life ain't lived in books, life's lived out in the world, on the open road. So put away your *How to be a Man for Dummies* before I shove it up your ass." He shot the dealer a look and tapped the table. "Hit me."

She snapped another card at his place.

A four.

He'd be safe as long as she busted.

The dealer flipped over her hole card.

A ten.

They were neck and neck.

Tuck wasn't a religious man, but at that moment he'd pray to any deity he hadn't pissed off to have the dealer draw another ten or a card from the court. Anything to get her as far over twenty-one as her age. Hell, he'd even offer her sexual favors if he thought it would help. Or, if he thought he could stomach it.

Her spindly fingers reached into the card dispenser.

Ten. Come on baby.

He held his face steady, but a bead of sweat launched from his temple.

She pulled the card out, eyeing him once more before flipping it over. "A six brings us to twenty-one, dealer wins." She pursed her fuschia-colored lips.

Son of a bitch.

"Would you like us to hold your seat while you get more chips?" Her words as smug as her old face.

Tuck tightened his fist; the need to hit something, someone, so overwhelming it trumped breathing. "You've had it out for me since I walked in," he growled.

"I just draw the cards." She shrugged. "I can't help if you make risky bets."

He looked up, the black dome of the camera stared down at him. "I want to see the tapes. I'm pretty sure you cheated there." His voice rose as he pointed up at the ceiling.

"Is there a problem here?" A man younger than all the other employees by a few decades sidled up to the table. It would be too much to ask that the casino's security be as old as everyone else.

Tuck knocked his knuckles on the table. "Nope, just saying my goodbyes." He downed the last of his complimentary shitty drink and pushed off the stool.

"Have a good day, sir," the old dealer called after him.

"Fuck you very much," he shouted.

Day had turned into night. The air was still, dry. He pulled out his phone and checked weather radars from around the country. Looked like there was at least a chance of something brewing up in west-central Texas in the coming week.

If he could avoid Jimbo until then he might make it through storm season with his kneecaps unbroken *and* all ten fingers.

7

Corporate housing was really a euphemism. When Armando first told Seth he'd be set up in corporate housing during the storm season, he'd imagined a decked out condo with a top-of-the-line surround-sound home entertainment system, a fully-stocked kitchen and a bed so comfortable it was like sleeping on a pillowy, cumulus cloud.

The apartment the Forecast Channel had rented for him and his cameraman, Rick, was the farthest thing from 'corporate housing.' It was more suitable for college kids. The kind who turned their clothes inside out to get another wear out of them before doing laundry and used empty pizza boxes as furniture.

Seth shuffled through the furnished apartment. The couch was covered in a velour flower print worn down on one side and pristine on the other. A faux leather recliner near a large window provided a beautiful view of the parking lot.

The linoleum in the kitchen had seen better days, most likely back in the eighties. A quick perusal of the cabinets revealed enough dishes for two meals, after that Seth and Rick would need to wash the dishes by hand, as the kitchen didn't have room for a dishwasher. He pulled open a door at the end of the kitchen, hoping and praying that a washer and dryer resided inside, but only a water heater stared back at him.

The bedroom off the kitchen was small and smelled like a wet dog. Lucky for him, the bed only held a mattress and box-springs. He'd happily spend his own money buying sheets, pillows and the thickest mattress cover he could find.

"Temporary housing, sweet temporary housing." He dropped his bag on the floor and a plume of dust exploded into the air. "It'll be a wonder if I don't get asthma."

His phone vibrated in his back pocket.

"Hey, Armando," he said, pulling open the beige refrigerator. His eyes watered at the tangy smell of pickle juice. The culprit sat on the bottom shelf in a wide, yellow-green, dried-on puddle.

"How're doing, Seth? Getting settled in?"

"Yeah, just, uh, checking the place out." He pulled open the oven. A charred cookie sheet sat on the bottom rack. "It's…" There wasn't an adjective alive Seth could use to be honest and not piss off his boss.

"Not the Ritz, I know, but the executives are being a bit conservative until the first season's ratings come in. Hope you understand."

He felt guilty at his internal pouting. "Sure, and with an active season I won't be spending much time here." He pulled open another door only to find it filled with shallow shelves. "Hey, by any chance do you know if this place has washer and dryer hook ups?"

His boss paused so long Seth looked to see if he dropped the call.

"Yeah, about that…Sarah in HR said there's a great laundromat just around the corner and you're welcome to expense your laundry charges."

Seth stared at the flaking ceiling, inhaling deeply and releasing it in a long, slow exhale.

He was still getting his career back.

Did he really expect them to roll out the red carpet for him? They weren't going to immediately give him keys to a shiny new apartment?

No, he was going to have to prove his worth one storm outbreak at a time.

He put on his best TV smile, the kind that reached his vocal cords. "Oh yeah, sure, no worries. Like I said, I'll be on the road most of the time. This is simply a place to crash between outbreaks."

"That's the spirit, kid," Armando said. "Rick should be there in an hour or so. In the meantime, get acclimated, get some rest. We're seeing some disturbances on the models that could kick up some action. Oh, and Seth, thank you for taking a chance on this."

He ended the call with his boss and fell into the faux leather recliner. The brilliant Oklahoma sun glinted off a car in the parking lot, making the dim apartment unnaturally bright.

Armando's words rumbled around his head. Sure, Seth had taken a chance on a new show and moved halfway across the country, but what choice did he have? Could he really have backed down from this? To say, "thanks, but I'm good watching radars overnight."

It was more than spending a few months in a dingy old apartment. He'd never been this far from his grandparents before. He'd gotten lucky when his college of choice in Florida had not only offered him a golf scholarship and a strong meteorological sciences program, but was also just a few hours from Gulf Shores. Same with Atlanta.

Oklahoma City was more than twelve hours away. Luckily, Grandma and Gramps were in good health, but it was that *what-if* that churned his stomach like a stormy sea. What if Grandma fell? What if Gramps had a heart attack? What if Seth's career collapsed even more?

A man sucking on a cigarette paced in front of his window. With a long exhale, the smell of tobacco flooded his apartment.

This new show is about as air tight as that window.

The man tossed the cigarette on the ground. Ascending footsteps clanged against the opposite wall. The door above him opened and closed, and what sounded like an elephant entered the apartment above his. Funny, because Seth had guessed he couldn't have weighed more than one-fifty.

He could still back out. They could get someone else to fly out, take his place and be the face of the show.

Seth flew through his demotion like a defiant teen running a stop sign. This crappy apartment in the middle-of-nowhere was a flashing *road ends, you're-about-to-drive-off-a-cliff sign*.

That same alarm was flashing when Julia had come on to him that night of the company holiday party. He should've known relationships that started after a boozy evening of eggnog and mistletoe make-out sessions—and would make Sarah in HR cringe—were destined to take a nosedive off the edge of the Grand Canyon.

He ignored that sign then and look where it'd gotten him.

Not this time.

Nothing was holding him in Oklahoma. The show hadn't started, storm season was barely cranking up. He could go back home. Not home to Atlanta, home to Alabama.

Gulf Shores was a small media market, but Seth didn't need to be on a national network. Being the local weatherman would suit him just fine. Aside from hurricane season, the weather was pretty calm. He'd have plenty of time to get back to his college golf scores, spend time with high school friends who told the same stories over and over, and he could even strike up a relationship with an old girlfriend.

Sure, he could do all that. He'd be bored off his ass, but he could do it.

He sighed and pulled his laptop out of his backpack.

Why should he decide? If the weather gods wanted him to take up residence in tornado alley, then they'd produce a storm system he couldn't say no to.

The computer program took a moment to wake up. At first, the southern part of the country looked like a sleepy summer day. After the second pass, a front dropping down from Canada like a falling star was on a collision course with rising gulf air from the south. The point of impact looked to be two days away, somewhere over central Texas.

He closed his laptop and drummed his fingers on the lid. Sure, he could return home and talk his way into a boring job, get a solid tan and find a nice girl to settle down with. Seth would then spend the rest of his life wondering, *what if.*

What if this was a bigger opportunity than sitting behind a desk? What if *Riders in the Storm* really made an impact in people's lives?

What if the sign ahead was a green light, telling him the road would likely be bumpy and curvy, but it was the route he was supposed to take?

What if saying yes changed everything?

8

Waking up in her childhood bedroom always made Elaina feel like the last several years of her life were a dream. The faded red curtains, tarnished medals and trophies, and curled edges of various weather posters tacked on the wall reminded her it'd been eight years since she slept in this room on a regular basis.

In her first moments of consciousness, she felt like someone else. It was an odd feeling of being unmoored.

Ever since that tornado, her grip on her identity felt loosened, like holding onto a weather balloon only to have it pulled out of her fingers and float away.

Elaina stretched and flipped the covers off her.

Nimbus grumbled beside her and stretched his long legs, smacking his lips before resuming snoring.

"Lazy butt," she mumbled. He answered her with a heavy sigh.

With her laptop tucked under her arm, she crept down to the kitchen. A note waited for her under the coffeepot.

Checking on the cows, then running into town. Back around lunchtime.
Love,
Momma

"Of course," she said before crumpling the paper.

Connie had avoided her since she'd questioned her about being in a tornado.

Her mother had always worked hard on the small farm, but seemed to work even harder in the two days since, waking up well before the sun and getting home after dark.

Her mom felt like a ghost. She'd catch a glimpse of her white hair out of the corner of her eye, or hear the creak of the hardwood floors outside her bedroom, only to disappear by the time Elaina got to the door.

Imagine if I'd asked about the little girl.

Her seat at the kitchen table waited for her. The smooth, cool wood welcomed her bare legs. It was strange feeling such a connection with a chair, but this seat had held her for as long as she could remember, supporting her through bumps and bruises and broken hearts, during homework and meals, and late night talks with her mom. The seat of the chair was practically velvet from all the years of Elaina sliding in and out.

She flipped open her laptop and launched her weather models software. A low pressure system was building over the Gulf. A high pressure was about to drop down from the north.

Elaina smiled into her cup. The perfect ingredients for super cell thunderstorms, with a possible tornado as dessert.

Her cell rang, dancing across the table as it buzzed.

"You seeing this?" She skipped the greeting when she answered Heath's call.

"Yeah, looks big. Could break out around north central Texas by tomorrow afternoon."

"I'll be back in a few hours."

Connie was still not home by the time Elaina was packed and ready to go. Her mom would've been just as happy with a text good-bye, given her recent behavior, but she couldn't bring herself to leave with whatever was growing between them.

She sat on the big porch swing, one foot tucked underneath her, the other gently rocking the swing.

Nim stretched out in the sun, first on his side before rolling over to his back, his blonde belly reflecting the bright, late morning sun.

Elaina studied the flat landscape, watching for her mom's SUV. The tension worried her. No matter what she'd done during her rebellious teenage years, Connie had never given her the silent treatment. Then again, the worst thing that'd happened was Elaina getting caught driving around with beer and several friends. Even then, the police had told Connie to go easy on her. She'd been the designated driver.

How could a simple question be worse than a minor in possession charge? What was so bad about trying to remember something from her childhood?

A cloud of dust billowed on the horizon.

Her dog bounced up and immediately began his someone-is-coming-to-see-me dance.

Elaina met her mother at her parking spot, pulling the door open before Connie could escape. She wasn't going to leave until they talked and everything was back to normal.

"Hey, baby," her mom said, pulling herself out of the car. "Is everything okay?"

"Oh yeah, really great, actually. A low is coming up from the Gulf, so Heath and I are hoping to catch some action tomorrow in Texas." Elaina caught Connie's gaze.

For the first time in the past two days, mother and daughter studied each other. Despite the unrelated DNA, their connection ran deep.

She remembered being little, and crawling into Connie's lap, resting her head against her chest, listening to the relaxing rhythm of her mother's heart, trying to make her own heart beat in sync. She'd never heard that heartbeat from inside her mother's body, but it didn't matter. She wouldn't have remembered it, anyway.

"I'm sorry," they said at the same time.

Connie's face mirrored Elaina's look of surprise and they giggled.

Her mother threw her arm around Elaina's shoulders and

started walking toward the house. "Let's have a quick lunch before you leave."

This time, the silence between them was one of comfort.

She pulled Pimento cheese out of the fridge, and Connie heated up the skillet. Her mom's grilled Pimento cheese sandwiches could actually be the secret to world peace.

"I'm really am sorry I upset you," Elaina said, swallowing a bite of gooey melted cheese. "It was just some stupid dream, and it felt so real that I couldn't help but wonder…"

Her mom put her sandwich down and wiped her hands on her napkin. She broke one of her favorite table manner rules and put her elbows on either side of her plate. "Baby, I should be the one to apologize. I worry about you out there. You have no clue the kind of injuries I've seen of tornado victims." Her eyes filled and she dabbed the edges with her napkin. "You're all I have, and the thought of seeing you like that—" Connie's chin trembled and her normally strong voice was reduced to a whisper.

She grabbed her hand and squeezed. For the first time, Elaina felt the stiffness of the joints and flesh that felt as thin as onionskin.

This woman—her mother—was also all *she* had.

"I'm careful. We always stay on the back end of the storm and we have computers and radars on our side. I do this so fewer people have injuries, and fewer mothers have to worry."

Connie pulled out of her grasp and stroked the side of Elaina's face. "I know, baby. You take care of everyone, but I just worry about who's taking care of you." They held each other's gaze moments longer before her mom broke the connection. "Well, you need to finish up and get on the road. I'll pack some food for your drive down."

The drive was long, but it was the perfect amount of time for her brain to chew on her mom's words. They were all each other had. Was it selfish of her to put herself in constant danger?

There were safer fields of study. Why did she have to choose the one that could kill her?

If she'd chosen botany, the worst that could happen was a rash from mishandling poison ivy.

The weather ran deep in Elaina's blood, as if part of her DNA matrix would include ozone from lightning strikes, water vapor, and positively charged ions. The weather spoke to her in ways that people didn't.

After five hours in her truck, her muscles were as stiff as concrete pillars. Her feet pushed on the sides of her boots, swollen from the constant pressure on the gas pedal. Normally, she loved driving. The freedom to go anywhere, the rhythm of the road, the control over her big mechanical beast at the wiggle of a toe.

Elaina shifted, hoping to reestablish blood flow to her butt. Today she could see the benefits of cruise control.

It took all of her strength to not kiss the ground when they arrived at the roadside motel Heath had booked outside of Stephenville. According to all of the models, the area outside of this town held the greatest potential for outbreak. Of course, they had to stay mobile; just because an outbreak started near them didn't mean it would stay.

The cracked parking lot was full. Judging by radio antennas waving in the wind and the number of vans sporting magnetic cling signs promoting various storm chasing groups, they weren't the only ones eager for some action.

Elaina wrinkled her nose at a Hummer and live truck duo wrapped in bright blue Forecast Channel propaganda. *The circus is officially in town.*

"Looks like the cold front's slowed a bit." Heath pulled his duffel bag out of the van. "Models still showing tomorrow afternoon, but we may be in more of a hurry-up-and-wait pattern. I need a shower and a nap." An oversized yawn punctuated his statement, and he slipped inside his room.

Her beloved yellow Lab raised one eyebrow at Elaina, as if agreeing with her research partner.

She let Nim into her room and walked over to the forgotten pool, half filled with emerald green water. A rippling under the surface made lazy, looping circles, but never betrayed the secret of what lay beneath.

The wind blew from the southwest and the familiar scent of her mom's cow pasture wafted off the water.

She faced the west. The sun slipped through high cirrus clouds, easing toward the cumulonimbus already building on the horizon. The clouds seemed to ignite as the sun touched them, setting off a firestorm of oranges and pinks.

Elaina closed her eyes and raised her arms overhead, reaching for the wispy strands of moisture licking the sky. Her back groaned and popped as it let go of the driving tension. Hinging at the waist, she dove down, gripping the toe of her boots.

After years of practicing yoga, the motion of sun salutations was automatic, almost prayer-like. While her body flowed with her breath, her mind played with that image of the man silhouetted against a blinding light.

It had to be a metaphor for something else. Weeks away from finalizing her research, perhaps it was her subconscious telling her that she was leaving childhood behind, moving into the unknown.

Elaina kicked back into a plank. Loose pebbles dug into her palms as she shifted her hips up and drove the heel of her boots down into a perfect downward facing dog.

She deviated from the flow of her practice to spend a little more time in her favorite pose, reveling in the floaty feeling of the blood rushing to her head.

Ready to move to the next pose, she fluttered her eyes open.

A man leaned on the gate behind her. His wavy blond hair reflected the fiery colors of the sunset. The crystal blue color of his eyes perfectly matched his polo shirt.

Elaina squinted, trying to make out the logo embroidered in white, frowning when the upside down words 'Forecast Channel' came into focus. "It's rude to just sit there and watch," she called out before hopping her feet between her hands and finishing the Sun Salutation.

"Didn't want to interrupt your yoga." His smirk morphed into a full smile. "What time is Pilates?"

Elaina tugged at the hem of her long-sleeved T-shirt and shoved the sleeves back up her arms as she walked toward him. "Studio's all yours. Enjoy your Kegels." Elaina reached for the gate, but he didn't move.

His hands covered the latch and the fingers of one hand curled around it, holding her hostage in the smelly, algae-infested pool.

His eyes stayed on hers, but she could tell they wanted to roam.

Then again, who knew how long he'd been watching her. He'd probably already got an eyeful.

Pervert.

"That sounded like an insult." The congeniality in his words was pulled tight over a challenge.

"You're smarter than you look." Elaina crossed her arms and narrowed her eyes. Challenge accepted. "It was definitely an insult." She shot her gaze to the latch and back up at him. "Do you mind?"

"Seth Maddux," he said, extending his top hand, but still keeping one over the latch. "Forecast Channel. I'm covering the outbreak tomorrow. Which tour group are you with?"

She scowled at his hand but didn't reach for it. Typical male MO, to assume she was a passenger, rather than a driver.

Her momma had taught her about boys like *this*.

"The one you need to avoid." Like a snake striking, her nimble fingers reached under his hand a flicked open the gate.

He stumbled back, standing aside as she pushed past him.

She was nearly back to her room when he shouted. "Hey, I never got your name."

"Nope," Elaina said over her shoulder. "You didn't."

9

The Texas air was tight with electricity. Heavy gray clouds greedily slurped up moisture, and fierce winds blowing from the north stirred a cauldron of hail and energy.

Elaina and Heath bent their heads over their computers, holding their breath and waiting for the moment of genesis.

"We may be wasting our time," his words blew out on an exasperated sigh. "The ingredients are all here, but the pot isn't boiling."

She looked up at the sky. The cold and warm fronts weren't clashing like angry gods; instead they were gently rolling around each other, like two old friends playing a lingering game of chess.

A tornado could still drop, but as the air stabilized, their chances of getting another data set dwindled. Along with her hope of getting another glimpse at whatever the last twister had revealed.

A blast of northerly wind brought with it a cold, hard rain. From the back of Heath's van, they watched through the open doors as the amateur tornado tourists shrieked and ran for cover in the safety of the various vans and SUVs. Radio static crackled with the lightning.

"Anything that happens will be rain-wrapped, so these tourists should just go home." Elaina wrinkled her nose as she muttered. "And the news crew, too."

Her partner laughed and shook his head.

"What?"

"You think these storms exist just for you, don't you?" His voice was light, but the words rested on the foundation of hard truth.

Her gaze left the rolling image of the radar and studied her friend's face. The storms *did* exist just for her. Folded into the layers of gray clouds was her future. Lying within positively and negatively charged molecules was the information they needed to finish their research. Spinning in the heart of every tornado was her purpose, to learn its secret so she could whisper it to others.

"Someone's going to get hurt." The words had to squeeze past the tightness in her throat. "If they aren't watching the radar or the sky. Or if they aren't paying attention to the road…" The image of her professor's legs forever locked into a wheelchair flashed across her mind.

The glow of the computers cast a green-yellow pallor to Heath's face. A quick tightening of his jaw was his only acknowledgement of her concern.

Elaina swung her gaze back to the world outside the van. Yellow headlights illuminated the falling rain. The motel sign danced and jerked in the rising wind. Everything was awash in gray; gray skies, gray parking lot, even the other vehicles all managed to look gray.

Except for the Forecast Channel vehicles. The Hummer and live truck were a beacon of bright blue.

The obnoxiousness managed to battle the storm.

As if someone let off the accelerator, the rain eased up and the growing puddles stilled.

The Forecast Channel reporter got out of his van with a golf club in hand. Holding the ends high overhead, he stretched, first one side then the other before twisting his torso and taking a few practice swings.

"That idiot is just asking to get struck," she said.

Movement on the other side of the parking lot pulled Elaina's attention away from the potential electrocution.

A man got out of the driver side of one of the tour vans. Unlike all the other tour vans in black, white or gray, this one was a deep maroon, pock mocked by years of hail dents. The gold lettering on the side, Tuck's Tornado Tours, made economy of the alliteration with each word sharing an oversized T.

He walked to the middle of the parking lot, hands in the pockets of his cargo shorts. With his face tilted up to the sky, he closed his eyes and outstretched his arms. The wind kicked up, whipping his shoulder-length gray hair across his face.

Elaina felt it then.

Something in the air had shifted.

Nim lifted his head and let out a soft whimper before sitting upright at her feet and staring hard into her eyes, as if to say, "Get my helmet, let's go."

A shrill whistle cut through the silence as the man made a circular motion with his finger and jogged back to his van.

"Let's go," she said.

"Where? We're getting some movement but no hook yet."

She scooted to the back of the van, not wanting to lose sight of the maroon vehicle. Something deep inside told her to follow the man.

It came from the same place that told her when the pressure dropped, the humidity rose, and the winds shifted. The instinct to follow was born in the same place where Elaina had learned to listen to Nimbus.

Her gut and her dog never lied to her.

"I don't know, just follow that van."

"Are you kidding me?" Heath looked at her with disbelief and concern for her sanity. "You want to follow the circus?"

"Trust me," she said, slamming the back doors of their van and opening the door of her truck. Nim hopped in first and she scooted in beside him, quickly snapping his helmet on before peeling out of the parking lot.

It was easy to follow the other van. The weather kept most of the people in this rural part of Texas home and tucked away.

The difficult part was keeping an eye on the horizon for

anything dipping down. On the northern edge of the Texas Hill Country, the land rose and fell more than the plains of Oklahoma.

A tornado could be just on the other side of the hill and they wouldn't know it until they got there.

The van pulled onto a dirt road abruptly, rocking onto its left side as if the driver never even let off the accelerator.

Elaina followed a quarter of a mile behind him. She watched as his brake lights brightened.

"We've got something forming, off to our left," Heath's voice came over the radio. "If we're going to get anything, we need to cut north. Looks like we've got a crossroad up ahead."

The road came into view and she turned. Of course the tour operator wouldn't take his guests into the heart of the storm, but somewhere safe on the back end.

"Guess we brought the party with us," Heath said.

Elaina looked in the rearview mirror. Behind them she could see the procession of headlights. Some stopped along the southern road to watch, others followed her and Heath to get closer.

Great.

Leaning over the steering wheel, she studied the sky. There was no wall cloud, no garish green tint, just a driving rain and debris flying from her left and her right. "Let's drop here and head back to the southern road," she told Heath over the radio.

Afterward, they turned and raced back to the other road. The hair on her arm stood with anticipation. Could she see anything in this weather? Would a rain-wrapped storm have the same affect?

They found a place along the highway with the rest of the storm chasers.

The maroon van's passengers clustered together, all waiting with cameras and recorders poised to capture the storm.

Seth's blond hair and bright blue rain jacket was easy to spot as he stood with a microphone in hand.

Anticipation and excitement, fear and bravery pulsed throughout the group waiting to see a meteorological wonder.

Like a stage queen waiting until her adoring fans were ready before making an appearance, the large wedge tornado showed itself. As guessed, it was rain-wrapped and faint as it sauntered. The low rumble of the storm was interrupted by whoops and whistles and rapid-fire camera clicks.

At this safe distance, everyone got out of their cars to watch, including Elaina.

Her feet pulled her toward it. Mud sloshed beneath her boots and the air was eerily still. Was she too far away? Would it happen again?

She moved closer to the storm, away from the sounds of the people.

Elaina closed her eyes, just wanting to feel the storm. Her skin prickled with cold air and warm rain. Her ears popped with the shift in pressure. She took a deep breath, inhaling the musky rain, her nose tickling with the woodsy smell of upturned dirt.

It's not going to happen.

She was still there, on a dirt road among strangers, her friend and her dog watching a lazy wedge tornado.

Elaina opened her eyes, but she was not staring at the field. She was sitting in a corner of a white room. Names were called over an intercom and a machine beeped an off-tempo rhythm to her racing heart.

"Mommy," said a small voice that felt both grounded and disembodied. "I want my mommy."

The white room faded into a gray rain cloud. The roar of the storm dissipated and cheers erupted in its place.

Elaina stood frozen, staring at the empty field. Hot tears heated her chilled face. Panic and confusion swirled around her stomach, but one thought emerged from the vortex deep inside her.

The mother she cried for wasn't the woman who'd raised her.

10

The tips would've been better if it weren't a wedge tornado. Endorphins made everyone feel generous, but if Tuck could've chased a sexier twister, the bills slipped into his hand would've been twenties instead of tens.

Once the air settled around them and the geeks and TV guys got their fill, his tour group was electrified with the find, even if *he* was utterly bored.

He'd been the first to call it, before the scientists and Forecast Channel flacks, with their equipment that cost more than his van. Nobody could read the sky better than Robert Tucker. That knowledge almost made the wedge tornado acceptable.

Almost.

Tuck looked at the ragtag vacationers and retirees in their sensible shoes and freshly-purchased rain gear. They had no clue that the man who ordered their lunches and held out a helping hand to their wives was a weather god.

"How much do you reckon we pulled in?" Biscuit asked, pulling out the barstool next to him and whistling for the bartender.

Biscuit had been his business partner for as long as he could remember. So long, in fact, that he couldn't recall the drunken night that'd resulted in his friend acquiring the nickname, Biscuit.

"About two hundred," Tuck said to his beer. "Cheap bastards." He was seven hundred short of what he'd lost in the casino, on top of the three hundred he'd hoped to make to pull together his payment to his loan shark.

Biscuit scratched the stubble on his chubby cheek and wrinkled his nose. "Not bad for beer money, I guess. Stop sulking and let's go entertain those cheap bastards, and see if we can turn them into drunk bastards."

He followed his friend over to the table where his tour group took up residence. Even if the faces changed, nearly every one of his groups looked the same. Father and son bonding team, a few sets of retirees in baseball caps and visors, and the international tourists getting away from the bustle of the city to get the "true" American experience.

It was a waste of time to remember their names. He focused on the roles they played.

"Y'all still doing okay?" Tuck asked. The buzz from the alcohol amplified the group's adrenalin and the collective excitement made him hopeful for another round of tips.

"There he is," slurred the man he'd called Father of the Year.

This nickname always went to the men who showed up with teenage sons hoping to pull the kids' eyes off their phones.

The teenager shyly took a sip of beer.

This father might actually get the award.

"Round's on me. That was so freaking awesome."

"What would you say that one was? EF4? Five?" asked New Hobby Retiree.

These guys were his bread and butter. Retired accountants, lawyers, or doctors who had the means and the time to throw themselves into a new hobby. He always made a point to remember their names.

"Well, Melvin, what do you think?"

The man beamed back. "That had to be an EF4, at the least."

Tuck laughed and nodded. "Man, Melvin, I better be careful or you're gonna end up being my competition." The storm had been an EF2, maybe a three, but he was willing to let corrections go to the wayside.

"Did anyone get good footage?" he asked. A few kind words on someone's photography could go a long way.

The cameras came out and Tuck *oohed* and *ahhed* like a proud parent. His hand reached into the pocket of his cargo shorts and fondled the change, cupping it in his hand, rolling it between his fingers so much that the metal heated up.

He chuckled. His old man had always said money burned a hole in young Robert's pocket.

"What's the closest you ever got to a twister?" asked the other New Hobby Retiree.

What was his name, Clyde? Kirk?

"Well, sir," he went with the safe formality. "We're professionals, and we take every precaution to keep y'all safe, so that means we stay on the back end of the storms and watch from a distance."

The man waved him off. "Enough with the liability and safety BS. Come on, you had to have gotten close once."

Biscuit nudged him. "Show them the scar."

Tuck took a long pull from his beer, purely theatrical. He had to make them beg for it. "Nah, man, they don't want to see that."

A chorus of "yes we do's" filled the air, and Tuck was reaching for the hem of his shirt.

"Let me start by apologizing to the ladies." He laid his hand across chest. "I mean no disrespect by showing you this." Modesty always resulted in a few extra dollars. He lifted his shirt and eight heads leaned in close, studying the puckered white scar that ran across his body like a fault line from just above his right hip up to his left nipple.

One of the wives pulled back, hand covering her mouth; another woman reached forward, one finger following its serpentine path from inches away.

"Cool!" the teenage boy said what everyone else was thinking. "What happened?"

He lowered his shirt once everyone got at least a twenty-dollar look. "Tornadoes are like women. There're the girls you can take home to Momma and make a life with: those are the ones where it's safe to take you folks out to see. And, then there are the fiery ones, redheads. Those are the ones you stay far away from."

Tuck drained the rest of his glass and had another in his hand within seconds. "This had to be a good twenty-five, thirty years ago. The weather was kicking up, and I was out getting some storm chasing practice. I was the only one out there, which was a blessing, believe you me.

"I was in the Panhandle when I saw the most perfect wall cloud. You could've used that cloud to hang a picture it was so straight. Then, she dropped down. All sleek with the perfect curves. If this twister was a woman, she'd be on the runway, no doubt."

He paused, letting the picture he was painting soak into everyone's head. "We spent an afternoon together, this twister and me. I chased her from Hereford into damn-near Oklahoma, until she almost got me. Now, you know the Panhandle is a bunch of cows and grain elevators. Well, this lovely tornado lured me to one of them elevators."

"Is that what caused the explosion?" Biscuit asked.

Their audience gasped.

Tuck nodded. "Yeah, the air pressure of the tornado ignited those tiny particles of grain and the elevator exploded. Remember the part about the red head? Well wouldn't you know it, but that tornado sucked up the flames, and she became a fire tornado."

Another collective gasp.

"Well, I'll be," said Clyde/Kirk. "I've heard they can happen, but they're rare."

"As rare as a unicorn," he said.

"How did you get the scar?" a wife asked.

"When you see a unicorn, you chase it. So I followed it, all snorting fire and smoke, seductive. If I'd died right then, I would've died a happy man. I tossed aside everything I knew about safety to get closer. I was about a hundred yards away when she hit some farm equipment. The last thing I remember was a combine headed my way. I woke up to a bright blue sky, birds singing and the worst burning I'd ever felt. I was stripped down to my skivvies and like the succubus she was, I was left with this to remember her by." Tuck finished his tale with a raised glass. "To tornadoes, may they dance across the sky but never across a man's body."

The clinking glass and hearty cheers ensured at least another hundred, maybe two hundred dollars before the night's end.

He fought the urge to scratch at his scar. Every time he told that story it itched, as if punishing him for the fable. In truth, he'd gotten the scar when he was fifteen trying to outrun the Sheriff after getting caught in his daughter's bedroom. A recent growth spurt had made him clumsy and rather than hurdle the barbwire with ease, he'd gotten all tangled up.

The group chattered, mesmerized by the secrets Mother Nature kept and how lucky they were that their benevolent tour guide survived this brush with danger.

Tuck reclined against the wall, studying the people of this road-side bar. Bikers and cowboys mingled and played pool. Everyone laughed. Smiles and good cheer flowed as freely as the beer.

Except for one table. He could tell by the long, curly brunette hair that it was the same girl he'd seen out in the field earlier that day. She'd walked toward the storm, her head held high and her small hands clenched in fists. It was an occupational hazard to notice anyone getting too close, but something about her posture told him she was in control.

He took another drink, studying the girl over the rim of his glass. Her face came in and out of view. The man sitting across from her fidgeted. A lot. His big head blocked most of Tuck's view. Finally, her companion got up from the table.

Her eyes were cast down, studying the remnants of a destroyed beer label. Long, wavy hair framed her delicate, yet determined, face. A thin, straight nose pointed down to Cupid's bow lips punctu-ated by a dimple in her chin. As if sensing being watched, her gaze shot up from the table and found his face.

His heart somersaulted before taking a free fall to his feet. He tried to shift his gaze, but everything was frozen, his feet, his hands, even his lungs burned from needing to draw in another breath.

The guy sitting across from her took his seat, breaking the spell her eyes cast on him.

"Is that it?" the teenager asked.

"What's that, son?" Tuck felt the words squeeze past the lump in his throat.

"Is that the only scar you got?"

"Yeah, that's it, kid."

It was a bigger lie than the tall tale of the fire tornado. He did have another scar, but he wasn't about to show that to no one. No matter how much money they offered.

11

The tarnished dancer twirled in loose circles below Elaina's rearview mirror. She watched until the momentum slowed to a standstill. She could relate. The momentum she'd felt after that wedge tornado had faded in the days since.

Like the first scene, it felt both solid and fluid. Frozen in time with the edges beginning to melt away. Maybe this memory was from having her tonsils removed. Or, had she gone to work with her mom and got lost in the hospital labyrinth?

Hell, maybe Heath was right. Maybe something had flown into her head and her brain was bleeding, slowly killing her.

As if sensing the thought, Nim whined beside her.

"Don't worry, Nimby, I'm not going anywhere." Elaina looked at the clock on her dash and jumped out of the truck. "Except to see Dr. Pierce. Come on, buddy."

A meeting with her advisor would screw her head back on straight, even if she was just catching him for a few minutes between classes.

These images were distracting her, not just out in the field but while she worked in the lab and graded under-grad papers. Her focus and attention impacted more than just her; Heath, Nimbus, her mom and all the people who may one day lie in the path of a storm she missed. A visit to the guru would put it back into perspective.

Her mind closed off the images of the scene in the hospital, but her heart wouldn't let go of the sensation of it. That was what clung to Elaina. Not seeing the room from the eyes of a child, but the jumble of emotion. Fear, sadness, loss and confusion.

Those were adult emotions, not a child's, right? Would a story that came from nowhere stab her stomach with the same ferocity?

Thoughts whirled around her head as fast as a cyclone and she let her dog lead her to the science building. It was a route he knew well, both from accompanying Elaina to the lab for the past couple of years but also because the science building was where they'd met.

Sometimes, she could still see him as she found him, a cold, wet bundle of yellow fur cowering against the heavy doors. No sign of other pups, or his mom, not another human being around. It was as if he'd appeared out of nowhere.

She shuddered in the warm sunlight. Did she appear out of nowhere, too?

Nim took his usual place on the top step, looking out over the campus, to relax in the sun.

Elaina was still swimming in thoughts and emotions when she approached Dr. Pierce's door, so lost in her head she didn't pause to knock or wait to listen for voices. She rounded the corner into Pierce's office and tripped over long, outstretched legs. "Oof," she grunted, catching herself on the edge of the desk.

"Elaina, are you okay?" Dr. Pierce wheeled from behind the table.

The offending legs hopped upright.

She studied his shoes, sturdy hiking boots with the laces double knotted, before moving up the jeans, a medium dark wash, past the bright blue polo shirt before settling on the white embroidered logo. Forecast Channel. *Does he have a million of these shirts?*

Her face warmed as her gaze found Seth Maddux's over-confident smile.

"I'm fine," she managed to get through her gritted teeth. Her mouth twitched, wanting to say more, but her filter clamped down hard.

"I'm glad you're here," Dr. Pierce continued, seemingly oblivious to Seth's self-satisfied face and her scowl. "Elaina Adams, Seth Maddux. Seth is a reporter with the Forecast Channel. Elaina is my brightest doctoral candidate."

Seth's smile widened. "We met, briefly, down in Texas. Thanks for that exercise tip, by the way, I feel tighter already." He punctuated his sentence with a wink.

"Oh, uh, yeah, um," the words tripped over Elaina's tongue. Sweat pricked at her forehead. She might be the first case of spontaneous human combustion by humiliation.

"Seth is here to learn more about tornados, his field of study was hurricanes."

I would've guessed his field of study to be himself.

"And, he's going to do a profile on me," her advisor continued, his eyes glancing down at his frozen legs. "But first, I must teach great minds, or a handful of half-decent ones. Freshmen. Elaina, do you mind showing him around campus and telling him a little about your research?"

A dozen half-baked excuses flashed through her mind, but Dr. Pierce ushered them out of his office before one rose to the occasion.

Seth and Elaina stared at each other, neither speaking until the elevator doors closed with her professor on board, and safely out of earshot.

"Well, this certainly makes my afternoon more exciting." He leaned against the wall, his arms crossing his chest.

She opened her mouth, but she was still too stunned to come up with a nasty retort.

"Nice shirt," Seth said.

She glanced down at her t-shirt. It felt appropriate for her mood. *I'm More Confused Than a Chameleon in a Bag of Skittles.* Did he see her as witty or juvenile? Did she care? "Come on, I don't have all day." Elaina turned and strode down the hall.

Seth caught up to her quickly.

She jogged down the steps, intentionally keeping her breathing normal despite her burning lungs, and he took the stairs two at a time.

Her eyes watered against the bright sunlight reflecting off the concrete.

Nim bounded up as soon as she burst through the doors, but he took a step back when Seth followed. Her dog had never met a stranger, but he likely sensed the frustration coursing through her blood.

"He's with me, Nimbus." As soon as she spoke, the few hairs that stood up on his back went flat and he pranced over to Seth.

The reporter fell to one knee and ran his fingers through her dog's thick coat. "Well, aren't you a handsome guy? I bet you have your paws full keeping Elaina out of trouble."

Her duplicitous dog yelped and whirled around, giving Seth a prime opportunity to scratch his butt.

"Should I leave you two alone?"

"You got any tips for me buddy?"

Elaina rolled her eyes and jogged down the steps. *One of those idiots will follow me.*

"You're jealous," Seth said, catching up to her with Nim following close behind.

"Of...?"

"That your dog likes me," he said.

His voice had a lyrical cadence to it that made her think of slow summer afternoons. Nothing like the indefinable accent she'd heard while watching his show. Not that she'd ever admit to watching him on TV, even if tied down and hot pokers were applied to her feet.

"He also likes to lick himself, but that doesn't mean I'm envious of his butt."

She intended that remark to shut him up, not make Seth double over in laughter. Elaina stopped walking and put her hands on her hips.

He laughed with his whole face. His eyes crinkled into tiny slits that barely let any of the blue show through, his mouth stretched wide and his nose twitched just a little.

Not that she noticed any of that, either.

"So, what do you need?" Elaina asked. "For your interview with Dr. Pierce."

Seth's laughter subsided, and his blue eyes opened up like the sky after a storm. With an outstretched arm, he let her lead them.

Her need to rush gone, she took a slower pace down the path. Patches of students dotted the lawn, taking advantage of the warming day. She'd never been one of those coeds. If the sky was blue, she had no interest in being outside. It was the gray, angry days that got her out of the lab and tilting her face up.

"Tell me about him." Seth's words were serious, yet gentle.

Elaina shrugged. "Where should I begin? He's my mentor. Taught me everything I know," she slowed to wait for Nim to catch up. "He's my biggest cheerleader, but doesn't sugar coat it if I miss anything."

"Does he miss being out in the field?"

"I'm sure he does." She tried to sneak a look at his face from the corner of her eye, but all she could see was that damn logo that reminded her he was out for ratings and nothing more. "But you would need to ask him that."

They walked in silence, Seth not pushing for more information on her professor and Elaina not offering it. She wasn't on a set path, just weaving through the buildings and students hurrying to class. It felt good to move, to be among people and outside of her head, away from the images of doctors and a white room, to distance herself from the fear and the suffocating sadness.

"So, the thing you need to know about tornadoes," Elaina said to fill the quietude that felt too comfortable. "Is to stay out of my way in the field."

"Does that include your yoga practice?"

Heat rushed her body at the smile in his words.

I hope I remembered deodorant this morning.

She stopped under the canopy of a giant oak tree. Its newly sprouted leaves gave her much needed shade to cool the sweat threatening to spill down her face. "Since you asked, yes."

He took a seat at the bench under the tree, patting the spot next to him. Before Elaina could sit, Nim jumped up and nuzzled the annoying reporter. *No treats for you for a month.*

"Your dog doesn't think I bite."

"My dog is a sucker for anyone who will scratch his ears."

"I'm pretty good at it. Want me to scratch yours?"

"I don't have time for this." She turned and took two steps back the way they'd come.

"Elaina, I'm teasing," Seth called out. "Lighten up a little. It's a beautiful day, the atmosphere is stable; nothing's going to happen."

Nimbus doggie-smiled at her when she sat on the other side of him, as if he'd joined *Team Seth* and celebrated winning a round.

"Tell me about your research."

Elaina took a deep breath. This was good practice; explaining it in very plain terms would help her with presenting their findings. "Not every supercell produces a tornado. It takes a very specific formula to get the air circulating like that."

"I know, you need a drop in barometric pressure, a clash of warm and cold," Seth gave her a lopsided grin. "I may not be weeks away from having doctor before my name, but I did study the science of it, Elaina."

Science he wanted, science he was about to get.

She mentally rolled up her sleeves and got to work. "Okay, fine. We believe there's a point in tornado genesis before the fronts collide and the storm drops," she looked across the quad.

Students passed by, some walking alone, some in pairs and small groups. "It's like love." She pointed at a couple walking together hand in hand. "Take them, what is it in each of them that made that connection? Just because two people are sitting together doesn't mean they'll fall in love. There's a catalyst in each of them." Elaina broke her stare when the couple's lips met, feeling her face warm for what felt like the eleventy billionth time that day. She glanced at Seth, checking to see if he was following her explanation.

The look on his face was intense, concentration and curiosity. "You're trying to find the butterfly theory for tornadoes," he nodded slowly, arching an eyebrow. "I'm impressed. We've been using that for years with hurricanes."

"Well, yes, but it's different, you have a week or more to prepare for a hurricane. It's like watching a marathon. Long, slow and boring."

He laughed. "Boring?" his voice raised an octave causing Nim to quirk his head. "There's nothing boring about sustained two hundred mile per hour winds and eighteen-foot-high storm surges."

"You have days to get people out of the way." She shifted on the bench to face him. "I have minutes, maybe an hour or so if we're lucky. And even then, things can change fast. Once that hurricane's on a track, it's on the track."

"You're right, but a tornado can affect no one or a handful of people." Seth turned to face her and leaned forward.

Nim hopped down on the ground as if trying to get out of the crosshairs.

"A hurricane can wipe out whole towns."

"There's nothing mysterious about hurricanes." Elaina's whole face was hot and her pulse pounded in her ears. She probably resembled an angry tomato. "What you see is what you get."

He reclined, crossing his arms and resting his right ankle across his left knee. "What's wrong with that?"

Were they still talking about storms?

She reclined and folded her arms across her chest.

Red stained his cheeks and the Forecast Channel logo heaved.

Their gazes were locked, and as much as she wanted to look away, his sky blue eyes held her hostage.

"Elaina!" Her research partner calling her name paid the ransom. Heath jogged up to them. "I'm glad I ran into you," he paused and looked over at Seth, recognition widening his eyes behind his thick glasses. "Oh, I know you. I really enjoy your show, man." He offered a hand.

"Seth, this is my research partner Heath Bryant."

Her friend joined the same time-out team as her dog and professor.

"Wish I could chat, but I got a class to teach," Heath turned to Elaina. "We're still on for dinner, right? Chloe is going to kill me if you back out. She swears you and Harrington are the perfect match." Heath started back-pedaling.

Was really heading to class or trying to outrun her?

"Six-thirty," Heath added.

She stared at the retreating figure of her friend. For someone so tall, he moved away from her at lightning speed.

"Harrington?" Seth mumbled.

Elaina flashed her winningest smile. She pushed herself up from the bench and stretched. "Now who's jealous?" Even though she moved back into the sunlight, she missed the cozy warmth of the bench. "Come on, Nim."

Her dog whined once before leaving Seth and jogging after her.

12

A force field around the doorbell prevented Elaina from pushing it. Soft jazz harmonized with voices, and wafted out the open window beside her. A warm yellow glow lit the stained glass window at the door.

Nothing screamed scary, intimidating, awkward. It was the whisper of expectation that made her fidget outside Heath and Chloe's door.

That, and the white eyelet dress she wore to appease her friend. She shuffled her boots, smiling at the little nuanced victory. Heath had said to wear a dress, but he didn't say anything about what shoes to wear with it.

Her phone rang and she fumbled through her purse.

The door flashed open just as her cell materialized and danced in the air like fish out of water.

Elaina caught it before it hit the welcome mat.

Heath's name faded from the screen as she looked up to see him staring down at her with his phone to his ear. "You thought about bailing, didn't you."

"I just got here." She stood, tilting her chin up to add a precious half-inch to her height.

"Liar," he whispered before opening the door wider. "I heard your truck pull up seven minutes ago."

Elaina's jaw dropped. Next time she'd have to park farther down the street.

Heath and Chloe's duplex perfectly defined them. It was simple, uncluttered, yet warm and inviting. Sweethearts since freshman orientation, it was hard to discern which pieces belonged to him and which were hers.

"Elaina." Chloe emerged from the kitchen with a frilly apron around her waist. The pretty blonde wrapped her in a tight hug. "I know you'd rather have razor blades under your fingernails. Thank you for trusting me," Heath's fiancée whispered in her ear.

"I may ask for those razor blades later," she whispered back with a laugh before breaking the embrace. "What can I help with?"

Before Elaina could escape to slice, dice, or julienne, an auburn-haired man entered through the swinging kitchen door with two glasses of wine in hand.

"This Bordeaux aged perfectly." The words rose and fell on his English accent. He paused and his cheeks reddened to the color of the wine. "Oh, hello, you must be Elaina. I'm Harry."

Harry handed her a glass of wine and leaned forward in an attempted kiss on the cheek, which she blocked with a shake of his free hand, but not before she tried to offer her cheek and instead collided with his forehead.

"Hi, yes, I'm the girl who was raised by wolves." Elaina took a long drink of the wine. If she was going to blush relentlessly, she might as well have a decent buzz to go along with it.

Embarrassed chuckles quickly turned into awkward laughter.

She took another drink and let her gaze dart around the living room, bouncing from a vase of peonies on the mantel to photos of Heath and Chloe before resting on the large mirror, reflecting an image she barely recognized.

Not only had Elaina put on a dress, she'd taken the time to bring out her forest-green eyes with makeup, and tame her long curls to frame her face. She had to admit, she cleaned up pretty well.

Too bad Seth isn't here to see it.

She frowned into her reflection above the fireplace. Why in the world had she thought *that*?

Elaina was supposed to be on a date with Harry. There was no room for Seth and his hurricanes-are-cooler-than-tornados nonsense.

"Dr. Harrington Preston, this is the future Dr. Elaina Adams." Bless Chloe and her proper Southern upbringing. "Heath, please help me in the kitchen."

Elaina and Harry each took another sip of wine, their eyes working overtime to avoid each other.

"So, come here often?" she asked, hoping to break the silence.

"Uh, no, it's my first time, actually."

Her mouth twitched, eager to call out that his sense of humor needed tweaking, but good manners cautioned against pissing him off before entrees were served.

"That was a joke, wasn't it." he mumbled into his wine.

"A really bad one." Elaina took a seat on the couch. "Scientists aren't necessarily the funniest people on the planet."

Harry collapsed next to her. "And Brits have their own wonky sense of humor."

They took another sip in unison.

"It's my first time too," she said. "I mean, I've been here a million times, but I'm not some special charity case. Despite the atrocious manners and inappropriate jokes." She looked at the nearly empty glass of wine. "Then again, maybe they keep me around for the entertainment value."

"Well, you look very nice this evening. The wolves would be proud."

Elaina laughed and studied Harry. His auburn hair had the first strands of gray dotting his temple. Rather than age him, it added to his British-ness. The camel-colored sport coat brought out the gold flecks in his hazel eyes.

Their shared nervousness melted the tension in the room and they chatted idly about his adventures in American driving.

He was handsome, in a very upper-crust, patches-on-his-elbows, and a pipe-in-his-mouth way. She tried to stay focused on his eyes, but hazel gave way to blue. His auburn hair faded to blond. His British accent sounded wrong in her ears, like it should have been from the south.

Dammit. She didn't invite Seth on this date. Why did he keep popping up?

She drained the last of her wine to keep the internal scowl from leaking out.

Relief softened Chloe's face when she called them to dinner. There was no doubt, that in addition to putting the finishing touches to the meal; her friends had been strategizing how to repair their disastrous matchmaking effort.

With plates full and glasses topped off, the foursome spent the first several minutes of dinner complimenting the roasted chicken and grilled vegetables.

"So, future Dr. Adams," Harry said, setting down his fork. "I hear you like to live dangerously." The second glass of wine had melted away his stiff upper lip, making room for his British charm.

Elaina's own second glass of wine coated the defensive wall she usually put up around flirtatious guys. It would be a slippery slope, but she deserved a joy ride every now and then. Plus, it'd be just what she'd need to shove Seth back into his box in her mind. "No need for the formality. You can drop the future and just call me Dr. Adams." She put down her own fork and leaned toward him. "It's only dangerous if you aren't careful."

"And, you're careful?" A serious note underscored his question, a bit of fear mixed with awe. "I mean, a strong gale could carry you off to Oz."

"Well, the flying monkeys should be very, very afraid." She tilted her head in his direction and lowered her voice.

Harry leaned in, the wine on his breath tickled her nose. "And for some reason, I completely agree with you."

Two sets of clearing throats broke the spell cast by the wine and the Brit's seductive talk of Elaina's favorite movie.

"You work with Chloe at the clinic, right?"

He nodded, swallowing his food before speaking. "Yes, I'm

collaborating on a project to study the effects of memory re-writing drugs and therapy on PTSD patients."

"What Dr. Preston isn't telling you," Chloe chimed in, "is that he practically wrote the book on this practice in the UK. So by collaboration, he means he's teaching us."

"It's nothing new, really. Psychiatrists both here and abroad have been experimenting with Rententamine for a couple of decades now."

Elaina propped her elbow on the table with her wine glass in hand. "Generations of twenty-somethings have turned to this right here for memory rewriting."

Three pairs of blinking eyes stared back at her. *I'm 0-2 on jokes tonight.*

"That was much funnier in my head," she said to her glass. "What kind of patients do you see?"

"The best candidates are veterans returning from the frontline, but really anyone who has been in a catastrophic event. Car crashes, assault victims, or, as you and Heath can relate to, storm survivors."

His words made the hair on Elaina's arms stand up, as if a chill blew through the room, but heat flushed through her. Was she having her own clashing of frontal boundaries? Was her nervous system having the hiccups? She was no biologist, but she was doubtful that nervous systems hiccupped.

"How does it work?" Heath asked.

"Today, we're finding that the perfect dose of the drug with specific and targeted therapy can render the fear moot," Harry said. "It isn't so much re-writing memories. That's a fallacy that clung to the treatment since its early days."

"How was it used then?" A voice that sounded very much like Elaina's asked, but she didn't remember the words escaping her mouth. She watched Harry's mouth move. His bottom lip was thicker than his top, making his face look a little bottom heavy.

"Everything from milder uses to more extreme doses combined with intense therapy."

"To do what?" Her words were listless, yet sharp.

His eyes shot from hers to Chloe's, as if silently begging his colleague to save him from the crazy blind date interrogating him. "You have to understand, that we don't use those methods today, and don't condone how they were used in the past."

Elaina took a deep breath. "To do what?"

Harry let out an exasperated sigh. "The brain isn't much different than a hard drive. In some cases, it can be completely wiped clean of memories, and then fed new experiences in its place."

"It was all done for the greater good, right?" Heath's question was meant to lighten the mood, but she couldn't help but shoot a glare in his direction.

"Sure, but it wasn't permanent. Sometimes those deleted memories start bleeding through. Like an old TV stuck between channels. And when they did, it sent those patients into madness. A depression so deep that some of them couldn't climb out of it."

The floor swayed beneath her feet and her stomach turned in on itself, forcing the wine back up her throat, burning her as she fought to swallow it back down. "Excuse me," she croaked, her fingers against her mouth to hold everything in. Elaina ran through the living room, burst through the front door, stumbled down the front steps before falling to her knees and vomiting in Chloe's potted geraniums. Another tide of nausea rocked her body, forcing her to drape herself over the plant.

Once she'd emptied her stomach of the evening's contents, she sat back on her heels. The full moon poked through a high cirrus cloud. Silvery light shone down on the dark red stains ruining her dress, and illuminating the clearest thought she'd had in weeks.

The scenes that flooded her mind, they weren't made up visions or images conjured by a head injury.

They were memories.

Her memories.

That someone tried to steal from her.

Another spasm twisted her stomach, forcing Elaina to double over.

If she couldn't find out what they held and why they were taken, it could very well kill her.

laina's eyes ached from the blue-white light of her laptop. Her phone had finally quieted after hours of incessant phone calls and texts from Heath and Chloe. She only responded after her partner had threatened to call the police for a welfare check.

The first websites she found pretty much said the same thing. Rententamine was used as Harry said. Coupled with intense therapy, it would render patients numb when faced with fear-inducing situations.

Then she found the darker sites, the ones that questioned the drug's initial use and called for its discontinuation. These websites told horror stories of people who'd lost all memory of their previous lives. In some cases mothers shunned their children and husbands left their wives. A person's whole essence was gone.

She sniffled and pulled her covers over her head.

Nimbus joined her in the cotton-sheet cocoon, panting but lying by his owner.

Elaina was going to spend the rest of her life there. Under the sheets, away from people who'd watched her puke her guts into a potted plant, without friends who tried to set her up with handsome psychiatrists who told her things that lived deep inside her. Most importantly, if she stayed locked in her house, in bed and under the covers, she'd never have to see her mother again.

Her mother.

Or, more accurately, the woman who raised her.

The websites got darker as she'd delved deeper into research. Some sites alluded to brainwashing techniques and hinted at the use of children as test subjects. Horror stories filled page after page of people becoming institutionalized or committing suicide once the drug wore off.

Elaina's stomach turned inside out. Was that in her future? Would she slowly go insane or would it happen all at once? Or had it already begun and there was no way back? Would she'd even know if she lost touch with reality? Had she already?

She kicked off the sheets and grabbed a notebook. She needed scientific detachment to determine what was reality, and what was potentially a false memory. A sharp line bisected the page. "Real" topped one column, "Lies" the other.

Her adoption had never been a secret. It went in the "Real" column. Her mother's reaction about being in a tornado went into the "Lies" column.

The image of being found in the rubble flashed across her mind. Where did that go?

Elaina closed her eyes and her hand drifted to the "Real" column.

She paced her bedroom until the sun rose, rubbing her temples, begging her mind to go all the way back to her earliest memory, but it was like a child's toy chest, half memories jumbled together with others.

Was her third birthday confused with her sixth? Which Christmas did she get the bicycle? When did she get her ballerina necklace?

Nimbus got up from the bed and looked out the window. He glanced over his shoulder, wagging his tail. His wise brown eyes bore into hers, as if saying 'Come on, let's get some fresh air.'

Elaina grabbed a pair of workout shorts and one of her favorite

T-shirts, *I'm Only Happy When it Rains*. It was the perfect shirt to wear on what most people would call a beautiful spring Sunday morning.

She needed a good thunderstorm to clear away her bad mood.

"Come on, Nim," she said, grabbing his rarely used leash. "Let's go for a run."

She yanked her front door open and took a step right into the chest of Dr. Harrington Preston.

He jumped back, lifting the two cups of coffee high overhead.

"So, you drew the short straw, huh?" Elaina crossed her arms and leaned against the doorjamb.

Harry shuffled on his feet and handed her one of the cups. "Something tells me you take your coffee black."

Elaina accepted the peace offering. "We were going for a run." She looked down at his sneakers. They were the kind one would wear to brunch or the farmer's market, not to run off the anger of finding out her whole life might be a lie.

"Would you settle for a walk instead? I'd like to talk with you." His voice was firm, clinical. The flirtatious inflections from the evening before were gone. He was all business.

Nimbus led the way. His yellow body wiggled as he greeted every tree, person, sign, and blade of grass.

They walked in silence for the first couple of blocks.

The coffee warmed Elaina's soul and calmed the cyclone of thoughts swirling around her mind. A light northerly breeze danced on her skin, the perfect balance to cool the warm rays of the sun.

She stretched to look up. High cirrus clouds were smeared across the blue sky. They were usually a sign of fair weather, but every now and then they indicated a change coming.

"One of these days I'm going to learn to keep my big mouth shut," Harry said.

"You're saying that to the girl who barfed in the geraniums."

He laughed. It was a nice sound, warm, joyous, relaxed.

They walked past a father and son playing catch in the front yard.

Nim danced his front feet, his tongue hanging out in excitement at the chance that a stray ball could land in his direction.

"How certain are you?" Harry's words were so low Elaina had to whip her head to the side to make sure his lips were moving.

"Would you call me crazy if I said very and not really at the same time?"

One side of his mouth tugged up into a smile. "Are you asking for my professional opinion?"

She took a long sip of her coffee. "I was adopted."

"At what age?"

Elaina chewed on the inside of her cheek as she tried to remember. She couldn't remember ever having the talk about the details of her adoption. She'd never brought it up, never wanting to risk hurting her mother's feelings at insinuating that she wanted something different.

"I always assumed as a baby."

"Could you ask your mum?"

Elaina shook her head. Before she asked about the storm, she would've brought it up without a second thought. Now, she feared what her mom would say more than she worried about her reaction.

What if Connie told her an obvious lie? Could they go back? What would happen to their relationship? Truth or lies, Connie was the only mother she had.

They turned the corner and arrived at the neighborhood park. It was what had attracted Elaina to this neighborhood. A jogging trail wove through the trees, picnic tables lay beneath ancient oak trees, and playground equipment filled the air with laughter.

This patch of green was heaven on earth. A place where young and old alike could be children.

"Maybe I can help," Harry said. "Will you share what you saw?"

She took a seat on the vacant swing set, pushing herself in haphazard circles with the toe of her sneakers. How much could she tell him?

Would patient confidentiality apply to the blind date who'd drank too much and embarrassed herself? Or would he share everything with Chloe and Heath? If that happened, would Heath then tell Dr. Pierce she wasn't fit for fieldwork?

No, Elaina couldn't take the chance of being sidelined. Not this soon into tornado season. Not this close to finishing her dissertation.

"I've made enough of a fool of myself in front of you." She drained the last of the cup. "I'm sorry about last night. But hey, you have a great story to tell everyone. I think Nim and I are going to have that run now." She pushed off the swing and walked toward the trail. The rustling leaves above her head applauded her decision.

"Elaina, it will happen again," Harry called out. "There's a trigger. If you don't want my help, that's fine. I understand. But you have to know that this will get worse, not better."

She dropped the empty coffee cup in the trash bin and turned back to study him. If she were someone else, someone who didn't make awkward jokes or run toward tornadoes instead of away from them, they could be happy.

The man sitting in the swing with the sun glinting off his auburn hair deserved someone who didn't mirror his patients.

"Thank you for the coffee," Elaina shouted. She and Nim jogged out of the park and down the street.

His four legs trotted at a comfortable pace, but she wanted to run faster.

It wasn't to run away from the handsome Brit who could entice her to share secrets or seduce her into a safe, boring life.

She ran because he was right.

There was a trigger.

It would happen again.

If the slight shift in the wind was right, she had to get home and check the weather models.

14

Their uncomfortable shuffling reverberated around the empty hall as they sat outside their professor's office.

The bottom of Elaina's sneakers squeaked on the linoleum as she swung her legs like a little kid.

Heath took several deep breaths, as if fueling up to say something, but the words never materialized, and his chest would deflate with an exhale.

The models were iffy on the chance of an outbreak that week, but she could feel it. Maybe much of the feeling was begging it to happen. She needed to see another tornado.

She needed to see if within it was another vision to tease forward anything that might be hiding in the depths of her memory.

Dr. Pierce would have to sign off on this chase, and with the computer models looking the way they did, it would take some convincing.

Elaina looked at Heath from the corner of her eye. The muscle in his jaw flexed and he shifted his gaze in her direction. *Dammit, this is ridiculous.*

"Let's pretend Saturday night never happened," she said.

"Works for me," he answered, his words tumbling out on top of hers. "But you do owe Chloe a pot of geraniums."

"Guess regurgitated wine probably isn't the best plant food," Elaina mumbled.

The air between them loosened to companionable silence as they waited for their professor.

"Are you okay?" Heath asked, concern underscoring his words. "I'm serious, Elaina, you've been a little off for the past few weeks." He shifted in his chair to face her. His lips were pressed into a firm line and eyebrows pulled so close it looked like a unibrow. "This isn't like you."

She smiled. Couldn't disagree with him. She *had* been off. Maybe this was like her. The real her. The person who'd been washed away in a deluge of psychiatric drugs. Elaina shrugged, as much as an answer to her own questions as his. "It's just all the pressure, I guess. But don't worry, this weekend was a wake-up call. I'm fine."

He opened his mouth to speak, but the squeak of Dr. Pierce's wheels interrupted him.

As soon as he rounded the corner, their professor's jaw jutted out, his lips stretched tight and his eyes narrowed. He pushed his chair forward with the force of someone in a race and skidded to a stop in front of his door. "Elaina, Heath," he spoke to the door as he flipped through his keys. "To what do I owe this unexpected honor?"

They exchanged looks.

"What did you do?" Heath mouthed.

"Me?" Elaina silently asked before shaking her head.

Had Seth said something about her snarky Kegels comment? Even if he had, Dr. Pierce would've laughed, not condemned her for it. Or had Harry reached out to him to express concern about her emotional wellbeing?

"Um, hi, Dr. Pierce, how are you?" Maybe friendly chitchat would melt away some of his iciness.

"I'm still in this godforsaken chair." His tone was flat, despite the bite to his words. He wheeled behind his desk and turned to face them.

Elaina and Heath hesitated outside his office door. She didn't want to be the first to enter, and apparently neither did her partner.

"I don't have time for you two to stand out there like idiots. What?"

Heath's Adam's apple bobbed as he swallowed. "Have you seen the models for later this week?" he asked, stepping forward into the dungeon of doom.

"Yes, typical spring forecast, something may happen, or it can be one hundred percent chance of boring blue sky."

She stepped forward, joining her partner. "Well, sir, we believe there's a strong possibility for an outbreak over the Oklahoma panhandle later this week. We would like to go out there now, to monitor the changes, see what we can get to further our hypothesis of tornado genesis."

"And what if you're wrong? What if the storms never happen? Or the outbreak is over Arkansas?"

They exchanged glances.

Dr. Pierce had never questioned her instincts before. Quite the opposite, he always praised her. Said she had a sixth sense for storm prediction. That she knew what the storm was going to do before the storm did.

"We're not," Elaina said. "I'm not. It's going to happen."

Their advisor thumbed through the stack of papers on his desk and pulled out a sheet peppered with graphs and red marks. From where Elaina stood, it looked like a homework assignment from Meteorology 101.

"You're running out of time and money." Dr. Pierce sighed. "You can't afford to make a bad call."

She lifted her chin and widened her stance. There was nowhere she'd rather be than with her back up against the wall. Fighting for her place in the world, for the scholarships she secured for college, and now fighting for her career. She only knew how to fight. Sometimes she lost, but most of the time she won.

If she didn't know better, she'd think that Dr. Pierce was intentionally stoking that fire.

Fine. A fight he wants, a fight he'll get.

"When was the last time I made a bad call?" Elaina took a step toward the desk. She paused, giving him a second to answer, but he kept his eyes on his papers. "Exactly. So when I say storms are going to fire up out there, they *are* going to fire up."

Heath froze beside her, a shallow gasp over her shoulder told her she'd gone further than he imagined.

Several seconds ticked by when the professor finally put the paper down and rested his elbows on the desk. "What exactly makes you so sure, Ms. Adams?" Even though his tone was condescending, there was enough of an undercurrent of belief to make Elaina smile.

She pulled her laptop out of her backpack and flipped it open, pulling up the weather models. "This frontal boundary is going to dip farther south, and this low pressure system is going to shift west. Give it three days, and they're going to collide." She hit play on the map she'd drawn up, and it showed the bulls-eye for the outbreaks firmly planted in the middle of the panhandle.

Her heart blistered as her eyes traveled to the east of the storm system. If she was right, if the storms formed where she thought and traveled their normal northeast path, her mother's house was right in the path. Her nose twitched, as if a sniffle threatened to escape.

Dr. Pierce studied the map while rubbing his chin. He took a deep breath and then reclined in his chair. For the first time since they'd arrived in his office, he looked directly at her. Strange shadows crossed his gray eyes in the low light of his office. It was a look of respect and envy, pride, and punishment. "You keep an eye on the models."

"We will," Heath chimed in even though Dr. Pierce's gaze was planted firmly on Elaina.

"The slightest variation suggesting a stabilizing atmosphere you get yourselves back here."

"Yes, sir," her partner agreed again.

Elaina crossed her arms. She wasn't used to rules in a fight.

"This isn't a game, Elaina. People get hurt out there. You are a scientist, not a thrill seeker. You gather data, you bring it back here and you analyze it." Their advisor paused, narrowing his eyes before continuing. "Do you understand?"

Her muscles released. Of course he'd be worried about their safety, but why push them forward and suddenly pull them back?

"Yes, I understand," her voice hardened, forming a tough outer shell to hide her true fears. Her fear that they'd get close to a tornado, and inside it would be another vision, another glimpse into something locked away in her mind. Inside this glimpse she might see something terrifying, something once brought to the surface would never again sink into oblivion.

Did she want to know? Was it worth taking the lid off the box? Elaina could look away, close her eyes.

But really, could she? Knowing what she knew, could she ever go back?

Could she forget what Harry had shared with her? Maybe try to re-write that memory herself, sans drugs, and just pretend it was a nice-enough evening with a nice-enough guy.

"Good."

Dr. Pierce stole her from her treacherous thoughts.

"You two get out of my office before I change my mind."

"Thank you, sir, thank you," Heath said, bowing slightly as he walked backwards out of the office.

Like kids escaping the last day of school, they sprinted down the hall and jogged down the stairs.

Her friend paused at the door, holding it closed, his brows drawn as tight as a stretched rubber band. "Are you sure about this?"

"Sure about what?" she panted.

"The models you drew up. They're pretty far-fetched." His lips were a thin line. "I mean, what if you're wrong. What if nothing happens? We're too close to make mistakes."

His words hit her with the stinging force of freezing water. Heath had never questioned her predictions before. She was always right. She never made mistakes. Well, aside from a pot of drunken geraniums.

"Is this about the other night?" Elaina folded her arms across her chest. "I thought we weren't going to talk about it. So I was nervous and drank too much."

"And interrogated Chloe's colleague about weird experimental drugs." Her partner's face softened. "Elaina, I know you well enough to know when something's wrong. What's wrong?"

She nibbled on her lower lip. What could she tell him? That she might have had a flash of a repressed memory brought on by a close call with a twister, and during her blind date when he spoke about his research something felt...right?

Heath had put so much faith in her. Faith that her dedication to their field would earn them their doctorates. Faith that her natural talent would carry them through even the most wild predictions. Faith that she had his back.

She pushed past him, popping open the door and escaping his doubt.

Heath's faith in her wasn't broken, but there was definitely a crack.

15

The highway whizzed by under Seth's Forecast Channel Hummer. His heart synced with the dashed yellow line. *Pump. Pause. Pump. Pause.* Always up for an adventure, his life on the road was turning out to follow the same rhythm as the lines. *Action. Pause. Action. Pause.*

He'd been hoping to add another variable to the equation when he went back to interview Tom Pierce. Even if he had to subject himself to another hour of Elaina's sharp tongue, it'd be worth it for the entertainment value alone.

Seth had a month's worth of witty retorts ready to lob in her direction. He kept his eyes peeled for her brunette curls, but the petite storm chaser was as elusive as a rainbow on a cloudless, sunny day. The professor's words had floated by his head, thoughts of Elaina's smile and dark green eyes kicked everything else out of his brain.

It wasn't until the interview was over, and he and his cameraman Rick were packing up when he learned Elaina was heading to Elk City in the Oklahoma panhandle to await an outbreak. A little professional flattery and he was able to learn where she was staying.

"The school parking lot looks like a good place to park the live truck," Rick Wise's voice came over the radio from the truck behind him.

Seth switched on the blinker and veered to the right, losing sight of the behemoth truck in the cloud of dust.

His back popped when he got out of the car. Life on the road was hard on his ass.

They stopped at the small city of Townsend, a little farming community hit by a storm system that'd produced a solitary twister just weeks earlier. It'd be good to have another human-interest story in the file in case the season hit a dry spell.

The humble high school was the only building that didn't have visible signs of tornado damage. Perhaps it was because the city's leaders didn't skimp on building supplies for housing their children. A church a little way down the street looked as if the bricks from one side had been siphoned off. Two pallets of bricks waited to be called into action.

Seth craned his head and looked down at the end of the street. The grocery store had taken a direct hit. Scary, considering the twister had hit on a late Saturday afternoon with the store full of shoppers. Aside from a few cuts and bruises, no one inside had been harmed.

"What's the plan?" Rick joined him, camera and tripod in tow. Like the good cameraman he was, he came armed and ready to shoot.

"Let's get some b-roll of the town, rebuilding, cleanup," he said. "I'm going to meet the mayor at City Hall and get some interviews lined up."

Seth jogged down the street and found the prefabricated building that served as city hall. He'd only just started up the path when the door opened and a man in dusty boots, dark starched jeans, and a plaid work shirt came out.

"Mr. Maddux? I'm Randy Sutton, Mayor of Townsend," he said with his hand outstretched. "We're real honored to have you visit us."

He grasped the mayor's hand. "Thank you for your help, Mr.

Mayor. The honor's all mine. Why don't you show me around, tell me about the storm?"

The sun beat down on them as they walked up Main Street. The wide blue sky was mostly unblemished, except for some thick cottony cumulus clouds blooming to the northwest. All the atmosphere needed was some cooler weather and a little bit of energy, and they'd be in for another outbreak.

"Where were you when the tornado hit?" he asked.

The Mayor squinted as he looked to the west. "I was out feeding the cows. I knew something was up when they started getting skittish, and my dogs were keeping them in a tight herd."

Seth followed the man's line of sight and tried to imagine what it must've been like to watch a funnel cloud heading for his town. What was it like watching something as uncontrollable as a tornado roll across the field heading toward something you love? Would his heart stop from fear? Would he speed up, pumping adrenalin through his body?

He swallowed hard and cleared his throat. Tornados scared him. The unpredictability. The picking of one home to demolish while allowing another to stand unscathed. The fact that a warning could produce nothing but a half-hearted watch could spin a deadly outbreak.

It felt wrong to hope one of these monsters would strike for the benefit of ratings when it could mean someone's world being torn apart.

But what about his world?

Julia had torn his world apart. She'd reached into his chest with her long, sharp, red talons and pulled his heart out for all the world to see. While he was put into career time out, the network had benefitted from some of the highest ratings ever, and Julia had shown up with a new Louis Vuitton bag just days later.

The network wanted the ratings. They wanted footage of crying babies and buildings being ripped apart. They wanted despair, red-rimmed eyes staring vacantly at what once stood.

What the network was going to get was truth.

They were going to get the raw power of the storm with the

knowledge of how to protect and survive. They were going to get honesty, hope, and healing.

Seth was going to speak like every person watching were his grandparents, urging them to safety, but giving them hope to not give up. "Well, Mayor, let's find my cameraman and get some interviews."

In addition to the mayor, they interviewed the minister who praised divine intervention for sending the storm before the monthly potluck dinner.

The general manager of the grocery store wove a vivid tale of rattling windows, bone-crushing pressure shifts, and how he'd seen into the vortex of the storm when a corner of the metal roof was peeled back. As Seth listened, the story felt more like a movie plot than what an EF1 could do.

The mayor and store manager walked him through the building. The smell of sawdust tickled his nose, and sparks from a bandsaw lit up the back corner of the building. As the only grocery store within an hour's drive, the contractor was working overtime to put it back together.

"Well, Mayor, I think we have everything we need," Seth said, pulling his sunglasses from the top of his head. "Appreciate your time today."

"Pleasure's all ours. Now you call me if you need anything else, you hear."

As the man spoke, Seth's attention was drawn to a little girl who sat on her bicycle, staring intently at the construction of the grocery store.

The girl looked like a specter sitting in the midst of rubble and heavy equipment. She was tiny, possibly no older than five, but in her big blue eyes, she carried an intensity most of her peers wouldn't see for more than twenty years.

"Who's that?" Seth wanted to make sure he wasn't the only one who could see the girl.

The mayor looked over his shoulder and swallowed hard. "That's Amy Wilson. She says an angel saved her after the storm."

"What's she doing here?"

He gestured to lead them down the parking lot toward their truck, away from the little girl who saw angels.

Seth sidestepped the man and took a step in Amy's direction.

The girl stared intently at the building, her eyes unblinking.

"Waiting," the mayor sighed. "She's waiting for the angel to come back."

"Come on." Seth turned to Rick, but his cameraman had already shouldered his camera.

Amy's straight light brown hair blew across her face, a few strands sticking in her eyelashes.

He really needed one of her guardians to sign off on the interview, but he'd cross that bridge later. Right now, he needed to see what Amy saw.

"Hi, my name is Seth." He knelt in front of her.

The girl craned her head to look around him, her gaze still intent on the building.

Seth looked up at Rick in silent guidance, but he just shrugged.

"Rolling?" he mouthed. "I heard you were in the store."

Amy nodded her head.

"Were you scared?"

This time one of her small shoulders lifted up. She ducked her head down, trying to not break eye contact with the building.

"Want to tell me about it?"

Another wind blew, this time covering her tiny face with her hair. She let go of the handlebars of her bike and shook her head while smoothing the offending hair.

Seth crouch walked out of the girl's line of sight to next to her, watching the store from the same perspective. Light from the descending sun glinted off the new metal roof, casting an ethereal shine from the building. No wonder the girl waited so intently for her angel.

"I saw an angel once," he said.

For the first time Amy's gaze shifted to his quickly before moving back to the building.

"I was about your age, and I lived down on the coast. I rode my bike too far from my grandparents' house, and a fog rolled in. I was so scared. I didn't know which way was up, and then suddenly out of the fog came this beautiful woman. She held my hand and walked with me back to my street. Once I saw my house, I turned to thank her and she was gone."

Amy's head turned in his direction. "Did you ever see her again?"

"Nope."

Big tears filled her eyes. "But I want to tell her thank you. And that Mr. Bear was okay." She reached down to touch the bear resting in her handlebar basket.

Seth looked over his shoulder to make sure Rick was still rolling. "Well, I have it on good authority, that the angels in Heaven watch my show, so why don't you tell her?"

When Amy nodded, the tears spilled over and streamed down her face.

"Tell me about your angel."

"She was so pretty and brave. She helped me find my meemaw, and she told a fireman to save Mr. Bear for me."

"Had you seen your angel before? Here in town?"

Amy shook her head with such ferocity that the stringy brown hair clung to her face.

He didn't want to break the connection, but he scanned the small town with his eyes. With a population barely over a thousand and the remoteness of this town, he couldn't believe that rescue crews would be on hand so quickly.

"What else do you remember about your angel?"

"She had long hair. It was so pretty and kinda curly." The little girl gnawed on her bottom lip and squeezed her eyelids as if trying to recall everything she'd forgotten about that terrifying day. Suddenly her eyes popped open. Like the sky after a storm passed, her smile was crisp, clean and pure. "I remember! She told me her name." Dimples pierced her chubby cheeks. "Elaina. That's the name of an angel, don't you think?"

Seth smiled at the girl. No doubt it would piss Elaina off if he ever called her that.

And he couldn't wait to do it.

16

One of Elaina's favorite aspects of meteorology was the equalizing effect. No one controlled the weather. The same rain fell on everyone. The same wind blew dirt into the eyes of the rich as much as the poor. The same sun beat down on the backs of women and men alike.

After spending a full day watching the weather radar not comply with her predictions, she wished she could control it. Not to prove to herself that she was right. To prove to her research partner that his faith in her was not misplaced.

Heath sat hunched over his laptop. After several minutes, he groaned a sigh and sat up straight, his popping back making her cringe nearly as much as the few words they'd exchanged since setting up.

She was mad at him for questioning her prediction models.

He was mad at her for being mad at him.

So Elaina had no choice but to be pissed at her partner for being angry at her for being mad at him.

She took a deep breath and hopped off the tailgate of her truck. She wound her torso to the right, studying the solitary oak tree among the golden sea of wheat. A twist to the left and her eyes followed the lolling power lines down the road until they vanished onto the blue-white horizon.

Like a child struggling to ride a bike without training wheels, the atmosphere fought to spin up anything worthy of a tornado.

Research-wise, the trip wouldn't be a total bust. They could collect data, compare it against other systems, and add it to their dissertation.

Personally, Elaina felt the all-too-familiar tug of disappointment churning in her gut. "I'm hungry," she said, needing to fill her gut with something else. "You hungry?"

Heath stared straight ahead at the computer, but she saw a flash of brown from the side of his glasses.

"I'll run into town if you want to stay here," Elaina added.

The rustling of the wheat filled the silence between them.

"My treat. I even promise not to poison it for you."

He snorted before a smile broke across his face. "Fried pickles do sound good. With extra ranch. But if I choke on one or burn my tongue, my blood is on your hands."

"I'll make sure to blow on them." She slammed her tailgate into place. "And cut them into pieces for you."

For the first time since they arrived, her shoulders relaxed and her face rested into a smile. Her truck bounced and rattled over the potholes in the country road. The ballerina hanging from her rearview mirror hopped and pirouetted along.

A few mountainous storm clouds blossomed ahead, but none towered high enough to be an immediate supercell. Those needed a little more heat.

If the rivulet of sweat running from her temple was any indication, they'd get the much-needed fuel. Eventually.

The parking lot of the convenience-store-slash-bait-shop-slash-diner was packed. Ham radio antennas quivered in the breeze, like metal wheat. The maroon van she'd seen outside of Stephenville, the one belonging to Tuck's Tornado Tours, was parked in the ditch at such a steep angle the passengers would have fallen out.

Juice Newton's *Angel of the Morning* greeted her when she entered. Elaina smiled at the memory of belting out that song to her mom when she was little. The thought assaulted her before she chided it. Like moss covering a rock, warm and fuzzy threatened to envelope cold and hurt.

"Afternoon." The man at the register tipped a non-existent hat in her direction.

She followed her nose to the back of the store.

Tile letters clung to a menu board, likely occupying their space long before she was born.

"I'd like an order of fried pickles, a cheeseburger, medium well, a large order of onion rings, and two large sodas," she said to the woman behind the counter.

The heat of the fryer combined with the woman's heavy-handed makeup application made her look like a Picasso painting.

"You got a wooden leg or something?" A gruff voice spoke behind her. A man sat half-perched, half-standing at a bar stool, his gaze focused on the phone in his hand, but Elaina knew he studied her as much as his screen.

"Second stomach." She crossed her arms and widened her stance. "I'm the nasty byproduct of human-bovine gene splicing."

One side of the man's mouth lifted up in a quick smile. "So do they call you Elsie then?"

"Not if they want to live."

The other side of the man's mouth lifted up adding a touch of symmetry to an otherwise uneven face. His nose was like a mountain highway, zigging right before sagging to the left. Wavy gray hair hung down to his shoulders, the ends a faded brown as if clinging to the last remnants of youth. Salt and pepper hair covered his face, not quite enough to call it a beard, but more than enough growth to call him sloppy.

He leaned against the chair and finally met her eyes. The maroon Tuck's Tours T-shirt confirmed what she suspected.

"We could call you Moo-Moo," he said, rubbing the stubble on his chin. "I knew a Moo-Moo once. And, despite the name, she was drop-dead gorgeous. She was crazy though, rumors she caught Mad Cow in the nineties…" His words trailed off as his gaze wandered up to the ceiling.

Elaina sighed and moved to the farthest table to await her order. The hiss and the steam of the deep fryer helped add to the distance she wanted to put between herself and the jerk who'd made callous jokes about women and cows.

She pulled her laptop out of her backpack and studied the radar. Some green pockets of rain were pulling together, but it would take an incredible amount of instability to shape it into a tornado.

I wish I could share some of my instability with the atmosphere.

A deeper, wistful sigh escaped her lips. What if she didn't see another tornado for the rest of the season? What if they had to be content with the data they had? Or, what if she *did* see another tornado and with no new memory?

What if the seepage of visions from the weakening drugs was suddenly stopped, as if psychotropic caulk filled the gaps?

"You're a chaser," the man said.

Elaina looked at him from the corner of her eye.

He was back to studying his phone. Every ounce of her being told her to ignore him, but the ember of curiosity was fanned by his hot air.

"I'm a scientist," she said. "I take it you must be Tuck."

"You say that like it's a bad thing."

"That I'm a scientist or that you're Tuck?"

This time a full-force belly laugh escaped the man's lungs. "You know, those science guys are usually pretty dull, but you, you're different."

She opened her mouth to make room for a smart-ass comment but he cut her off.

"And I ain't talking about the lady parts."

"Tuck, your order's ready." The melted make-up lady screeched over a microphone, even though she could've just called out his name.

He propelled himself off the barstool and picked up the white paper bag, the bottom of it already saturated with grease. "You'll want to set up on FM 586," he said as he gathered three handfuls of napkins. "It'll drop to the southwest."

Elaina flipped over to the online map as he carefully filled his bag with condiments. "That's the wrong way, the tornado would move away from it."

Tuck walked in her direction. His gunmetal blue eyes studied her.

Tested her.

"It's going to turn. Backdoor twister. You drop your stuff and get the hell out of there." He took a long pull from the Styrofoam cup. "Anyway, he who follows conventional rules won't see the end of the day."

The odd man brushed past her, and Elaina felt her heart freeze. The certainty with which he spoke. Familiarity mingled with the foreign. Tuck spoke a truth that lived deep inside of her.

"So if I can't call you Elsie, what can I call you?" Tuck spoke from behind her.

She was still absorbing everything he'd said, and his words drifted by her. Could she convince Heath to decamp, move, and set up again? How would she explain her conviction? Some storm chasing tour operator told her?

"Elaina," the woman spoke over the microphone.

What if he was wrong? What if *she* was wrong to trust him? They could completely miss everything.

No, she had to follow science. Science never let her down.

"Elaina, honey, your food's ready."

She turned, remembering she owed Tuck an answer, but he was gone.

17

During the entire ten-minute drive back to Heath, she contemplated following Tuck's advice and moving positions, but to go where he suggested was a forty-minute drive out of the way.

The sky had grown dark while she'd been waiting for the food. Dark clouds swirled like a boiling soup. When she turned onto the dirt road, the hair on her arms was standing at attention. The air was thick, electric, ready for something to happen.

"You got back just in time, I think we'll have genesis in no time." Heath shouted over the lifting wind. "Are those my pickles?"

Elaina handed him the bag with her cold, forgotten hamburger and now chewy onion rings. Indecision gnawed at her stomach and stole her appetite.

Science said they were right where they needed to be for tornado genesis.

Her gut said there was something different in the air. Perhaps Tuck was right.

Science argued Tuck wanted the "science guys" out of the way for his paying customers.

Gut countered, if that were the case he would've told her nothing was going to happen.

Science pouted and said this guy was nothing more than a carnival barker.

Gut agreed and said maybe, but this guy had spent more time in the field than she had, and nothing beat experience.

Science stuck its tongue out and said shut up.

Movement up the road to her left caught her attention. The blue Forecast Channel trucks moved into position to the northeast. The large antenna rolled into position and Seth hopped out.

As his cameraman got the equipment ready, he studied the sky and twirled a golf club in his fingers.

Tuck's Tours flew past them, heading to the southwest. Elaina's feet shifted, as if they wanted to chase after the van.

"I'm starting to see a bow," Heath shouted over the rising wind. "Seriously, I think something's going to happen right here. Are the pods ready?"

She pulled the equipment out of the back of the van and worked as quickly as her shaking fingers allowed. Storms never scared her, mostly because she always knew with absolute certainty where it was going. But Tuck got into her head. Made her question if she *really* knew what she was doing.

Seth's blue jacket drew her gaze like a moth to a light. He spoke and gestured to his colleague, the man's head covered by the camera on his shoulder. The jacket billowed in the wind.

"Are you ready?" Her partner's voice was insistent and reminded her she was nowhere near ready.

"Um, almost."

"Not almost, *now*."

A piece of the cloud broke off and fell to the ground. Still tethered it sucked and syphoned energy from above. Like a foal learning to walk, the tornado wobbled slightly but then stretched and took its first strong steps.

Elaina's ears popped and her braided ponytail thumped against her back. She reached out to the side of her truck to steady herself. The unmooring reality slipped away like a naughty child hiding from punishment. Something else waited to move into its place. She begged for it, wanting to see what hid in the darkness.

Then, the storm turned.

"It's turning," Heath shouted. "This is fantastic."

Aside from having to squint against the flying dust, they were safe. Her eyes followed the new path of the tornado to its target.

The Forecast Channel van.

"Shit." She ran around to the driver's side and hopped in, ignoring her partner's shouts. She could make it there in thirty seconds. In about fifteen, the storm would hit the Forecast Channel crew.

If her past experiences with Seth were any indication, she'd need that entire time to convince him to move.

Elaina popped the truck into park before it came to a full stop, and ran the short distance to the two men.

Seth's back was to the storm, his blond hair whipping up in one large gelled piece.

She couldn't hear what he was shouting into the microphone over the rising wind, but she was certain he was reveling in his positioning.

"It turned," she shouted as she got within earshot. She was on the cameraman's right side. "You have to move, it turned."

The man couldn't hear her through the wind and camera.

Elaina ran to his other side, but an earpiece clogged his other ear. "Seth, you have to move," she shouted.

His eyes drifted in her direction, but he kept on talking. "This tornado just touched down moments ago. Folks, if you're in the town of Pecan Pass, this is heading in your direction. Take cover immediately."

"No, it's not," she shouted. She glanced in the direction of the storm and felt as if the ground was rolling beneath her. Darkness blended with the gray, the image of a pitch black highway merged with the field in front of her, like the afterburn of a picture.

A flashback threatened the present.

"No," Elaina said to the image.

The tornado grew larger behind Seth. If he turned and saw it, he might think the storm grew, rather than turned toward him.

She tugged at the cameraman's sleeve, but he just waved her off.

A large piece of sheet metal flew several feet behind him, taking flight as easily as a bird.

"It turned, Seth," she took a step in his direction, but the cameraman pulled her back. "Dammit, listen to me!" She broke free of his grasp and strode toward Seth. She could hear him speaking clearer now.

"The winds are really kicking up and my ears are popping." His eyes widened as they focused on her face. "Again, if you are in northwestern Oklahoma take immediate coverage, storm shelter, interior room... Elaina what're you doing?"

"I said the storm turned, you idiot."

All of her frustration, the embarrassing date with Harry, missing the turn of the storm, the lost flashback that might've held the final clue to what was hiding. All of that traveled from her heart to her right fist, which balled into a tight knot, begging for release. When it collided with Seth's cheekbone, there was a gratifying pop and a sting and numbness traveled back down to her heart.

Then everything went still. The air, the wind, Elaina's heart. Had they been sucked into the vortex? She'd been too late.

The field behind them was empty. The storm had vanished back into the sky.

Seth held his cheek, the microphone dangled in his left hand.

"Um, we're still live," the camera guy ducked his head away from his equipment.

18

"You've gone viral," Heath said. His thin shoulders rounded as he sat hunched over his phone.

Elaina's stomach twisted. What an appropriate word. Viral. She felt sick. Contagious.

If Dr. Pierce caught wind of what she'd done on live TV, on live *national* TV, he'd kick her out of school.

She'd be done. DOA.

"Ugh." She slumped deeper over her untouched beer, her nose practically in the foam of the pint glass.

After the sky had cleared, literally, the reality of what she'd done washed over her. Shock rained down on her, Seth, Rick the camera guy…and the viewing audience of the entire country.

An apology bounced around her mouth but never managed to materialize. Tears threatened but rather than let them fall in front of him, she'd run to her truck and sped down the soggy road back to Heath.

His face had been pinched in anger. Her distraction had caused them to miss the drop. This tornado was one of the rare storms that'd turned, and they had little in the data set for it.

Once Heath realized she'd just been trying to save someone, he'd transformed back to her soft-spoken, slightly geeky best friend.

Elaina was ready to head back to campus that evening, but he suggested they spend one more night in the field.

She could use a drink.

Or ten.

The bar was dark and smoky. Perfect for hiding from the rest of the world. A handful of lights cast glowing beams throughout the bar. She'd intentionally chosen the table under the burned-out light.

"It could have been worse," Heath said, soft and teasing, but a quiver of worry trembled his voice.

The vacuum of air from the opening door pulled her attention away from her warming beer.

Seth entered, pausing to shake hands with a few chasers by the door. A raspberry-colored bruise shadowed his right eye.

She groaned and mimicked her partner's slouched posture. "Dying sounds better right now."

The reporter wandered up to the bar. The sea of people waiting for a drink parted, and he was given free passage to the Promised Land. His mouth moved as he reached into his back pocket, but a chorus of shaking heads argued about who would buy his drink.

I risked my life saving his ass, and no one offered to buy me a drink.

Elaina's right hand gripped the glass. She winced as pain flared out and up her wrist. Somehow, she *knew* before she'd hit him that Seth had a hard head.

Heath laughed as he read some of the video comments aloud, but the classic rock tunes from the jukebox drowned out his words.

The worn wooden tabletop was a roadmap of the town's history. Relationships carved in the top were soft to the touch. Did some of these romances last "4 Ever"? Did the children of JM + LP live nearby, visiting this table with their parents to learn the story of how they met?

She wanted to lose herself in the lives of these anonymous vandals. To fall into their stories. Trip over their lives. Barge into family vacations and holiday traditions. Anything to keep her out of the black hole of her future.

Or her past.

Her imaginings of the ghost carvers' lives was interrupted by the thumping of two ice-filled bar cloths as they dropped in front of her.

"If your hand hurts as much as my face," Seth said, sinking into the chair next to her. His shiner looked worse at close proximity. The skin puffed up like a marshmallow and was an ugly mix of reds and blues, with a half-inch-long cut sitting square in the middle. "You're gonna need this."

Heath's phone lit up with Chloe's picture. "Well, I'll leave you two alone."

If they were in a cartoon, dust would've floated in his wake as her friend hurried from the bar.

Seth grabbed his ice bag and held it against his cheek. A long sigh escaped his lungs as he reclined.

Elaina stared at its twin. "So," she said. The cold comfort was too much to fight, and her hand inched toward it. "This is where I say I'm sorry." An icy flame of relief cooled the burning pain of her knuckles, and she matched Seth's sigh with one of her own.

"Are you kidding?" He lowered his ice pack. "My name's trending. The network hasn't had this kind of attention since, well…" His voice trailed off, and he looked down at his beer, arching his neck back again with the bottle at his lips. "Not to mention, you saved my life. Rick's life, too. I'd rather be beaten up by you over a tornado any day." He offered the neck of his beer in her direction.

She clinked her glass against it and took a long drink while letting her gaze float around the bar.

The front door pulled open again, and the man from the convenience store, Tuck, entered through a haze of cigarette smoke. Like earlier, he wore the maroon T-shirt advertising his company, tan cargo shorts, and worn sneakers. He had a slight paunch in his middle, as if in the early phase of growing a beer belly. His shoulder-length hair flared behind him as he strutted toward the bar with a man in a similar shirt and a more advanced beer gut following behind.

How in the world did he do it? He'd called everything about the storm. Where it would touch down, that it would turn. Everything.

Something both drew her to him and repelled him. As if he were filled with magic, but she was afraid it was dark magic. Yet curious nevertheless.

"I feel like I've learned so much about you in just three encounters," Seth said. "You practice yoga. You're getting your doctorate under the direction of a weather god. You have a dog with amazing taste in friends, and you have a mean right hook." He took another drink and squinted his blue-green eyes at her. Or at least the left more than the right since his mouth quirked in a quick wince of pain. "What'm I missin'?" Seth's accent went back to his lyrical roots.

Slow. Southern. Sexy.

Idiot, why did you think that? She shook her head to argue with herself.

"Social media superstar?" Elaina shrugged her shoulders.

"International social media superstar."

"International?" Panic strangled the word.

He pulled his phone from his pocket. "Yeah, you've been mentioned in Canada. We should start a hashtag for you. I was thinking #boxingelaina. Too corny?"

Laughter erupted from her lungs, taking with it fear and panic and embarrassment, leaving in its place relaxation and peace. Sure, her methods had been a bit rash, but she couldn't stand by and let two men be killed.

"You know so much about me," she said. "All I know about you is you're from somewhere in the south, but you mask it when you're on the air."

"Good ear," he smiled. "Alabama, Gulf Shores." He dropped the ice bag he was holding. Seth's gaze darted to a spot above her head, but he wasn't looking at the wood-paneled wall behind her.

"Tell me about it."

"The sound of the waves. It's a heartbeat. Anyone who grows up by the ocean lives by that pulse like our own. And when it's gone, it can feel like death." His gaze floated down from his memory and met hers.

Elaina had never seen the ocean, but she could almost hear the rhythmic rushing, the thud of the waves breaking and the lull as the water was pulled back to sea.

"The air's thick with salt, and while some people hate it, to me it's like being wrapped in a warm blanket."

As if by suggestion, she could feel warm moist air on her bare arms.

"Are your parents still there?"

He took another long pull of his beer. "Grandparents. And, yeah, same house where I grew up."

Elaina opened her mouth to ask about his parents, but he grabbed her good hand. His sudden touch made her feel like a stormy sea, turbulent, full of rushing energy. Her stomach frothed and churned.

"I've always wanted to learn how to two-step." Seth stood and pulled her to standing. "Teach me."

She was afraid her knees would betray her, but she managed to land on functioning legs.

He waited for an opening in the twirling dancers and put his hand around her waist, still holding her left hand in his.

Elaina put her right hand on his shoulder, inches from the matching wound on his face. "Are you sure all your friends in the bar won't think this is another fight?" she asked, glancing at the people trying not to stare.

"As long as they can see your hands we should be good."

They hung on the outer edges of the dance floor, and she showed him the steps.

In no time, Seth picked up the rhythm, and they made one turn around the dance floor with little incident. He guided them deeper into the center of the floor, directing them perfectly among the other dancers, nodding at those who eyed them warily.

More tension released from her shoulders and Elaina felt herself move a little closer to him, her gaze studying his jawline.

He smelled of electricity, the same scent that permeated the air right before a crack of lightning splinters the sky. Electricity and a woodsy scent, with a bit of yeast from his beer tickling her nose.

When Seth's hand tightened on her waist, the voice in the back of her mind awakened.

What are you doing, Elaina? You don't have time for distractions. Research. Memories. Not boys. Focus.

She pulled back slightly, but he didn't release his grip.

The spell he was casting threatened to overcome her.

Elaina turned her head, watching the cast of characters rush by as they circled the small dance floor. Most would glance in their direction briefly before turning back to their conversations and drinks.

Most.

Except for one.

Each time they spun back to the side closest to the bar, she could feel Tuck's eyes on her before she saw him. His expression was blank. If he took a drink, it was a quick sip, not tilting his head back to risk losing the lock with her eyes.

"I have to ask," Seth said in her ear. "Were you and *Harrington* the perfect match?"

The memory of her disastrous blind date swirled around her stomach. Why would he ask if this was just a dance lesson?

Elaina glanced at the space between them, or the lack of space. This wasn't just a dance lesson. Unless she wanted it to be.

Did she? Did he?

"Like dance partners with two left feet," she said. As much as she liked Harry, it just wasn't there.

Seth spun her in two quick turns before dropping her to a dip, his face just inches away from hers. "Good," he sounded a little brighter.

One song ended and a new one started.

Neither made any indication to leave the dance floor. "How did you do it?"

"Do what?" she asked, feeling three steps behind in the conversation, instead of the dance.

"When the twister turned. You had to have known it was going to happen before it did. How else would you have been there so quickly?"

They approached the bar side of the dance floor, this time her back was to it. Tuck was there, she could feel his stare between her shoulder blades.

"Do you see the man at the bar? Mid-fifties, maroon Tuck's Tours shirt? He's the one with the shoulder-length hair."

Seth's chin jutted up. "Yeah, what about him?"

"Know him?"

This time he shook his head. "Seen him around. Why?"

Other scientists would've seized on the praise and acknowledgement that the change in the storm's direction was her call, but Elaina couldn't take credit for someone else's discovery. The thought that someone would steal her work, her intellectual capital made her cheeks heat. There was no way she'd do that to someone else. Even if he just ran a sightseeing tour.

"He told me this afternoon," she said, keeping her eyes on Seth's chin. Her gaze threatened to wander to his lips, but she kept it anchored. "I ran into him while picking up lunch. He told me right where it would drop and where we needed to be because it was going to turn."

Seth's right hand squeezed her even tighter, nearly on the verge of causing her pain, and he fell half a step behind. "How? What type of radar was he using?"

"I don't know. That was the extent of it, and then he was gone."

They'd circled back to the opposite end of the floor.

He spun her, keeping her back to the bar, and his chin lifted again, this time higher, as if he tried to look over the ocean of bodies lying between them and Tuck. "He's staring a hole in you." The warm accent was gone. He was back to his TV voice.

"Yeah, I've noticed."

Seth's chest billowed out, closing the chasm between them. "Want me to go talk to him for you?"

Elaina stopped and he stumbled into her.

"What?"

She dropped her hand from his shoulder and pulled out of his grip. That was all it'd taken. One little sentence with so much weight behind it.

The magic between them broke. The secrets her mother held from her, the deadlines that leered, the embarrassment that burned her, the desire to find out what her mind was trying to tell her all crashed into her with the force of a tsunami.

"What?" the reporter asked again.

"I should've known." She started to push past him, to be out of the claustrophobia of the bar, but he moved in front of her.

"Should've known what?"

"I don't need a fixer, or to be fixed, or to have someone ride in on a white horse to save the day." Elaina's throat strained as she shouted over the music.

"I didn't say you did!" Seth matched her shouting.

A few couples around them stopped dancing, no doubt waiting to see if she'd throw another punch. Others kept on two-stepping, as if a couple fighting on the dance floor happened every weekend. Which it probably did around these parts.

"Of course you did." She raised her voice even more. "And what's sad is you're such a chauvinist you didn't even realize you did it."

"That's ridiculous. I was just trying to help."

"Well, I didn't ask for your help." She lifted her chin and braced her hands on her hips. If she didn't hold on to something, she'd end up punching him again.

"Neither did I, Elaina. Thanks to you, I'm going to be toting concealer around with me for the next two weeks." Seth leaned over her, his mouth just inches from hers, but his eyes were ablaze with anger.

"That will go perfectly with your Kegels." Elaina pushed past him and through the crowded dance floor.

The air outside was cool, dry, and welcoming. She paused and closed her eyes, listening to the muffled sounds of the music, waiting for it to rise with the opening door.

It didn't.

The apology on her lips floated away.

19

T uck wasn't shocked to see Jim Wagner standing there when he lifted the heavy metal garage door. The money rolled up in his pocket would only partially placate the loan shark.

The same way a flake or two of cocaine would hardly appease a raging junkie.

"Mornin' Jimbo," he said before taking a sip of coffee. "I was just about to fry up some bacon and eggs. Join me?"

Jim narrowed his eyes. The loan shark had the strength of a martial arts expert with the smarts of a top-of-his-class Harvard lawyer tightly packaged in five feet and two inches of total badass.

Tuck glanced around the parking lot of his warehouse that doubled as his business office and tripled as his home. He exhaled into his cup.

Jim was alone. Which meant he wouldn't need a believable story and a trip to the ER later that morning.

"You know I hate that name," Jim said. "And I like my eggs over easy."

Tuck led Jim through the garage, casting his eyes up to thank whoever was the Patron Saint of Losers.

"Busy storm season," the guy added. It was a question without the question mark. He had a way of speaking that constantly put Tuck on guard.

Questions were framed as statements. Statements delivered with the authority of two periods. Exclamations were punctuated with a fist.

Lucky for Tuck, his dealings with Jim had mostly been ellipses. Then again, he hadn't been this late on that much money.

"We've had some good groups out in the field," he said, filling Jim's coffee cup. "The retirees are feeling better about the stock market, their pensions are strong, and their tips are generous."

The frying pan hissed when two yolks made contact. He watched as Jim wandered around the open space of his living quarters.

The crumpled bed sheet hung off the futon shoved against the wall. A decade's retrospective in laptops and video equipment was heaped on a bowed particleboard desk. The dirty clothes pile and clean clothes pile commingled in a laundry basket. If he needed to, Tuck could be packed and on the road in fifteen minutes. Pueblo, Colorado was a small enough town that he could escape its city limits in less time than that.

He used this advantage mostly for quickly forming storm systems, but it'd come in handy for starting over a time or two.

Tuck looked around at his meager belongings. Reinvention was a lot like peeling back an onionskin. Superficial layers came off first, but the skin was harder to shed closer to the core. Eventually, the only thing left would be the stinking, slippery center.

"We had this storm the other day." Tuck shoved bacon around the pan. "She dropped down and while all the news guys and science dweebs were following it one way, she turned the other and my group had the most spectacular view."

Jim thumbed through Tuck's bookcase. Secondhand science textbooks gave way to biographies and the occasional true crime novel. "I've long questioned your income ability under this line of work." The loan shark spoke to the books and moved on to the desk.

His heart skipped like a stone across the water. It was common knowledge if Jim asked a question it was as good as putting a bullet in the chamber. Questions were wildcards, and the man only gambled if he could see all the cards everyone else was holding. Tuck hoped his bluff could hold for a little while longer.

"I offer a chance to feel alive. For mankind to put his finger on the pulse of Mother Nature," he said. "I give people a front row seat to life. We've solved all the mysteries, but I give people a chance to find one more thing to gaze at in wonder."

Jim lifted his hand, halting the rest of his argument. "And I gave you this opportunity, did I not?" He bent over and picked up a sweat-stained Tuck's Tours t-shirt, holding it on the end of his finger.

The loopy script of the words made Tuck dizzy, so he stayed focused on the shared *T* of the words.

"I'm impressed. Even if the branding is rather basic." Jim dropped the shirt on the floor and wiped his finger on his pant leg.

Pressure squeezed at Tuck's lungs, forcing the shallow breath out. If it weren't a clear, pleasant day outside he'd swear a funnel was about to touch down.

As the loan shark walked around his living quarters, the man's presence formed ripples in his wake. Everything he touched trembled long after his finger left. Even though he walked with the finesse of a cat, vibrations from his footsteps rattled Tuck's knees.

Grease from the burned bacon sizzled on his wrist. He shoved his hand in his pocket and was reminded of the ace of spades he kept hidden away. He palmed the roll of money from the last tour group.

The tips had been pretty decent, but would've been better if he could've kept his focus on his group and not that brunette.

Tuck watched Jim over the rim of his coffee cup as he drained the final, cold dregs.

The man was alone, but it didn't mean that someone wasn't lurking outside. There were still two more months left in the storm season, and he couldn't damn well chase while recovering from a bullet in the kneecap. Biscuit wouldn't understand.

"Oh, Jimbo," Tuck pulled his hand out of his pocket and

wiggled the wad of money between his fingers. "That reminds me." He tossed the money across the room, which Jim caught with ease.

The man wrinkled his nose at the money, eyeing it and turning it over a couple of times before shoving it in his pocket. It barely covered the interest. Jim knew that.

He knew that Tuck knew that.

"Let's speak frankly, huh," Jim said. "Let's say, you have a tour group about to load up." The loan shark stalked across the room. His ice blue eyes never left Tuck's as he stepped over dirty underwear and delivery pizza carcasses. "You've got one guy on the tour who can't pay, but hey, he's a nice guy, you like him." He shrugged and held his hands out to the side, Christ-like with a devil-may-care attitude. "Hell, you'd have a beer with him if things were different. What would you do?"

"Jim, buddy—"

"How many free seats do you give away on your—what did you call it? Front row to life, I believe."

"It's not that—"

The man leaned up on the Formica countertop, adding another inch to his height that suddenly made him seem like a giant. "But it is *that*, Tuck. It absolutely is *that*."

Tuck shifted and looked up at the ceiling. There was no such thing as a free ride when chasing storms. He'd had a fair share of sob stories. Retirees who were on a fixed income. Cheap dads trying to explain that the price of a tank of gas wouldn't be different if their kid came along for free. Terminal illnesses who wanted desperately to see a twister before they died.

They all were met with a sympathetic face and an equal sob story of him having to take care of a sick parent or a kid needing braces.

"You'd let one of your precious tornados Hoover them right up, wouldn't you," Jim came around the counter and grabbed a handful of Tuck's shoulder length hair. The man's hot breath tickled the inside of his ear. "I want my goddamn money, or they'll find you so bloodied, they'll think a storm got you."

In a swift movement, he shoved Tuck's head down, his face hovering just inches above the crackling bacon.

The heat warmed his face and bubbling grease clung to his beard. One large bubble of grease directly below his eye heaved and bulged.

"Next time you hear a tornado siren…" The loan shark's breath was back in his ear. "Instead of getting a freakish hard-on, I want you to piss yourself, because that means if you don't have my money, you're gonna get sucked right down to hell."

The grease bubble stretched and groaned, and just as it was about to pop, the pressure on Tuck's head was gone. He looked up and watched Jim's back moving to the open garage door.

"I want half of what you owe me by the end of the month," the man said over his shoulder. "And the other half two weeks after that."

A slamming car door jolted Tuck upright.

Biscuit came around the parked Tuck's Tours van, nearly colliding with the retreating little ball of hate.

"Hey, hey Jimbo. You come for breakfast?"

"I fucking hate that name!"

Tuck cringed. There was an exclamation point. He really hoped his best friend wouldn't get shot because of it. Instead, Jim slammed the door of his Mustang harder than necessary and peeled out of the parking lot.

"He's crankier than usual," Biscuit said, helping himself to a cup of coffee. "Hey, so wanted to see if I could get my share from the other day. Got a big date tonight."

His stomach felt like it was filled sand. Sand that threatened to choke him as it bounced up his esophagus. "I had to make a payment to Jim." Tuck burped and acidic coffee burned his mouth. "I'll double you next time, buddy."

Biscuit's chubby face went slack, but he nodded and shrugged. "That's okay. If she's gonna like me, she'd like me anywhere I take her."

His friend's good-natured reply splintered his heart. Borrowing money was the only way he could get his business going, but it wasn't fair that his only employee should suffer because of a slow start.

If only he could get a windfall, something that could wipe his debt to Jim Wagner clean, then he could get ahead.

This time, he'd manage his money better. He'd live on as little as he could, put everything else into savings. He could avoid the tables, tell all the poker games he was out for a while.

Biscuit filled a plate full of burned bacon, but Tuck's eyes watered from nausea, and he had to turn away from the smell.

He studied his bookshelf, a sticker on the spine of a physics textbook shining out at him like a beacon.

There was a reason he couldn't get the brunette out of his head. It wasn't just her heart-shaped face with a slightly off-centered dimple in her chin, or her forest green eyes or thick spirals of hair down her back.

It was the OU T-shirt she was wearing. A perfect match to the textbook staring at him across the room.

Tuck had spent only a little time in a science lab, but he knew for a fact no one would notice an instrument or two going missing. "Eat fast, Bis. We're going to take a road trip to Norman."

20

E laina paused the footage of an EF5 wedge tornado. She'd seen this video, taken nearly ten years earlier in Nebraska, at least a dozen times. The twister was nearly half a mile wide, dropped from a perfect wall cloud, and had stayed on the ground for two hours, crisscrossing country roads and dancing in cornfields.

It did nothing to evoke a flashback.

Aching eyes threatened to stay closed with each long blink, but she fought it with a coffee and energy drink chaser. It was stupid to spend her precious time in the lab chasing ghosts. How did she know these memories were even real to begin with? They could be dreams. Elaina'd had plenty of vivid dreams that never actually happened. Or, maybe she was remembering a show she'd seen. Could it be images from an old, forgotten childhood movie?

She closed the video and slumped in the chair. The white ceiling tiles stared down at her as she swiveled back and forth.

They were quickly approaching the peak of tornado season. Not to mention, the due date for their dissertation. Because of her, they'd missed a whole storm's worth of data. Because of her, they weren't going to have the luxury of a few extra weeks of storm season to check their findings.

Once the atmosphere stabilized, she had a feeling her life would hit serious turbulence.

The chair sprang forward, launching Elaina nose to nose with Seth on the screen. She grimaced as she studied his unblemished face. It would stay that way as long as she didn't hit play. As long as she didn't hit play, she wouldn't see the twister drop down and crawl away from him, only to change its mind and double back on itself. As long as she didn't hit play, Elaina wouldn't watch herself come into the frame and throw a right hook in his direction.

Of course, if he walked into the room, she'd give him a matching bruise under his left eye.

"Forget him," she said to the monitor as she clicked past that video. "No distractions."

No matter how good he smells.

She scrolled through the video library until she found another large and equally menacing storm. This time, she turned the volume of the roaring twister as high as it would go. With her eyes closed, Elaina imagined herself in the field. She could almost feel the piercing sting of the wind as it whipped around her, threatening to peel her skin off. Her ears filled with the jarring pressure shift. She gripped the desk tighter, her quickening pulse thudding in her fingertips.

Like a scared puppy, a faint glimpse of an image peeked out of the corner of her memory. Blurry and sepia-toned, she looked down at a chubby hand holding a gold necklace with a ballerina dangling. Unlike the dancer that hung from her rearview mirror, this one was shiny, new and untarnished. The room spun, not from dizziness but because she could feel her body twirling, arms out as she tried to replicate the on-point stance of the tiny gold dancer. Torn vinyl furniture, a thin Christmas tree, aluminum-covered windows, and a busted-out TV whirled in her mind.

The wail of a tornado siren sliced across Elaina's torso. The coffee and energy drink roiled in her stomach, pelting her with a wave of nausea so strong she had to open her eyes to ground her in the present. Goosebumps broke out on her arms as cold sweat trickled down her temple.

She was back in the dark lab.

Elaina looked at her hand. It was empty. The little necklace she'd long considered to be her good luck charm wasn't hanging from a small fist. It was now hanging from her rearview mirror.

The room with the tree, it was all wrong. It wasn't where she'd grown up. Her mom always had a grand Christmas tree next to the fireplace. Connie never owned vinyl furniture and would never have put aluminum foil over windows.

This was the first memory that grounded her in a place. But *where* was she?

Elaina pieced together what she'd seen so far. A man helping a scared toddler out of a hiding space. The smell of upturned dirt and musky rain lingered long after that image, then morphed into the next. Tucked into a corner in a hospital room, she stared out at cold metal poles guarding her with snaking tubes filled with pulsing liquids. A disembodied voice bounced off the linoleum floor. Shadows stalked beneath the door, pausing then moving away.

She rubbed her temples. There was a stark difference between the first two and the most recent flashback. The first two she'd been afraid. In the new memory, even though she hadn't seen another person as she'd twirled, deep within her heart she felt a presence.

Happiness, joy, and love pulsed from the center of her body. Had she and her mom lived somewhere else? Was there a time in her life she'd been in the hospital? Maybe sick with some childhood disease her mom would rather forget than have to replay every time she looked at her healthy, grown daughter?

As much as she tried to reason that these images were part of her known past, there was still that voice awakened the evening with Harry. She could lie to her friends, her teachers, and her mom, but she couldn't lie to herself.

It knew the truth. The voice stood across a chasm, calling her to come to it, to not be afraid of crossing the narrow, shaky bridge of her mind, but that it was a one-way trip. As soon as she crossed the gap, there'd be no going back.

Elaina couldn't go it alone. She needed to know what was on the other side.

The only person who could tell her was her mom. It didn't matter if Connie tried to avoid her or would clam up tighter than a locked door; she wasn't going to let it go until she got some answers.

What were those images? If they weren't memories, what were they? How far back did they go? And why now? Why did a tornado make them come back?

Her mind replayed Harry's words. Rententamine. Memory rewriting. Experimental.

"Enough," Elaina said through gritted teeth.

She shut down the computers and grabbed her backpack. The forecast was clear for the next few days. A quick trip to her mom's wouldn't coincide with anything bubbling up in the atmosphere.

Quite the opposite. A nice talk with her mom would be as cleansing as a spring rain, washing away the dirt, making everything look new and green.

Or it could unleash a flash flood.

"Shut up," she said as she pushed open the door. A thud boomed through the silent hallway, and the door pushed back at her.

"Oof." A man grunted on the other side.

She peered around the door.

One man leaned against the wall, his head tilted back and blood gushing down his chin.

The other man had his back to her and was talking to him in a soothing tone, pinching the bridge of his friend's nose. "Hold it right there, buddy. I'll get some paper towels for you." He turned, and recognition flashed across his eyes.

Elaina's hands went cold. It was the man from the convenience store, the one who'd told her the storm would turn. The one who'd then watched her every move on the dance floor.

He paused, the muscles of his face working to change his emotions.

"I'm s-so s-s-sorry," she stuttered under Tuck's glare. "Are you okay?"

"I'm fine," the man answered through a very stuffy nose.

"Well, hey there, Moo-Moo. Is this another one of your nasty side effects of cow-human genome splicing?" This time he wore a Hawaiian shirt, but she would've recognized him anywhere. "Super human strength. You might've broken his nose."

"Nah, it's all good," his friend said. The river of blood slowed, and his color was coming back.

"Why don't you go wash up, Biscuit?" Tuck said without taking his eyes off Elaina.

Without a word, he walked down the hall, ducking into the men's room.

From inches away, Tuck looked older than the other times she'd seen him. His face was the color of leather, with wrinkles in the corners of his eyes. The hair hanging down to his shoulders looked unwashed, greasy. A faint yellow colored a patch of fabric on his shirt above the right pocket.

"Elaina," she said, eager to break the silence. "My name is Elaina Adams. Is Tuck your first name or your last name?"

He broke eye contact and looked over her head, blinking twice before nodding. "Neither. Both," he said before taking a deep breath and meeting her eyes again. This time, his gray-green eyes were warm and friendly. "I'm glad to see you minded what I told you about that twister."

She crossed her arms over her chest. "How did you do it?"

He shrugged and opened his mouth to answer, but Biscuit's return cut him off.

The other man's face was wiped clean, but a cut across the bridge of his nose glared at her.

He was the second man she'd disfigured in a week.

"An old storm chaser's secret," Tuck said with a wink. "But really, it was a tail-end Charlie. That south cloud was bound to break away from the herd and raise its own hell."

Elaina nodded as his words sunk in. "What are you doing here?"

"I'm here to see Tom Pierce. I've got a standing invitation to come check out some of his latest toys in the lab. See how the other half lives." He chuckled and cut his eyes to Biscuit.

"Dr. Pierce isn't on campus today, but he'll be here tomorrow. Want to come back then?"

Tuck pursed his lips and glanced down the hall. "Nah, I gotta head down to Fort Worth tomorrow, and I won't be coming through this way for some time." He put his hands in his pockets. Coins clinked together under the rustling of fabric. "Man, he was really excited to show me some of the new equipment y'all just got."

"I have an idea," Biscuit chimed in. "Think she can show us?"

"She's busy, Bis," Tuck's voice was a harsh whisper. "I mean the way she came out of that room, she's obviously running late to something."

Elaina's face warmed. With no window into the hall and a door that opened outward, she should've exited the room slowly, peeking to ensure no one lurked on the other side. She'd been too lost chasing ghosts to pay attention to the world around her.

It could've been worst. Rather than a man with a broken nose, it could've been someone's life.

All because of those damn visions.

"No, no, I can take you down there. It's okay." She pulled her key card from her backpack.

"Are you sure?" Tuck asked. "I don't want to make you late to class."

"I'm a doctoral candidate. I don't have class, just field research." Elaina pointed down the hall. "Come on." She led them down to the basement lab. This late in the afternoon, it was quiet and empty.

"What are you studying?" Tuck asked, his eyes glancing over all the equipment.

"Tornadogenesis. My research partner and I are trying to figure out how far out we can make tornado predictions. Why some storms form funnels and why some don't, even with a strong tornado warning."

"Fascinating. What drew you to meteorology?"

"I don't know. I guess it's just always been there. Thunderstorms amaze me. The power, the electricity that pulses through the clouds.

Driving rain. All of it. And then there's the other part of it, the part that wants to give families as much warning as possible. And not quantity, but quality. We know that if we cry wolf too many times people will start to ignore us."

The old storm chaser glanced up from the various pieces of equipment lining the room. His mouth quirked up to a serene smile, and his chest puffed out. "You've got a good heart, Elaina."

The words were honest and warming, and she smiled back at him, suddenly feeling affection for this odd man with dirty hair, mustard stains, and a friend named Biscuit.

"Uh oh." His friend's voice pulled her out of basking in Tuck's approval. Blood dripped onto the countertop. "I'm sorry."

"It's okay." Elaina rushed to his side, and Biscuit tilted his head back again. "Tuck, you just wait here, I'll run him to the bathroom."

The man mumbled apologies all the way to the bathroom.

She waited outside the men's room, opening the door every few seconds to see if he needed assistance.

When he emerged, pieces of toilet paper hung down from each nostril, and his face was pale green.

"Maybe we should get you to a doctor," Elaina said, walking back into the lab while clinging to the stumbling man.

Tuck jogged over to the other side and took over leading his friend.

"I'm so sorry, let me come with you guys," Elaina said, her stomach gnawing on a ball of dread.

"No, no, we've taken enough of your time. I'll take care of him," Tuck said, not meeting her eyes, but pulling his friend toward the door. "Thanks for the tour."

She followed close behind. "Are you sure? I can come with you guys to the campus medical clinic. Explain that it was all my fault."

"Nah, he just needs a burger and a beer, and it'll be all better." Tuck led them to the elevator, hitting the up button with his elbow.

"I don't think a beer is such a good idea."

The elevator dinged, and the door opened. Tuck pulled Biscuit in and hit the button for the ground floor.

"Do me a favor, Moo-Moo," he said as the door was closing.

"Don't tell Pierce I came by. I'd hate for him to feel bad for missing me. See you in the field." His hand traveled back to the pocket of his shorts. This time, the jingling had a different tone.

21

The warm Gulf air welcomed Seth the moment he stepped off the plane. His sunglasses fogged over, but rather than curse and wipe away the moisture, he closed his eyes and let the salt penetrate his pores. Gulf Shores was as comforting as a gentle mother wiping away tears.

His duffel was light. Armando hadn't fought him when he wanted to take a couple of days off during the storm season, but a missed storm was missed coverage. Missed airtime. People were talking about him, albeit because of Elaina's punch, but he'd take it.

The small airport terminal was quiet. No one to stop him, to ask if it was really him. Again. He didn't have to wear a ball cap pulled down low with dark sunglasses fortifying against the glares, the sideways whispers, and the head shakes of pity.

The old rust-red Chevy was parked at the curb, the silhouette of his grandfather's head visible. Seth couldn't tell if it was a trick of his imagination, or if the great bear of a man sat lower in his seat. Years on the Gulf oil rigs aged a man, and although his grandfather was in his late sixties, he carried himself with the weight of a much older man with a life full of sacrifice. Forced retirement had gotten him back to the shore a few years ago, but not before giving him forearms that would rival Popeye's, deep crevices in his face, and a permanent hunch.

"Hey, Gramps," he said into the open window, while plopping his bag into the truck bed. "Thanks for picking me up."

"Good to see you, son," his grandfather said, his face breaking into a wide grin. "Your grandmother's been worried sick. It'll do her some good to see you in one piece."

Seth hung his arm out the window as they drove home. His fingers flexed and grabbed as if trying to capture the salty wind to bring back on the road with him. Coming home to Gulf Shores always felt like traveling back in time. He saw past the new buildings into what had stood there before, into the glory of the old under the veneer of age. Here he was no longer a thirty-year-old man with more of a past than a future. Here he was forever a teenager with barely a past, an anxious present and the wide-open ocean of a future.

The truck roared once more before Gramps shut if off in front of Seth's childhood home. As a boy, the stilted home loomed over the adjacent canal like a giant, but now it just felt like a home with too many stairs for his aging grandparents.

"Fresh coat of paint?" he asked, admiring the teal green clapboards. "I could've come down to do this for you."

His grandfather waved off his concern. "Paid someone to do it. Marnie won't let me change a light bulb these days."

As if on cue, Seth's grandmother jogged down the steps, her long white braid bouncing down her back. Even though she seemed thin under her clothes, the woman possessed a strength he dared not to challenge.

She tugged him into a tight hug and for the twentieth time that day, his thoughts rushed to Elaina. That was what drew him to the petite storm chaser. She reminded him of his grandmother. Fearless strength and unrivaled beauty.

"You're choking me, Gram." He managed to get out on the last breath of air in his lungs.

"You deserve it," she said. "What're you thinking, going out there in all these dangerous storms live on TV so your poor grandmother has no choice but to watch and worry?" She took a step back and studied Seth's face. With lightning fast reflexes, she pulled off his sunglasses and narrowed her eyes at the shiner. "That little girl did a number on you." His grandmother grabbed his jaw and pulled his face down to her eye level. "I like her."

He sighed. Knowing better than to roll his eyes or argue, admitting he liked her too would only result in Gram spending the entirety of their time together hassling him about making things right. No, he had to hold steady. Seth was here to get his head straight.

"Marnie, how's the boy going to explain that new set of bruises?" Gramp's spoke from behind him.

Gram let go and stroked his face. Her soft, chubby fingers smoothed away the stress and tension that the Gulf air couldn't touch. "Go get settled and clean up. We'll have shrimp and grits for supper."

The smell of simmering spices called to him from the kitchen, but she shooed him up the stairs.

His bedroom was exactly as he'd left it. The faded patch at the foot of his blue plaid bedspread was even more obvious. Years of late afternoon sun hitting that same square had made it almost transparent. A treasure trove of golf trophies held varying shades of tarnish.

Seth sat at his desk and stared out over the canal. On clear days, he could nearly see the oil rigs dotting the southern horizon, but the air was as thick as his head felt. His grandmother had already shown what was on the agenda for dinner conversation.

Elaina.

He just had enough time to prepare for the Q & A.

Seth watched the water flow beneath him and imagined sitting between his grandparents at their modest kitchen table with the wallpaper bubbling from years of moisture. The barrage of questions would be tough, pointed. He had to have his armor firmly in place, or a wild shot might pierce him.

"Who was that girl?"

"Elaina Adams, she's a researcher, studying tornadoes."

"Why did she hit you?"

"She'd been trying to get my attention to tell me the storm had turned. It was headed right for me."

"Wasn't she putting herself in danger herself?"

"Yes, she was, especially because she was set up where it was safe. Elaina put herself in the path of the storm for me."

"She must like you."

"I think so. I thought so. I asked her to dance and it felt like it, but then she got mad at me and left."

"And what did you do, Seth?"

The sun lowered itself into the water of Oyster Bay while he considered his answer.

What *had* he done? He stood there, stared at the door she ran through. The couples dancing around him twirled and spun like a rising tornado, and all he could do was stand in the dizzying vortex.

The winds of emotion tore at him.

Elaina was different.

She was the same as Julia.

They were all just like his mother.

He was afraid that if he looked down he'd see the tattered cloth of conflict covering him.

"Seth, honey, dinner's ready." The conjured image of his grandmother faded away at the real one's voice.

"Showtime," he said to the final burst of the sinking sun.

As predicted, a place was set for him between his grandparents.

His grandmother filled a tall glass of milk at his spot, and his grandfather countered it with a sweating bottle of beer.

He'd been dancing around his grandparents' dueling drinks for so long his eyes teared at the briefest thought. One day he'd come to the table to only one beverage.

Seth dug into his bowl, letting the spices burst on his tongue and warm him from the inside out. After a few bites, he noticed a place setting across from him. An empty bowl sat between an unused fork and a full glass of water. Something else was missing from dinner. Conversation.

Gramps was even more hunched over his food, lifting his body just enough to pull a sip of beer before diving back in.

Gram's loose cheeks were flooded with red, and the color seeped down her neck and faded into the collar of her old denim shirt.

Seth was just about to ask about who they were expecting, when his grandmother got right to her questions.

"How long have you been seeing Elaina?" Gram asked.

His fork quivered, knocking its precious cargo back into the bowl. He expected a warm-up of questions, not going right into the final play. "We're not seeing each other."

"Yet." She stabbed her fork in his direction. "She cares for you or she wouldn't have hit you." His grandmother's tone was tight, as if it were holding something back.

"Let me guess, you had Gramps in a headlock before he asked you out?" Seth turned the charm up to eleven.

His grandfather laughed, his body draping more over his bowl before lifting up. "Nah, boy, she used that rolling pin of hers. First cooking for me, then beating me over the head when I didn't realize that was flirting."

"You lyin' fool." Even though Marnie's lips were tight, her eyes were teasing. "I had to use a rolling pin to fend you off. Still do."

Gramps straightened as much as he could and gazed down the table at his bride.

For a moment, Seth felt as if he'd disappeared, and all that remained was a lifelong love between two people.

That was what he wanted. A love that grew stronger each day. That was what he'd wanted with Julia, but she'd crushed it.

That same desire stirred within him when he touched Elaina, but she'd run from him.

Maybe having that love was just as fleeting.

"Why do you have that place set? Is someone else coming over?"

The warmth between his grandparents iced over.

Gramps hunched back over his food, and Gram's cheeks reddened again.

Only the clinking of her fork and the thud of his beer answered him.

"Lisa's been coming around," his grandfather growled into his bowl.

The hold Seth had on his beer loosened, and the bottle slipped right through his fingers and landed sideways on the table. Amber liquid trickled out, but no one made the move to wipe it up.

"She's cleaning herself up." Gram's voice had the pleading undertone of an argument made more than a few times. "She's been sober for nine months now."

"How is that different than the other times?"

He sat between his arguing grandparents, staring at the empty seat. Of course, it was meant for his mother.

Seth had more memories of her empty seat than her filling it. The Christmas pageant when he was eight and played one of the Three Wise Men. His high school baseball games when he was named All-State MVP at first base. His golf tournaments. Graduation, both high school and college with honors.

The last time he'd heard from Lisa was when she'd called to tell him how much he'd embarrassed her after his on-air meltdown. Rather than list all the times the woman had humiliated him by showing up high, he'd simply hung up and added that call to the long list of blocked numbers.

"She's his mother," Gram said.

"She's the girl who gave birth to him." Gramp's voice climbed to a near-shout. "You're more his mother than she ever could be. We're just lucky she had the good sense to leave him with us."

His grandmother sniffled and stared down at her plate.

Gramps was right, his grandmother had assumed the role of Seth's mother without any hesitation. Lisa had tried, at least that was what Gram told him. His mother had feigned surprise when she'd gone into labor, in the middle of the night, swearing she hadn't known she was pregnant.

Lucky for Seth, his sixteen-year-old mother had held off on the hard drugs and alcohol until after he was born.

Gram had taken care of Seth so she could finish high school, but it'd become obvious quickly his mother was skipping school. She'd started disappearing for days at a time around his first birthday.

By the time he was four, she'd left for months. When he started first grade, his grandparents had completed the paperwork to be named his legal guardians.

Because Lisa had sworn she didn't know she was pregnant, she'd also sworn she didn't know who Seth's father was. He never dwelled on that much, but there was one summer in high school when he'd worked at the local hardware store, and he'd studied every man who came in, hoping to see his green-blue eyes and square jaw.

"When did you see her last?" he kept his words steady and hard.

Gram's gaze darted to her husband before shifting back to him. Her chest heaved as she took a deep breath. "Two weeks ago. She saw you out chasing a tornado and was worried about you. She called after that one storm. Said she wanted to call you, but you keep blocking her calls."

Seth opened his mouth to argue, but his vibrating phone interrupted him. He pulled the phone from his pocket. Someone from the station was calling him.

The weather was clear across the country, and the models showed nothing churning. Whoever it was could wait.

"It's probably because the boy doesn't want to see her."

Years ago the lines had been drawn. His grandparents were on Team Seth, but somewhere along the way, Gram had defected to Team Lisa.

It wasn't that his grandmother was flying his mother's flag; it was as if she'd assumed the role of peacekeeper, eager to draw up a treaty to end the war. Both Gramps and Seth were wary of any promises made by Lisa.

Once again, he began to speak, but his vibrating phone cut him off. Forecast Channel again, but no voicemail was left earlier.

Who in the world keeps calling?

He sent it to voicemail again. He couldn't help it if whoever was on the other line couldn't get the message.

"I'm not the little boy who goes to bed crying when his mom lets him down," Seth said, setting his phone on the table. "If Lisa wants to see me, she can. I just won't believe a word that comes out of her mouth."

For the third time, his phone lit up with his employer.

"This is the third time they've called. I need to take it."

Seth escaped the rising tension of his grandparents' kitchen and went out to the backyard.

The screen door clattered as it bounced off the doorframe. Singing bullfrogs paused briefly, but picked up their chorus.

"Hello?" He turned his back to the kitchen to look out over the dark canal.

"One would think you'd answer a call from the station on the first ring."

The bullfrogs stopped again at the sound of Julia's cold voice coming through his phone.

Could they sense the predator on the other end?

Shrimp, grits and beer churned in his stomach at the sound of his ex. *Great, first my mother, now my ex. If Hitler were alive, he'd probably show up next.*

"What do you want?"

Like boxers between rounds, the station kept them in their corners. Seth adhered to the forced separation, but Julia broke free from her keepers. He braced himself for her first punch.

"Don't be mean."

He could almost hear the pout.

"I wanted to check on you."

"I'm fine, thank you. Goodbye." Seth ended the call. He looked over his shoulder at the battle in the kitchen.

His grandfather gripped the end of the table, and his grandmother was shaking her head.

Going back in where his grandparents fought over his head was less appealing than speaking with Julia.

His phone rang again. "You've just confirmed what I've long suspected," Seth said as a greeting. "You really are a witch."

"Stop being so juvenile."

"Guess you should start dating men your own age." That was a punch below the belt.

Julia was so well preserved no one would have guessed she was twelve years older than him, and she worked hard to keep that little fact from slipping out.

He walked down to the edge of the canal.

The houses on the opposite bank were quiet. Lapping waves slapped the boat docks. He could almost imagine his ex taking a long sip of chardonnay.

"Seth, sweetie, I hurt you. That much is obvious." Julia turned on Miss America voice, clear, confident, warm and endearing with a baseline of I-will-claw-your-eyes-out. "When I saw how close you came to… It's so dangerous out there, even without obsessed fans attacking you during a stand-up."

A slamming door pulled his attention away from the dark canal and even darker ex-girlfriend.

His grandfather shuffled down the steps and hopped in his red truck.

Gram braced herself at the sink, the crown of her head staring out the window at him.

How had their argument escalated so quickly? Unless it wasn't a new argument, but the continuation of an old one.

Seth started back toward the house, nearly forgetting that he still held a phone to his ear.

"It made me realize what a good thing we had," she continued. "I miss that. I miss you. Us."

He stopped and looked at the phone. Yep, the number was still the station.

"You're working late, Julia."

"You blocked all my numbers."

That really was his favorite feature on his phone.

"Look, I can't talk right now."

"I screwed up, Seth." Her words were running together. The bottle must be half empty by now.

"No, Julia, you screwed Benjamin. With your mic open. While I was on the air."

He could still hear the sounds.

Julia had excused herself from the control room for a bathroom break. At first, he'd thought it was a joke, but then he heard that little moan in the back of her throat. Seth was the only one who could do that to her.

Thank God someone in the control room had cat-like reflexes, or he would've had the FCC on his back once he'd entered forbidden words territory.

A little voice in the back of his head had told him it was a bad idea to date his co-anchor all along.

He needed to give that little voice more credibility in the future.

"Please give me another chance."

"Another chance to do what? Ruin what's left of my career?"

"You're not being fair."

He drew his arm back, ready to chuck his phone into the canal, but he took a deep breath and tightened his grip.

"What's not fair is listening to you screw another man while I've got a camera on my face. What's not fair is me taking the fall for calling you a slut in front of all of America when we both know damn well that was the nicest thing I could say about you." Seth turned back to the window and watched his grandmother wipe tears from her eyes.

What's not fair is watching Gram's heart be broken by her daughter time and time again.

"Don't ever call me again, Julia. If you see me at the station, pretend I'm a ghost."

He switched his phone off and went inside to comfort the woman who'd raised him.

22

E laina watched the sun come up in her bright living room. The tea in her cup had grown cold over an hour ago, but she didn't notice. Sleep avoided her as much as *she* wanted to avoid the impending conversation with her mom.

But she couldn't.

A door opened. A peek inside, and suddenly she saw her world through a kaleidoscope. Fragmented. Distorted.

Confusing.

She kept refreshing the weather models on her computer, begging something to show instability in the air. Anywhere.

Anything to give her a reason to avoid driving to her mom's house and asking her questions she wasn't sure she wanted to have answered. Could she handle another turn of the kaleidoscope?

During a final refresh, an email from Dr. Pierce flashed across her screen.

Elaina,

Can you join me in my office this morning?

Great. Not necessarily the instability she was looking for. She'd made it three days since the storm that'd turned. Being summoned was bound to happen sooner than later.

"All right Nim," she said as her dog stretched. "Quick stop by the school, and then we have to go see Mom."

The campus was bustling when she arrived. The final stretch of the semester. A frantic energy pulsed among students and teachers hurrying between buildings.

Elaina's heart pounded against as she walked to the building.

Nimbus slinked beside her, his long body close to the ground. Tense, as if he was ready to spring into action at the first sign of his owner's distress.

She crawled up the stairs. Heath wouldn't have betrayed her. Then again, he didn't need to. Clips on replay across the country showed her leaving her post, her partner. Abandoning her research, her career. Punching a minor celebrity.

His office door was open. Darkness poured out into the bright white of the hallway. Quick, sharp strikes of the keyboard clicked a melodic beat.

With a deep breath, she propelled herself the final two steps into his office. "Hi, Dr. Pierce." She tried to make her words light and carefree, but instead it sounded squeaky and tight, as if it were held together by a stretched-too-thin rubber band. "You wanted to see me?"

"Elaina. Good. Yes, sit." Her advisor darted his eyes in her direction, then shifted them back to the computer. "Give me one minute."

The key strikes sounded more like gunfire at close range.

She busied herself with picking at the hem of her *Back to Your Regularly Scheduled Madness* T-shirt. It felt like the most appropriate shirt for today.

"Okay," he said. The light from his computer monitor cast strange shadows behind his glasses. "Sorry about that. Thank you for coming in on short notice." He wheeled around his desk, but stopped at the side rather than come beside her.

Judging by the two feet of wood between them, she was in serious trouble.

"Of course. Anything I can help you with?"

"How are you doing, Elaina?" Dr. Pierce's voice was disarmingly warm, genuine.

"I, uh, I'm good." Her words tripped over her tongue. "How are you?"

He rolled forwarded another foot and into the light streaming in from the hallway. "This is a critical time. I've seen many students falter right here. Doctoral studies are not a sprint. It's a marathon. A very hard one, with unexpected twists and turns. This is not for the weak, mentally, physically, or emotionally."

Was he calling her weak? Had he just questioned her emotional wellbeing? Her mental state had never been up for discussion in the past.

"I know. I've been preparing for this since I was an undergrad. Even when I was in high school."

"There's no playbook for being in the field." His words struck like his fingers hitting a keyboard. "It takes one hundred percent focus. Dedication. Without it, you'll have failure."

Elaina's heart plummeted, but her rising anger caught it. *Failure* was never a word used in her presence. All the nights spent studying, chasing storms, forgoing the typical college rites of passage, that was not for failure. Dr. Pierce knew that. He was mad.

But he was also right.

"I know why you're angry. I couldn't let them get hurt." She straightened her spine and scooted to the edge of the chair.

"And I commend you for that, despite the fact that our university president was less than thrilled to have one of his own known more for her brawn than her brains."

"Desperate times…" She shrugged. She wasn't going to let him take her down the path of self-doubt and regret.

The storm had turned. Elaina had made the decision to warn Seth, no matter what would happen next. It was a decision she'd defend for the rest of her life. Even if he had another punch coming to him.

"Yes, yes," Dr. Pierce waved her off. "I know what you see out there. The toll it can take when you're watching Mother Nature's monster come crashing down on someone's home and family. I know what lies in the vortex, possibly better than anyone else."

His words were likely meant to console and encourage, but instead doused kerosene in the pit of her stomach and idly tossed a match on it. Flames licked up from her belly and warmed her neck.

What would he say if she told him what she'd seen in the storm? In that fleeting glimpse of whirling winds and damaging debris, Elaina had witnessed a past that didn't exist but felt as real as the ground she stood on. Images and feelings blurred together like a nightmare she couldn't wake from.

Dr. Pierce saw what was superficial in the storm. He could never understand what *she* saw. Even if she attempted to explain it, he'd send her directly to the campus medical clinic, suggesting an overzealous workload had contributed to her delusions.

"I thought you would understand," Elaina said. "Of all people, I thought *you* would get it."

He blinked. Half of his face was flooded in light, the other half hidden in the darkness of the office. In the bisection, he looked complete, as if the two opposing sides made one convincing whole.

Who was he? The question whispered to her from a corner in the depth of her mind.

Who are any of us but the sum of our lives until that very moment?

Sitting in his dark office sliced by fluorescent light, Elaina saw Dr. Pierce for who he was, a brilliant man who'd become a completely different person in a shattering second.

Did everyone have that shift? That moment when everything changed and they ceased being who they were, and become who they would be? Had Elaina's happened earlier in her life? Or was it happening now?

She glanced down at his immobile legs. Dr. Pierce would never run again. He'd never climb the two flights of stairs to his office. Feel the sun on his calves.

How much did he yearn to go back? Was it selfish of her to want to go back to that moment? To understand what *she'd* lost? Would digging to her foundation cause everything else to collapse?

"Do you miss it?" As soon as the words were out, she wanted to draw them back. It was the circus elephant in the room. Flaunted when he controlled the message but avoided by all others.

Her advisor turned his face away, first staring into the darkness before whipping his head toward the light. "Very much." His voice trembled before he cleared his throat. "And that's why I want *you* to be careful out there. All it takes is one one-hundredth of a second. One mistake and you are forever changed."

The fire in Elaina floated up to her eyes, tears threatening to douse the welling emotion.

"You're special, Elaina. Storms speak to you in a way I've seen in no one else. Warning Seth Maddux, yes, that's exactly why you're out there." He looked down at his legs, gazing at them with the detached curiosity of a cat with a bug. "I'll have to let you go one day. Sooner than I'd prefer, but until that moment, bear with me as I serve as your concerned professor." An easy, relaxed smile crossed his handsome face.

Waist up, Dr. Tom Pierce was still the good-looking, charismatic tornado expert he'd been before the accident. Yes, his life had shifted in a direction that was unforeseeable, but it didn't change who he was.

They smiled at each other, sharing a moment of student and teacher, mentor and protégé, the future and the past.

Dr. Pierce cleared his throat again, more to break their spell than to make a path for words. "Well, then," he said, maneuvering his chair back behind his desk. "That's all, Ms. Adams."

Elaina took a deep breath and gathered her backpack. She stood and started for the door before a thought struck her. "Oh," she said, whirling around. Even though Tuck told her not to say he'd dropped by, it was worth mentioning so her professor wouldn't think the man had ignored his invitation.

Dr. Pierce looked up from his computer. "Oh."

There was the awkward pause between two people who'd spoken at the same time.

Elaina motioned for Dr. Pierce to speak and his gaze darted back to his computer screen.

"Were you in the lab three days ago?"

Her knees loosened, and her heart skidded to a stop. Three days ago, she'd been watching videos in the media library, trying to force another vision. Why was this even a question? "Yeah, I was in the media library looking at some old storm footage." Elaina was surprised at how clear and strong she sounded, because her heart pounded with the ferocity of a hail storm. "Why do you ask?" She knew why he asked, but was afraid if *she* didn't ask, it'd be a sure sign of guilt.

"A circuit board from one of the pods came up missing. It wasn't large, probably just got misplaced," he said, his eyes still focused on his computer screen and his fingers tapping away with the rhythmic rapping of a rainstorm. "Your ID was used to get into the lab. Thought maybe you'd noticed something...off."

She'd never tried so hard in her life to be normal. *Breathe in, breathe out. Don't tremble. Blink naturally. Swallow back that rising tide of guilt.*

That little voice of intuition, the one that told her which cluster of water vapor would mingle with cold air to produce a storm, the one that told her the images she saw in tornadoes were real enough to upend the relationship with her mom for answers, told her Tuck was no long-lost friend of Dr. Pierce's.

"Yeah, I was looking for someone. Just ducked my head in."

"Did you see anyone in there?"

She smiled and shook her head.

Her advisor leaned forward, his strong forearms resting on his withered legs. "Elaina, you know if you need anything...If money is an issue..."

She was far from rich. Barely clinging to middle class if truth be told, but money was never an issue.

The air in the office tightened. What was going through Pierce's head? Did he think she was a junky? Spending money on uppers to keep her going through to the end? "I've gotta run. Going to see my mom." Elaina fled his office without a glance at her mentor's disappointed eyes.

She waited until the violent tapping of his keyboard receded before she broke into a run. Never in her life had she felt so duped, vulnerable, used.

When she burst out of the door of building, Nimbus jumped up from his patch of sunshine and whined.

It was time for Elaina to take back control, and it didn't matter who had to be shoved out of the way.

23

T he sweat trickling down her neck did nothing to cool Elaina. If anything, it only made her that much angrier. Did Pierce accuse her of theft?

Who did he think he was, telling her she wasn't mentally strong enough to finish her dissertation? Had Tuck sought her out for the sole purpose of stealing from the school? Or, was that a bonus for her accidentally breaking his friend's nose? Was all of it an elaborate plot, or was it just more of her own messed up cerebral cortex that caused her to draw conclusions with the accuracy of a clumsy toddler?

With each question she mulled over on her drive to her mom's house, her foot pressed a little harder on the accelerator, driving her closer to the biggest question.

What was locked away inside her mind?

Nim hung his head out the window, his long tongue flapping in the wind as she sped down the dirt road.

The late spring sun was high overhead when Elaina pulled up to her mom's house.

She parked her truck behind her mom's SUV and hopped out with Nim following close.

They both hesitated. She looked down at her dog, and he looked up at her.

Something was off. They both could feel it. Nimbus lifted his nose higher into the air, sniffing big gulps of scent before turning and trotting to the open gate of the pasture.

Lucky for Connie and Elaina, none of the small herd of cattle seemed to notice the open door to freedom.

"I got it, Nimby," she said, latching the gate close. "I'm not sure what Mom was thinking."

Her footsteps seemed louder than usual, as she climbed up the large wooden porch. The anger that'd boiled in her body since leaving Dr. Pierce's office burned down to a small, smoldering pit of ash sitting heavy in her stomach.

Connie usually met her by now. No matter what she was in the middle of, hands covered in dirt, kitchen caked in flour, boots heavy with muck, all of it was worth interruption to greet her daughter.

"Mom?" Elaina called. "Are you here?" She stepped all the way into the house and was hit by blowing cold air. Goosebumps broke out on her arms and a 7.0 magnitude shiver rocked her entire body.

Elaina trotted to the thermostat. Connie had it set at fifty-five. It was definitely one of the warmer days so far this spring, but the temperature had still not crested the mid-eighties.

"Nimbus, where is she?" Before her dog could answer, Connie's voice came through the wall from the family room.

"Elaina? Is that you, honey?"

Her mother was sitting up from the couch. One side of her braid had pulled loose and her cotton shirt was rumpled.

Had her mom been napping? To her knowledge, Connie had endless energy from sunrise to sunset.

"It's freezing in here. Are you feeling okay?"

Connie's eyes were unfocused and her gaze swept the room before settling back on her. "Yes, I'm fine. A bit warm and tired today. Probably a little spring cold is all." Her words were slow and thick, as if they traveled through quicksand to reach Elaina's ears. "What're you doin' here?"

She exhaled when her mom took three confident, strong steps in her direction.

She's a nurse. If it's anything more than a cold, she'd know.

The answer sat on Elaina's tongue next to the argument and accusations. They sat there, but like little kids at the top of the high dive, they were afraid to leap. The pool could be deep, warm and inviting, or empty and decayed. "I, uh," she started, but the words scrambled back down her throat.

Connie wrapped her in a quick embrace and she inhaled the scent of her mom's apple spice shampoo. "You *are* freezing," she said, rubbing her hands on her Elaina's arms. "I guess I went a bit overboard with the thermostat. Let's get some hot tea to warm you up, and let's catch up."

She followed her into the kitchen and braced against the counter while Connie filled the teakettle.

This woman was no Judas. She was a saint who as a single woman adopted and raised Elaina.

Who was the real Judas?

The tea canister fumbled in Connie's fingers.

Elaina reached for it, popping it open with ease, trying to ignore her mother's murmuring about getting older and needing to be checked for arthritis.

The water in the kettle bubbled and boiled like the apprehension in her stomach. If she didn't do this now, she'd just go home filled with remorse and resentment. Rip off the Band-Aid, that was what Connie would tell her. Just say it, lay it out there and see what happened.

It may not be that bad.

Then again, it could be worse.

The shriek of the kettle signaled it was time.

"Mom, something really strange has been happening to me, and I really need your help understanding it." Elaina didn't look at her as she spoke. She studied her shoes and the tiniest crack in the linoleum running between her feet and under the fridge. As a girl, she often traced that line with her finger, imagining it opened to a magical world under their house filled with fairies and unicorns. She wished she could fall into that world now.

When Connie didn't answer, she dragged her gaze from the floor to the counter and her mom's trembling hands. Water sloshed out of the cup and onto the counter, steam rising in the cool air.

"Here, let me." Elaina reached for the kettle and finished pouring. "You sit I'll clean this up. Are you sure you're fine?"

"Yes, yes, just a bit worn down with this cold." Her mom took a quivering sip of tea. "You were saying…"

She took her own sip, hoping to warm her vocal cords for the words to pass. "Have you heard of Rententamine?"

Connie's mug landed on the table with a soft *thud*, splashing hot tea over the side and onto her hand.

"You have, haven't you?"

"I've heard of a lot of drugs in my day." Her mom wiped her hand on her shirt. Her voice had changed. The motherly warmth from just a few minutes ago frosted over into sharp edges.

"Over the past few weeks, I've had visions, out in the field when we're chasing storms."

"Elaina, I've told you, I don't want to talk about you out there in the storms. It worries me." Connie pushed herself from the table and reached for the cupboard beside the sink. Bottles of medicine kept company with spices, and her mother rummaged through them all until she found the one she was looking for. "Can we talk about this later? My head is splitting." This time her mom made several attempts at flipping the cap off before succeeding.

"No." As much as Elaina wanted to give in to her mom, half the Band-Aid was peeled off. She couldn't put it back on. "We're going to talk about this now."

Connie slammed the open bottle on the counter and white pills rained down, pinging on the counter like hailstones. "Why, Elaina? Why are you doing this?"

"Because I have to know. I see stuff, when I'm out there, in the tornado."

Her mother flinched, as if struck by her daughter's words, but it only fueled her anger. Despite Connie's obvious distress, her own far outweighed anything her mom was experiencing.

"I see a man standing over me, finding me after a storm, except it's me as a child, during a time I should've been here with you." She paced, as if the argument needed to take up more space than the little corner of the kitchen where she stood. "And then I'm in a hospital, and I'm scared, except I was never in the hospital. Was I? But it feels so real, it's like watching something through a sheer curtain. It's there. I can see it, but there's a haze over it."

Elaina stopped her pacing and her chest heaved. Wild exhilaration coursed through her veins. Adrenalin, combined with finally getting to say everything built up inside her, made her feel lighter, almost giddy. Laughter threatened to burst from her lungs, but she swallowed it back with a big inhale. "Mom, you're the only person who can help clear the haze." Her voice was softer, gentler now. "That's why I'm doing this."

Connie was a statue in front of her. The web of blue veins under her vellum skin seemed more noticeable, as if her mother were made of parchment.

Then she saw it. The corner of her mom's left eye drooped. With it, her cheek sagged, and the left side of her mouth turned down, like a sad-faced clown.

The parchment withered. Before her eyes, Connie was melting.

Her mother's lips moved, as if trying to grasp the words on her tongue. "You were so tiny. So scared. Forgetting was the only way —" Connie swayed and reached for the counter, but only her right hand made purchase. Her left arm jerked up only slightly before falling back at her side.

"Mom!" Elaina braced herself under her mother's left side, fighting against her full weight to keep them upright. "What's happening? Tell me what to do."

Her mom's head lolled back, her eyes searching for something on the ceiling. Her tongue moved back and forth, as if trying to shape words, only to have them slide back down her throat.

Her mother's weight grew heavier, and Elaina's own knees loosened too. A fast, heavy pulse thumped in the kitchen, maybe her own, maybe her mom's.

They both went down.

The sharp corner of the cabinet cut into her back as she braced her mom, clinging to her, doing whatever it took to absorb the impact of the fall. Pain shot up from her tailbone when they landed. She cradled her mom against her chest, rocking her, whispering apologies.

She'd never lived inside her mother's body, but when she was little, she'd tried to make her own heart beat at the same strong rhythm of her mother's.

Now, Elaina hoped the beat of her own heart could carry her mother just a little further.

24

The tinkling fountain in the corner was meant to calm nervous families. To call up images of tall grass blowing gently on a warm day next to a bubbling creek. It was intended to break the hushed silence so lurid that ears would ring just to ensure they still worked.

All that thing succeeded in doing was making Elaina squirm against the pressure of her overflowing bladder.

There must be a chapter in an interior design textbook on how to decorate a hospital waiting room. Muted colored chairs, comfortable yet not too cozy. A machine belching out bad coffee.

The TV with chipper talk show hosts, the audience on a hushed laugh track. A piece of thought-provoking, yet non-offensive art.

And the damned fountain.

But she couldn't leave. Not even for a bathroom break.

The doctor had promised he'd be out with an update as soon as possible. After four hours, *soon* had to be getting close. And if he came out while she was gone, who would he update?

There was no one else. They only had each other.

Elaina leaned her head back on the chair and let another round of tears pool. It would be great if her bladder was tied to her tear ducts, and she could just cry it out.

Grit still coated her face and neck from when the medical helicopter had taken off, leaving her alone to watch the diminishing vessel carrying her mom.

Once she'd realized her mom's heart still beat and her lungs filled with air, everything had laser-focused clarity.

Her cell phone was close at hand in her back pocket. She'd told the 9-1-1 operator her mother likely had a stroke, and they quickly dispatched transport to take her to Oklahoma City. No matter how much she begged, there'd been no room for her in the helicopter. Connie had looked alien, pale, listless, shrunken, as they rolled her past Elaina.

Why did she have to do it? It could've waited. She could tell her mom was sick, but she chose to push it. Her selfish drive to understand what was behind the visions had blinded her to the fact that her mom was ill.

Connie was lying in a hospital because of Elaina, and for all she knew, her mother could have exhaled her last breath, forever having the angry accusations as the final words to penetrate her brain.

She balled up a fist and pounded her thigh. Pain rattled her bone.

Good. I need to hurt. I need to look as ugly on the outside as I am on the inside.

Elaina switched to the other thigh, beating it with the same ferocity.

The whoosh of an opening door jolted her upright.

Heath paused before catching her gaze and running toward her.

She attempted to stand, but when her boots hit the floor the pain of a thousand needles flared through her feet.

"I'm so sorry." Her partner pulled her into a tight hug, holding her up long enough for the stinging to subside. "Can I do anything?"

She inhaled her best friend's scent, a musky shampoo with his cinnamon gum topped off with the lightest touch of Chloe's perfume, as if the tiniest notes of it clung to him after her hug and kiss goodbye that morning.

"Nim?" She'd had nearly forgotten about her other best friend.

He was scared away by the helicopter.

It was only when she'd looked up in her rearview mirror, and saw him sprinting after her truck that she remembered he'd been with her. That was the second layer of guilt, the thought of accidentally abandoning her dog.

"I already asked Chloe to pick him up on her way home." Heath pulled back and held Elaina at arm's length, studying her through his thick glasses. "You look like hell. Why don't you go wash your face? I'll wait here for the doctor."

In the bathroom, she accommodated her throbbing bladder and studied her reflection.

On the outside, she looked mostly the same, but she felt the beginning stages of a metamorphosis bleeding through. Her jade green eyes were cushioned in purple pillows. Long wavy hair was tangled in a mess that had begun the day as a simple braided ponytail.

A fine layer of red Oklahoma dirt covered her olive complexion, with parts washed away by tears.

No one who knew her would see the monster that lurked inside. The ugly beast that had driven her mother to a stroke by asking questions better left unanswered.

She had wanted to know who she was.

Elaina looked away.

The answer stared back at her, but she wasn't ready for it.

When she returned, Heath stood next to a man in faded aquamarine scrubs. Her friend had one arm crossed, the other covering his chin and lips.

The doctor's back was to her, so whatever words were leaving his mouth and entering her best friend's ears was as hidden as his reaction.

When Heath saw her, he dropped his arms and a faint smile brightened his face, as if to coax her to join them.

"There are two things that a trip to the bathroom will cause, the waiter to bring your food and the doctor to come see you." Elaina tried to stretch her lips into a smile, but the gesture felt as inappropriate as her joke.

"You must be Elaina."

He was younger than she'd imagined, but his eyes carried the exhaustion of a man who had lived many more years.

"I'm Dr. Parker. I've been taking care of your mother since she arrived."

"She's okay?" She needed to know if her world was blown off its foundation, or if something still stood, no matter how cracked or warped it may be.

"She's stable, breathing on her own, and her heart's steady and strong." The doctor paused, as if giving her time to absorb the good news. "Connie had a substantial stroke, and from the scans, I think she had some smaller ones recently leading up to this, although she likely saw it as just migraines coupled with exhaustion and forgetfulness."

Her breath hitched, and her eyes watered. She should've been there earlier, not to confront her mom but to just thank her for the life she'd given her. If she had been there, she would've noticed the headaches, the tiredness, and even the absentmindedness. "I should have…" Elaina whispered.

There were too many should haves to list.

"Actually, your mom is alive because you were there," Dr. Parker said, as if reading the guilt written across her face. "We have her in a medically-induced coma, so we can let our medicine do its job. We'll keep an eye on her, monitor for any changes. The good news is, at this point, I don't foresee surgery so she only has to heal from the stroke."

She nodded, shaking loose the knot in her throat. "Stroke," she said, repeating the word, even though it'd been uttered more than a few times. "That can be debilitating." She took another deep breath, building up to ask a more loaded question. "Will she walk, talk?"

"Unfortunately, we won't know the extent of the damage just yet." His voice was soft and apologetic. "There's only so much we see in a scan. Until Connie wakes up, we would only be making a guess." He glanced at the buzzing phone in his hand, tapped a quick reply, and slipped it back into his pocket. "Get some rest tonight, we'll call you if there's any change." Dr. Parker retreated with quick, smacking steps down a hall, closed off by heavy pneumatic doors only opened with the magic of a key card.

Her mom was safe, protected from her.

Had Connie muttered final instructions before slipping away into a deep sleep? Had she begged the doctors and nurses to keep her demon daughter away from her?

"Pierce will understand if you want to take a break." Heath squeezed her shoulder.

Elaina felt hollow under his touch. If he squeezed tighter, she might crumble, turn to dust and blow away in the wind.

Without her studies, without her storms, she'd be completely empty inside.

"No," she said. "I'm going to do this. I have to do this."

They stood there for several long seconds before Elaina worked up the energy to speak again.

"I think I'm going to go home soon. Do you mind calling Chloe? She doesn't have to worry about Nimbus."

His grip on her shoulder tightened before leaving her completely. "Are you sure? We don't mind taking care of him."

"Thank you, but I think I need him right now."

Heath nodded. He pulled her into another tight hug and pressed his lips to her forehead. "Get some rest, and call us if you need anything."

The trickling fountain drew her to its corner. It was a fairly simple design. Galvanized brass stood between two endplates with large river stones frothing the water at the bottom. Man's attempt at creating a waterfall, capturing the essence but losing the spontaneity of nature.

Acting on their own, her fingers reached out to interrupt the water's rivulets. It was cool, the brass backdrop was slick. Water splashed up her arm as Elaina mindlessly traced figure eights.

One loop. She was a traitor for demanding something her mother couldn't give her.

Another loop. Or could she?

Had Connie been about to tell her everything she needed to know before a weak vessel in her brain had called it quits?

Forgetting.

That was the last word her mother had spoken to her. So was that what the images were? Were they her body's attempt at remembering?

She plunged her entire right hand under the electric waterfall, splashing water on her shirt and the floor. She couldn't hover on the surface, seeing what was below but not diving deep to capture it. Her left hand joined the right, disrupting the water even more, driving large currents of water onto her jeans.

Elaina jumped at the sound of the fountain's motor, whirring and choking like a fish out of water. Only a few drops remained. Most of the water covered the front of her clothes; what wasn't on her pooled on the floor around her feet.

She'd already gotten wet. Made a mess of everything. There was no other option but to jump right in, dive into her work, finish her dissertation.

No matter how dark the waters and what kind of creatures lurked there, she had to uncover who she truly was.

25

The rising sun burned Elaina's eyes. It was the first one her mother was not awake for, so she had to catalog every changing hue, how the sun peeked over the eastern horizon, like a shy child making sure it was safe to come out.

The deep blue sky turned into purple. Streaks of orange danced with pinks. One last star winked goodbye before letting the sun have center stage over the empty parking lot.

She had to remember it all so she could tell her mom what she missed when she woke up.

If she wakes up.

Elaina reached into the paper bag next to her and pulled out another chocolate donut. Her legs dangled off the tailgate, swinging so quickly she was afraid her boots would come flying off.

Sugar, guilt, exhaustion, caffeine, adrenalin, and determination coursed through her veins.

If the drugs made her forget, there had to be drugs that could make her remember.

A lifetime of tornadoes might never show her what she needed to know. She'd never have to bring it up to her mom ever again. When Connie woke up, it would be as if it never happened.

She could fix this.

Sitting outside Harry's clinic waiting for him to arrive was the first step to repairing the hole in her soul.

Elaina peered into the bag. There was one donut left, and the coffee she'd picked up for him was growing cold. From Chloe, she'd learned Harry was one of the first to arrive, but she probably meant after sunrise.

Just as she reached in for the last donut, headlights swept across the parking lot and a navy blue BMW swung into the parking spot next to her.

"Elaina?" His accented voice had the measured tone of someone trying very hard to act normal. "This is a surprise."

She jumped off the tailgate and held out his coffee and donut. "I brought you coffee and donuts. Well, *a* donut. I ate the rest. And your coffee might be a bit cold, but if there's a microwave inside I can warm it up for you." Elaina looked down at her chocolate covered fingers. "Oh, sorry, I think I got chocolate all over your cup." She gasped. "But you're British, I bet you drink tea. I don't know why I didn't think of that. I could get you some." The words were a crutch holding her upright. If she stopped speaking, she'd breakdown right there in the parking lot.

Harry held up his thermos, and his eyes scoured her face.

She could see him running through the diagnosis in his head.

Rumpled clothes worn for twenty-four hours. Once-braided hair filled with grit and oil. The muscles around her eyes twitching, begging to close but propped open by too much coffee.

Elaina hoped he'd hear her out before calling for the straitjacket.

Finally, his body relaxed, and he exhaled. "Something's wrong."

"I need your help." The words hurt as they squeezed through the lump in her throat.

Harry turned his head. His face was illuminated orange with the rising sun, and the muscle in his jaw flexed and loosened. "I had a feeling I'd see you again." He spoke to the sun. "And not in the way I'd hoped. Come on, let's go inside where we can talk."

He gathered his briefcase and led her into the two-story clinic. He deactivated the alarm system while Elaina studied the lobby.

Indoor trees sat potted in corners next to muted colored chairs with lamps offering illumination instead of harsh, overhead lights. It was warm and cozy, a good place for people to relax before they had to crack open the scabs over their psyches.

"Follow me." Harry gestured over his shoulder. He flipped on lights as he led her down a narrow hallway.

Closed office doors gave the names of his colleagues.

When she passed Chloe's, a nervous chill wrecked her body. How would she explain her presence?

In his office, Harry's movements were precise, automatic. He booted up his computer and clicked on lamps.

Elaina took a deep breath. Mentally, she flowed into a sun salutation, feeling her body reach overhead to welcome the day. She inhaled peace, patience, grace, and tried to exhale anger, guilt, fear but her breath hitched in her throat, and she burst into a coughing fit.

Anger, guilt and fear weren't giving up that easily.

The psychiatrist took a seat in an overstuffed leather chair and nodded to the adjacent couch.

She studied it, chewing on the inside of her cheek.

Do I lie down on it? Sit next to him, in the middle, at the far end?

"This is where you sit," he said, patting the corner next to him.

Sit, not lie down. Good.

If Elaina had lain down, the exhaustion might win out, and rather than get help, she might get some sleep.

"My first appointment is at 7:30, so we don't have much time," Harry said, his voice becoming heavy with regret.

"I'm sorry for just showing up, but I needed to see you." She spoke to her folded hands. Harry's cologne battled against her sweat, dirt and car exhaust perfume. "About the Rententamine."

"I don't mind you showing up unannounced. I guess I just hoped it was for me and not my work."

She could hear the smile in his words. At another time, she could've countered that she was interested in him. But any attempted spark only whirred with the slur of a dying car battery.

"Trust me, you'll run in the other direction after you hear what I have to say." Elaina took a deep breath and looked at her watch. Twenty-five minutes. She had to get it out and get his advice in twenty-five minutes. Now or never. "You said there's a trigger. You're right. And it's happened more than once." She paused, and her eyes focused on his bookshelf behind his desk, but that wasn't what she saw.

Rather, what she saw was what she'd never seen. A baby picture of herself. Connie wasn't always the sentimental type, so there were few pictures around the house.

"Elaina?" Harry pitched forward. "You're starting to worry me."

She blinked back into his office and flashed a weak, but well-meaning smile. "I'm okay, I just—anyway, a few weeks ago, I got really close to a tornado and something happened. I blacked out, I think, or something." The words struggled to come out, as if they didn't believe themselves. "Instead of being there, I was somewhere else. Maybe even *someone* else." A shiver flashed through her body even though his office was warm and stuffy.

Harry remained quiet beside her. He didn't ask questions or encourage her to go on. He recessed into the chair, as if he'd become chocolate brown leather himself.

"In my head, I was small, three or four, and it was dark outside —nighttime maybe—even though that funnel was in the middle of the afternoon. Rain bounced off something over my head, and I was cold, wet and alone." Elaina closed her eyes and straightened her back. There it was. She was back there. "I heard voices, and I wanted to scream for them, but every time I tried, I'd get water in my throat and choke. And then, something above me lifted and there was a man. I didn't know him, but I knew he would help me." She let the memory end, but the emotions lingered.

She was safe, but the fear was rooted so deep inside, it overpowered anything else. Even now, sitting on the soft leather couch, fear pulsed with each beat of her heart.

"That was the first." Elaina cleared her throat. "There was another one. I was in a hospital, sitting on the floor, trying to hide behind my bed. In that one, it was the lights I remember most. This unnatural brightness that burned. I remember feeling there was nowhere I could hide because of those lights."

The final memory was queued up, like a photo ready to click onto the screen, but she couldn't push the mental button.

The feeling in this one was joyful, safe. Love. It would lighten the weight in the room, but it felt as if she'd betray something, *someone*, to share this memory.

"Is that it?" Harry thumbed his lower lip.

Elaina nodded. "I went to ask my mom about it, but—" The words were stubborn. How could she explain she'd caused her mother to have a stroke? Would Harry feel that the same would happen to him?

"She was no help."

"You could say that."

They sat in silence while she watched the time tick down.

When eight minutes was left before his appointment, the handsome Brit pushed himself off the couch and looked out the window. "Why are you here?"

"I told you. I need your help. There's something locked away in my head that wants to come out. I feel like I'm looking through a dirty window. Help me brush aside the dirt so I can see what it is."

"The brain is fascinating," he spoke to glass panes. "But, we're only just beginning to understand how it works, especially in regards to repressed memories. They act as a sort of circuit breaker, to protect you from getting overloaded."

"I get that, but I didn't repress the memories. Someone did it *for* me."

Harry turned and looked at her from the corner of his eye. "Do you know that for a fact?"

Elaina joined him at the window. The coffee was wearing off, leaving only the exposed nerve of her desperation. If he didn't help her, what would she be left with? Forcing memories with every tornado warning across the country?

She'd do it. If that's the only way, she'd gladly walk into the line of a twister.

"Well, no, but when you mentioned the drug, it felt right."

"Just because something feels right doesn't mean it is." His voice was soft and low, and his eyes were filled with sadness.

It was written all over his face. However right she'd felt to him before she'd arrived, it turned wrong. *This* was the kind of man her mom would approve of, but like everything else she'd touched lately, it'd turned septic.

"Okay, forget that. Forget that anything was done to wipe away my mind and my past. You mentioned repressed memories, people use hypnosis to remember them, right?"

Harry sighed and faced her. "Elaina, don't." His expression was soft and pleading. "You're a beautiful, smart, vibrant woman. You're clever and witty, and someone I'd like to spend more time with. Please don't mess with your mind. It's who you are."

"Who I am? That's what I'm trying to figure out. How am I to know who I am with these images bleeding through? How can you say you want to spend more time with me when I may not really be who you think I am?"

"Who you are is who you always were. Who cares if you can't recall your first steps? Very few people can remember the first years of their lives anyway."

"It's more than that. It's not what I forgot," Elaina gasped.

There it was. The anemic Christmas tree and dirty apartment.

It was never about the what.

Her body shook with the force of an EF5 bearing down on her.

"It's the who. I want to remember *who* I forgot."

26

Pawnshops sit at the junction of one person's past and another's future. Tuck always marveled at what caused one to sell something as mundane as a toaster. Were they just that down on their luck they couldn't even afford bread? Did the four dollars they get in return buy them a hot meal or cheap wine?

Most importantly, how much more in debt would he have to fall before selling *his* toaster?

He couldn't even fathom what the do-dad he'd swiped from the university was used for. It didn't matter. Its value made it worth the risk of being caught by Elaina.

Elaina.

His feelings toward her pulled at his gut. She was establishment. The straight and narrow. To her, rules were made to be followed. A world that only saw things in blue skies and thrashing thunderstorms, no gray, overcast days. Her world had thrown him out, like storm debris.

Yet some internal compass tugged at him, pointing toward her as if she were true north. That dark wavy hair made him face something scarier than an EF5 barreling down on him.

His chest squeezed like rising barometric pressure when he'd met her dark green eyes. Twice, a protective wave had slammed into him at the sight of her, prompting him to warn her about the turning storm and forcing him to stare down that TV reporter.

A strange magnetism had pulled at him when he saw Maddux's hands at Elaina's waist. It'd been a long time since he'd wanted to punch a man simply for the fact that he existed.

Tuck pulled at the cigar box under his sink. One edge of the warped lid popped up, offering a peek-a-boo into the secrets it held inside.

He didn't come to this box often. Once, he'd visited it daily, flipping through the odds and ends of his past, trying to hold on to who he was.

Longer chunks of time passed between visits, and when he did peek inside, it felt foreign, as if the artifacts belonged to someone else.

In a sense, they did.

Tuck closed his eyes and imagined the contents as they were the last time he'd seen them. The old coins, his grandfather's money clip, a modest diamond ring and a simple gold band that belonged to a different time.

A different man.

The cigar box joined two old textbooks, a clock radio, and an electric toothbrush, a step above selling a toaster, but still grazing the bottom.

A temperate breeze blew through the open garage doors and into his tiny living quarters. The air wasn't warm with a lick of moisture, nor was it cool with a slice of dryness.

It was fine, which meant if a storm system didn't break out in the next few days, *he* wouldn't be fine. Jimbo would come collecting and the box of bric-a-brac sitting on the kitchen counter wouldn't come close to appeasing him.

Tuck gripped the edges of the box. The science guys had shunned him and made predictions from behind computers. He'd been reduced to selling old books and an electric toothbrush to pay off his loan shark.

His forearms tensed, and the desire to throw it across the room pulsed in his veins like a drug. His heart beat a rhythmic "do it."

Do it. Do it. Do it.

Junk. That was what it was. What he really was. He'd tried to climb the survival ladder like everyone else, but the rungs were slippery. This junk gave him just a little bit of traction.

Tuck passed three pawnshops on his way to the outskirts of town. He'd been to each of them enough times to know they were run by good, honest men. Men who kissed their wives every day before work and were home in time for dinner. Men who asked all the important questions and whose eyes could see directly into someone's soul.

Today wasn't a day for a good man.

Today, he needed someone who lived by the credo, "Honor among thieves."

A dust devil spun up as he pulled into Dee's parking lot. Tuck smirked.

Good sign.

The chimes above the door crashed together. His boots thudded against the dusty hardwood floor as he passed crap no one in their right mind would buy: a doll with all but one tuft of hair ripped out, a taxidermy monkey, a set of dentures. He paused at the full prosthetic leg.

Now that SOB must have been really low.

There was no doubt Dee was one fucked up dude. He was just the man Tuck needed to see.

He made it all the way to the back of the store, but no Dee. It was entirely possible he'd missed him, which the man always used to his full advantage. "Dee," Tuck called. "You here, man?"

"Robert Tucker," the high, nasally voice came from his left. "Didn't I tell you to never come back here?"

He flashed his smile, almost willing his teeth to gleam. "You didn't mean that. I liven the place up."

A sound somewhere between a cackle and a cough came from around the back side of a shelving unit.

After years of coming here, the sight of Dee still gave him a shudder. The man was short. Not in a dwarf sense, but in a way that made Tuck contemplate if Dee simply stopped growing when he was ten years old.

It wasn't just his short stature. Everything about the man was stunted. His face was soft and smooth, without the gristle of a beard. His arms and legs were thin and gangly, never having a chance to come into their full potential. Hidden beneath his uniform of a black turtleneck was a missing Adam's apple.

Tuck always swallowed the many questions on the tip of his tongue. Had Dee really stopped growing at ten? Or, was he a vampire? How was his sex life? What kind of girls were into a forty-year-old ten-year-old?

Had the guy ever thought about getting his testosterone checked?

"Make it quick, Tuck," Dee said with impatience snapping at the end of words. "As you can see, I'm busy."

He glanced over his shoulder at the empty pawnshop filled with crap that hadn't moved in years. Tuck sat the box on the counter and Dee scooted a step ladder in front of him and leaned over the goods.

"Garbage, crap," he mumbled as his fingers touched his possessions. The diminutive man flicked open one of the textbooks, squinting and bringing the book nearly to his nose. "This book was published in 1987. Why should I buy something this outdated?"

Tuck sucked in a big gulp of air, hoping the extra oxygen could fuel a good line of bullshit. "Well, you know how hipsters are always making new shit out of old shit."

Dee ignored him and moved on to the cigar box. "What's in here?"

"Some old coins, gold band, money clip and a diamond ring." The words fled his mouth faster than usual. "I'll sell you that whole cigar box and everything in it for a hundred." His fingers reached inside the pocket of his windbreaker looking for some change to jingle as his gaze bounced around the eclectic shop, looking for anything other than that box to focus on.

Instead of coins, Tuck's fingers found the gadget he'd swiped

166   KIMBERLY PACKARD

from the university's lab. He wasn't keen on shooting his silver bullet this early, but he needed something to keep Dee from opening that box. "Oh, I nearly forgot about this." He pulled the tiny circuit board from his pocket, turning on his five-hundred-dollar smile. At least, he hoped that thing could pull in that much.

"What is it?"

"What does it look like? A computer thingmabob." He shrugged. "It's got to be worth at least five hundred dollars."

The man grabbed the instrument and studied it from various angles before handing it back. "Twenty-five."

Tuck snorted. "Twenty-five? That's an insult, man. Four-fifty."

No expression crossed Dee's face as he continued to rummage around the box. "They mass-produce those in China. Twenty-five is being generous."

A flush of sweat broke out on his temple. What else could he sell to get the money he needed for Jim? Plasma? Sperm? Although he couldn't imagine a happy, yet reproductively-challenged couple picking *him* from a catalog.

What about things he had two of? He could live off one kidney. Perhaps he could talk Dee into selling him that prosthetic leg cheap, and he could sell his other.

"Dee, man, look." Tuck leaned an elbow on the glass case and lowered his voice. "I can sell you this whole lot," he waved his arm over the box. "For five hundred dollars."

The pawnbroker rubbed his chin and pursed his lips. "Three hundred."

Desperation pooled around his feet, threatening to claw its way up his leg and wrap a tight fist around his throat. He swallowed, pushing that feeling away.

Desperation was like blood, and pawnbrokers could smell it like sharks.

"Four seventy-five."

"Three hundred."

"Four-fifty." Tuck reached into his pocket, trying to grasp anything that would give him hope, but found his pockets completely empty.

Dee looked up from the box and cocked his head to one side and then the other. Gray eyes narrowed as if studying him like a piece of art hanging on a wall. "Ah, so that's your magic number. You owe someone five hundred dollars."

Shit. He caught a whiff of blood.

"Just some business investments I need to make." Tuck tried to keep his words light, nonchalant. He even added in a back stretch to make it seem as casual as getting out of bed.

"Go to the bank for a loan then." The tiny man started putting his junk back into the box.

"Would *you* loan me five hundred dollars?"

A lopsided smile crossed Dee's face. "I wouldn't loan you a Kleenex." He hitched his hands on his hips.

Tuck could see a decision in process, the weighing of options, considering the pluses and the minuses. He cheered on whatever side tilted in his favor.

"You remind me of my uncle."

Ah, there we go.

"Sounds like a great fella. What's the resemblance, my charm or rugged good looks?"

"My uncle was a miserable bastard who could never do anything right. Everything he touched turned to shit."

He licked his lips. His ego wanted to scream and kick and deny and shout *nuh-uh.* Reality quietly said, *sounds about right.* Ego pushed back, saying he was better than that, and this was slander, but Tuck swiftly kicked his ego in the teeth.

His ego had gotten him into this mess to begin with.

"Well, yeah, I guess you could say I've had a patch of rough luck."

"My uncle used to say that, too." Dee stepped off the ladder and reached over to the register. "Four-fifty, but I get the entire box, that thing, and you promise to never come back here again."

Tuck shook his head. "Scout's honor." He crossed his heart and held up two fingers. It seemed like a scout honory thing to do.

Dee handed Tuck a stack of bills without counting them out.

Oldest trick in the book. Short change someone a twenty and call him a liar when he comes back for it.

He wasn't going anywhere until they counted it all out.

"Who are they?" the guy asked, interrupting Tuck at two-sixty.

"Who's who?" He looked up and saw the flat rectangle covering Dee's entire palm. He tried to pull his gaze away, but a searing pain froze his body in place. The money felt hot in his hands. A droplet of sweat burned like lava flowing down his face.

Tuck finally tore his attention back to the money, but not before ivory skin, raven-colored hair and chubby baby legs ripped open the scars he kept hidden away.

"No one." He shoved the money in his pocket and turned to leave. It didn't matter if Dee had shorted him a full hundred—that dusty, smelly pawnshop was closing in on him.

"What? She break your heart? Course, that means you'd have to have one." Dee's voice went up even higher. "I didn't know you had a daughter."

His lungs seized on the noxious air.

If he didn't get out of there soon, he'd suffocate.

"I don't," Tuck croaked.

He had his hand on the door before Dee called to him. "What should I do with the picture?"

"Burn it."

27

The machine was there to monitor her mother's heart, but Elaina felt her own synced up with the consistent beeping. It was strong. Steady.

On the screen, the cadence spiked with sturdy peaks and fell to deep valleys. It was the perfect heart, warm, loving, willing to take in a child and raise her as her own.

Her own heart felt like a racehorse behind a starting gate. It wanted to sprint. Lucky for her, listening to the beeping machine had the same effect as a donkey in the barn. It calmed her, made her breathe slower breaths, think clearer thoughts. Even unconscious, Connie still managed to mother her.

In the three days since the stroke, time was measured in nursing shift changes. Nothing else had changed. Her mother still lay there, the beige blanket tucked under her arms, a thin cotton gown sprouted wires out of the top, and her long white hair flared out on the pillow.

"You should talk to her," a nurse said after checking vitals. "There's a lot of science behind comatose patients being able to hear their loved ones."

Elaina lifted her gaze to the young nurse with kind eyes. Eyes that witnessed people's most desperate moments. Moments of complete loss and helplessness. The warm brown eyes that absorbed so much grief and gave encouragement in return.

"What if she's better off without me here?"

The nurse's mouth pulled up into a bless-your-heart smile. "Sweetie, whatever happened before doesn't matter now. You're here, I'm sure all is forgiven." She finished checking the IV bag and tugged at Connie's sheets. "I'll leave you two alone. Call if you need anything."

She counted one hundred heartbeats before she could find the courage to speak. It wasn't that she hadn't tried before. In the past three days, every time she'd open her mouth, tears would strangle the words.

What if her mom knew she was there, even if she couldn't tell her? What if she thought that Elaina's silence meant anger, not remorse?

Another storm of guilt thundered in her heart. She couldn't let another day pass without speaking. Just because Connie was stable didn't mean she wouldn't slip away in the middle of the night, dying of a broken heart.

"Mom." Her voice cracked and she could feel the familiar sting of her tear ducts. She cleared her throat and closed her eyes. No, this wasn't going to happen. Not now. "Mom, it's me, Elaina. Your daughter."

She wrinkled her nose.

Of course she knows I'm her daughter.

Why was it so hard to speak to someone who wasn't going to interrupt you?

"I'm sorry, let's just go ahead and get that out of the way." She took a deep breath, feeling better with the apology. "I didn't mean to push you so much. I just—"

She just what? She just wanted to find out who she was. Looking down at the woman who raised her should be answer enough. She was Elaina Adams, daughter of a nurse, Connie. She was a meteorologist, drawn to the worst storms as if there was a secret held inside them.

It always felt as if the secret was purely scientific, decoding Mother Nature, discovering why tornadoes dropped to the ground and destroyed lives.

Was it more? Had her life somehow ripped apart at the seams, only to be sewn back together by this woman she'd nearly pushed into death?

"I feel like I just dropped out of the sky and landed in your life. And you've never made me feel like I didn't belong, but I think that was always there, in the back of my mind. This intense need to understand where I came from."

Elaina's phone buzzed on the table next to her. A text message from Heath.

Northeast Arkansas firing up. Leaving in 30. You coming?

Every cell of her being wanted to go, to see what other memory could be teased from her brain, but her heart reminded her that was what had gotten her into this mess.

"And as much as I want to put it back," Elaina continued, ignoring the text and the pull to get back into the storm. "I can't. It was all neatly packed away before, but now it just won't fit back in."

Another buzz pulled her attention away from.

Pierce antsy. This could be big. Trying to stall but he wants you to go.

She typed a quick response back. *Visiting Mom. You go, I'll catch up.*

"It's Heath. Storms in northeast Arkansas, but don't worry, you're safe here. Boring blue skies outside. You're probably wondering what I've seen. I'm trying to understand it myself. The first one was me, as a little girl, and I was inside some storm debris. That's why I asked you if we'd been in a tornado. The second was me in a hospital." Elaina glanced around the room, a shudder rattled her teeth. "It was a room like this. I was hiding and scared."

She took a deep breath. This last memory was the hardest to speak about. Her heart knew what her brain didn't want to comprehend. The woman in *this* memory was most likely her biological mother. The emotion accompanying it wasn't one of fear or being a burden. It was love, unequivocal, unending, and bigger than life itself.

"I just need to know if there's someone out there looking for me.

Not to replace you or leave you, but to let her know that you did an amazing job."

Her phone rang this time.

"Hi, Dr. Pierce," she whispered into the phone, as if not to disturb the unconscious woman lying there.

"Have you seen the models?"

All she'd noticed from the last glance was a frontal boundary was forming, and there was a good chance of storms forming to the east.

"Uh…"

"Things are really intensifying west of Fayetteville. Heath is about to hit the road, I really need you out there with him."

There was an urgency she'd never heard before. The words came out faster, coated with the hard edge of demand.

"Okay, I'm with my mom. She's in the hospital."

"I heard. Condolences. We're talking potential for several EF5s with some of these staying on the ground for a sustained period," her advisor paused. "Need I remind you that you have a deadline looming, and thus far you haven't completed your research. It's a three-and-a-half-hour drive, and you needed to leave an hour ago."

"Well, if I'm that far behind, why don't you just have Heath do it?"

"Since when did you let someone else take control of your future?" His words dripped with judgement.

Since my mother nearly died because of me.

That thought was shushed by ambition and the desire to make her professor and mentor happy.

"I'll get on the road and catch up."

Dr. Pierce responded by ending the call.

If the storm was really as dangerous as he'd said, was it safe for them to go out? For the first time ever, apprehension spun in Elaina's gut like a twister, picking up fear, dread, and anxiety like storm debris. What would happen if she called Heath, told him her concerns, explained how dangerous it could be, questioned why their advisor, of all people, was pushing them into what could potentially be a deadly storm?

Would her partner agree they needed to stay away? Or was he as eager to finish their dissertation and willing to take the risk?

No, she couldn't let Heath down. They'd been working toward the same goal since freshman year. Partners, colleagues, best friends. He was the brother she'd never had.

Elaina had already let enough family down to last a lifetime.

"Mom, I have to go. Work. But before I leave, I need you to know, that this was never because you weren't enough. You're more than enough. I just hope I never let you down. I hope you never regretted picking me as your daughter." She kissed her mom's soft forehead. The skin cool beneath her lips. She inhaled the breath of life still pulsing beneath the surface.

It took no time to catch up to Heath on the highway. The lumbering van was loaded down with heavy equipment. The sky ahead of them was an ugly gray-green with a misplaced double rainbow luring them forward.

"Do you get the feeling we're driving into hell?" Heath's voice came over the radio.

"What gives it away? The cauldron of green clouds or the rainbow asking if we want any candy?"

His chuckle broke through the static as a streak of lightning zinged down to the earth. If there were weather gods, they weren't just angry, they were *pissed*.

"I really don't like this," Heath said after several minutes. "We're not going to get there in time. It's going to be cutting it really close to drop everything and get back to safety."

"Why is Pierce pushing us on this? I mean I know we're close to the end of storm season, but we have the summer to calculate and finish the paper. Over."

"I was asking myself the same question. It doesn't feel right."

They continued down the interstate for several more minutes. The storm they drove toward seemed to fill more than just the sky, it felt as if the dark clouds and static electricity invaded the inside of her truck, causing the hair on her arms to stand.

Elaina had never had this reaction before. Rather than the thrill of the chase, she was full of dread and regret. Regret at leaving her mother's side. Dread at the thought of what lay ahead in the storm. Assuming they could even get there in time.

The van in front of her heaved forward, and she locked down her brakes, swerving to avoid rear-ending their equipment.

"Sorry," Heath said through the crackle of static. "Gridlock. Apparently everyone else is smarter than us."

She rolled down her window and stuck her head out. The air was cool, wet, and heavy with anticipation. A trail of red taillights dotted the path to the storm ahead.

"I'm going to get off the highway," her partner added. "Follow me and let's see if there's a back road."

They pulled into an abandoned restaurant to check maps. What little cell service was available that far out was overwhelmed with the number of people calling, texting, and weather-checking.

The GPS on Elaina's phone simply churned a spinning wheel rather than give her any clue as to which way to go.

Heath dug the map out of the glovebox of the van, and they bent their heads over it.

Her finger traced the various lines, like trying to figure her way out of a maze. Finally, they settled on a path, and she took the lead.

The minute they turned down a one-lane road, the rain came down in sheets. Her gaze swept the clouds, trying to see anything that indicated ground truth, the moment a twister touched down. Elaina already knew her ground truth. She'd left her comatose mother behind to chase after a hot mess of a storm. What did she need to see to prove that?

She watched the odometer tick off three miles, but the left-hand turn she'd expected was nowhere to be found.

"Did we pass it?" Heath asked over the radio.

"No, it has to be up here, just a little farther."

She slowed again to study the map in the dying daylight. The supercell was still to the northeast of where they were. If they didn't turn soon, they'd be too far south of the storm to get into place.

Elaina's truck lurched forward again, and within minutes, a red reflector of a turn lit up in her headlights. Relief washed away the tide of self-doubt that threatened to drown her. "Here it is."

The two vehicles turned, but doubt slammed into her when they came upon a house sitting nestled at the end of a long driveway.

"Shit." She slammed her palm on her steering wheel. Sweat tickled her neck. A chill slivered down her body.

"Should we just drive right through their back pasture?" Even though Heath was teasing, she could hear the undertone of concern.

They backed out and retraced their drive. Somehow the turn magically appeared this time, and they headed east.

The sky ahead of them darkened into a yawning maw. A swirling black hole, illuminated only in bursts by yellow lightning. Her windshield wipers were flailing themselves back and forth, but made hardly any impact on the rivulets of rain. Wind rocked her truck from the right and then again from the left.

As far as Elaina could tell, they were the only ones out in the storm.

Her foot lifted slightly at the first tinge of fear. Not fear for her own life, but a cold, noxious breath of death blew in through her cracked window and stroked her cheek. What if Connie woke up and learned she'd died out here, in a storm, chasing after an apparition. "We have to hurry," Heath's voice broke her thoughts. "It's moving really fast."

As if to punctuate her partner's eagerness, a flash of lightning lit up a perfectly shaped, monstrous wedge tornado miles ahead of them.

Adrenalin kicked concern to the curb. One side of Elaina's lips lifted in a smile as she pressed on the gas. Just seeing the shape of the twister reminded her *why* she was on the earth. So what if she dropped from the sky. It meant there was no one better to ride the storms.

"Don't lose me," Heath crackled over the radio.

She glanced into the rearview mirror to see his headlights a hundred yards behind him and slowed. Sparks of light ahead of her beckoned.

The monster was devouring transformers, leaving little illuminated bread crumbs in the dark path ahead of her.

"Elaina, it's moving too fast, and it's too far," her friend said. "I don't think we're going to make it. Over."

"No, we will get there," she said, not bothering to press the mic open on the radio. She flexed her foot on the accelerator again and felt the back end of the truck sway in the water-filled ruts. The lights behind her faded to barely visible pinpricks.

"What are you doing?" The fear in his voice bounced around her truck cab. "Stop!"

Elaina took one hand off the wheel and reached for the radio. "No, we can make it."

"No we can't. I'm looking at the radar, the storm is moving into open farmland, and there are no roads to get us in front of it." Heath paused. "Let it go Elaina, we didn't catch this one. We can get ahead of the next one though."

She stared at the radio in her hand, fighting between agreeing with him and arguing his point. If Nim were with her, she'd know what to do. A flicker of lightning reminded her she was still speeding down a dark country road in the middle of a storm.

She looked up just in time to see a Buick heading in her direction. Not with wheels gripping the road like her own vehicle, but sideways with its roof pointed right for her.

Elaina ducked and slammed on her brakes. The car hit the ground twenty feet in front of her but tumbled on its side as if a petulant child had tossed it. Her old brakes squealed in the wetness and refused to react.

A head-on hit would surely kill her, but cutting the wheel could put her in a similar rollover.

With every bit of strength she could muster, she slammed her left heel hard on the parking brake while her right hit the other brake. The engine grunted and she felt the truck heave forward. The seatbelt cut into her shoulder as she bit hard on her tongue, gagging on the bitter taste of copper.

The car tumbled toward her. Side over side. A tumbling dice. White top, black axles. White top, black axles.

It rocked up on the side once more, but the momentum was

gone, and it teetered back on its wheels, bouncing twice as if an unseen energy radiated through it.

Her truck came to a stop, its front bumper just kissing the passenger door of the formerly flying car. She leaned forward, peering through her windshield wipers, holding her breath. Elaina exhaled. The car was empty.

Another flash of lightning showed the storm slipping away from her. The dark green roiling clouds reminded her *she* was merely a child's plaything.

When the storms tired of her, they'd discard her like the car. Whether the storm told her all of its secrets or not.

28

The supercell stretching across northeastern Arkansas painted a dramatic backdrop for a stand-up. Seth and his cameraman traversed the country roads in the lumbering live truck, searching for the perfect spot to capture the roiling clouds.

Trees with fresh leaves bowed down for the oncoming storm. The contrast between the warm, welcoming air of Gulf Shores and the electrified, clashing of cool and warm fronts was whiplash to his senses. Goosebumps rose and fell on his arms with every shift of the wind.

The roads were filled, both with cars trying to escape from the oncoming storm and those rushing toward it.

Seth sat up in the passenger seat, searching for a faded brown truck driven by a petite brunette who scared him more than an EF5 barreling down on him. It took him getting a thousand miles away to realize Elaina was *nothing* like Julia.

His ex struck with the unpredictability of a cat. She'd curl up, purr and snuggle only to strike and draw blood the moment he let his guard down.

He was more of a dog person anyway.

Especially loyal yellow Labs owned by pretty girls with long, curly hair and could give Mike Tyson a run.

He shook his head. In the field with a deadly storm bearing down on them was not the place to fantasize. Searching for Elaina in a sea of storm chasers was purely professional. She had a knack for being in the perfect place at the right moment.

Keep telling yourself that, buddy.

A few fat raindrops pinged off the windshield. He refreshed the screen on his laptop. The colorful depiction of the storm outside the van showed what he suspected; a bow echo was forming to the west. The ingredients were all present. Now the weather just needed the right chef to whip up a tornado.

"We've got some action," Seth said. "I'm going to switch on the dash cam for a while." He switched on the camera. "Seth Maddux, with *Riders in the Storm* here in northeast Arkansas on the trail of a supercell. Folks, this giant is dangerous, so please, *please* don't try this at home. We're trained meteorologists and take every precaution out in the field." He smiled into the expressionless glass eye staring back at him. Most people ran from the camera, but the camera was always friendly, never judged him, never lied to him.

Never cheated on him.

He picked the camera up from the mount and pointed it out the windshield. Through the screen, the light gray morphed into dark gray, blue became green only to become blue again. Lightning splintered the scene and thunder laughed in response. The weather gods were having fun this afternoon.

Two maroon vans sped past the live truck, soaking the windshield with dirty rainwater.

Seth turned off the camera and reclined, staring at the departing words of Tuck's Tours.

"That man is as arrogant on the road as he is in person," Rick mumbled. "People really pay him for this?"

"A sucker is born every minute. Follow him. If this thing fizzles, I can at least get an interview with him."

Ex-girlfriends aside, Seth always considered himself to be a good judge of character, and something about that man had irked him since dancing with Elaina. It was a look of curiosity and contempt. It was a look of temptation and threat. And something that baffled him; it was a look of possession. Maybe a good interview would help him peel back the layers of this enigmatic man.

The computer in his lap beeped and he looked down. The hook was getting more defined. It was only a matter of minutes before showtime.

Tuck's two vans pulled over, and Rick slowed, pulling off to the side just ahead of them. Between the thick clouds and the near-dusk setting sun, a preternatural darkness settled over the road.

Lightning illuminated debris flying across the highway and just out the driver's side window, a spindly rope tornado slinked out of the storm and flirted with the earth.

At the next lightning flash, cars around them collectively hit their brakes. The twister danced in a field to their left, as if listening to some wild, enchanting song. Up, down, forward. Right, up, up.

Vehicles sat immobilized as the twister crossed the highway a half mile in front of them. That was smart for all the moms and dads taking their kids to soccer practice, but Seth could feel his flailing career running out of gas.

"We have to get around this and follow it," he told Rick.

His cameraman eased the heavy truck onto the shoulder, two wheels on concrete, the other two sloshed through the mud.

Lights flared behind them. Tuck's vans followed suit.

Rational thinking told him the man was following the storm, but a niggling irrational fear flared down Seth's spine.

"A little further up, and then let's film a stand-up. Maybe get some of the twister in the background."

Rick glanced at him from the corner of his eye. "You sure about that, man? I don't see Elaina out here to save you if you get too close."

"I'm not going live. Let's just get some footage of the twister, I'll talk along."

The cameraman put the truck in park and reached for his equipment, while Seth checked the radar once more.

The storm was moving away, but he couldn't help but hear

Rick's apprehension echo in his mind. After all, his colleague was the one with a wife and kids. Seth just had an ivy waiting for him back in Atlanta. Assuming he'd remembered to ask someone to water it.

"On second thought," he said. "You stay here, keep an eye on the radar in case it turns, I'll jump out and get some footage."

Without giving Rick a chance to argue, Seth hopped out. The wind clawed at his pants and jacket, whipping him around to face the headlights of Tuck's parked vans behind him.

Expressionless heads watched him from behind the flickering windshield wipers. He'd never been much of an egomaniac, but the little bit of ego he did have was at risk if he didn't at least get *some* footage.

He pushed off from the van and took five steps out. His ears popped, and fine, sharp rain pelted him in sporadic drops. Seth wiped the water from his face and pressed record, focusing the camera on the tornado ahead of him.

"You're looking at a rope tornado," he shouted over the din of the wind. "This storm is probably about a mile, maybe two miles, away, but as you can see from the trees, there's some pretty serious winds even here."

As if to reinforce his words, what looked to be a wall flew a hundred yards in front of him, tumbling as if it were nothing more than a weed.

Shit.

"That shed wall probably weighs a hundred pounds, and you can see how it was just tossed in the air," Seth paused, letting the sound of the wind, rain and tornado have a starring moment. "I know I've said before, but I'm trained to chase storms. I'm not in the path of the tornado. I know it's hard to tell but it's moving away from me."

He heard someone shouting his name and turned to look behind him.

Tuck was motioning him forward. "We have to go," the man shouted over the wind. "The atmosphere's too unstable. Something's going to drop behind us."

Seth jogged toward him, the wind equally pushing him forward and pulling him back.

Tuck's face was hidden under the hood of his raincoat. He couldn't rely on looking him in the eye to see if the man told the truth or was simply trying to get him out of the way.

"What do you mean? We're on the backside."

"Did you go to school to just look good on camera or for anything useful?" the guy snorted. "You ain't on the backside of shit until you see blue sky."

He opened his mouth to argue, but Rick rolled the window down and shouted his name. "We've got another hook forming behind us. We gotta go, buddy."

"Now you believe me?" Tuck's gravely voice was full of I-told-you-so. "Follow me."

The three vehicles made awkward U-turns and sped back to the interstate.

Seth kept his eyes on his laptop the whole time, marveling at the radar's seeming obedience to Tuck's wishes. How did he do it?

Everything science told him said they were in the clear. This man was clearly in possession of some knowledge beyond what the Forecast Channel had in its arsenal.

Seth only looked up when he felt the van turn into the parking lot of a gas station behind Tuck.

The storm was fully past them now. The sky to the west was a layer cake of black from the trailing clouds to blue-black of the horizon to orange of the last remnants of the day's sun. The air was cool and damp.

There was always something about the moments immediately following a storm that made him feel grateful for everything in his life. It was as if God told him He could take it all away if Seth wasn't careful.

Rick pulled up to a pump behind Tuck's vans.

Seth approached with his hand outstretched.

"Hey man, I really owe you for back there."

The man pursed his lips, his gaze shifting down before meeting Seth's hand with his own calloused palm. "Think nothing of it." His weathered cheeks pulled back into a grin. "I couldn't let these kids see you get hurt."

As if on cue, a swarm of Boy Scouts fled the vans, hyper chatter competing with the distant thunder.

"They were getting their weather-safety badges," Tuck added.

"I'd say they just learned a lot."

The boys overtook the sleepy convenience store, an equal number lining up for the bathroom as raiding the drink coolers.

"Hey, so let me make it up to you. If you've got a few minutes, can I interview you for my show?" Seth asked.

Tuck rocked back on his heels and popped a toothpick in his mouth while his other hand worked some change in his pocket. "Well, I don't know about that." He leaned up on his toes, breaking eye contact to look over his head. "I'm a pretty private person. You know, staying off the grid and stuff. You see Lainey out here?"

"Who?" Seth couldn't help but look behind him, as if the man's roving gaze was an indicator of a sneak attack. "Look, is there really such a thing as being off grid? Anyway, this will be great for your business. You can tell people the services you offer. Who was it you were asking I'd seen?"

The man shook his head, droplets of water escaped his shoulder length hair, like a dog shaking off the water. "Sorry, I meant Elaina. You seen her? And my business does just fine."

He crossed his arms in front of his chest and straightened his back. The nickname set off an alarm of protectiveness deep inside of him. He'd never heard anyone call her *Lainey*, not Heath, nor Pierce.

She'd never introduced herself as that or suggested *he* call her that. Of course, there were plenty of douchebags out there who belittled women with unprovoked nicknames, but his alarm wasn't at a watch level. It was at a warning level.

"An offer like this doesn't come along very often." Seth's words had a sharpness he thought had gone dull. "Trust me, you'll be begging me for this later."

Tuck met his posture with his own crossed arms. "I appreciate the offer, and I can promise you I won't be begging you for anything."

The air around them froze. Even the chirping crickets sensed the tension forming and went silent, out of fear and curiosity as to what would happen next.

Tuck's blue-gray eyes stayed locked on Seth's. The toothpick bobbed back and forth, and the sound of the damn change in his pocket jangled over the din of the interstate.

The older man was no match, but that didn't lessen the sensation of malice that pulsed from him.

With empty bladders and full sodas, the Boy Scout troop ran out of the store and back to the vans, breaking the bond between them.

"Seth, ready?" Rick asked. "Everything okay here?"

"Yeah, everything's fine." The assurance squirmed through his tight jaw. "We're done."

He'd tugged the door open and was about to crawl inside when he heard Tuck's voice again.

"You better watch your back out there, boy." The man didn't look at him, instead he gazed up at the sky.

"Is that a threat, old man?"

"Nah, just a warning. Out here in the field, a storm can be a man's accomplice."

29

Heath was waiting for Elaina on the steps of the science building. His gaze flashed over the rim of his glasses, briefly making eye contact before he stood and walked ahead of her into the building.

This summons from Pierce was different than before. Most of the time, getting called in was a collection of mild warnings of stormy weather ahead, but this one felt like they were about to walk into a rare, mythical fire tornado.

With each step up the stairs and down the hall, the air tightened and her cheeks flushed as if she was getting too close to the sun.

Their appointment was for two o'clock, and they arrived at ten minutes before, just on the verge of being late in their advisor's mind.

Elaina could feel her professor's awareness shift as they hovered outside awaiting an invitation to enter. As usual, his office was dark except for the blue-white glow of his computer screen and the yellow light of the fish tank.

Frustration simmered within her gut. Every minute she stood outside waiting for Dr. Pierce to finish whatever it was he was doing, was time away from her mother. Never mind that she'd missed an important consultation with the doctor while chasing that hot mess of a storm in northeast Arkansas.

Never mind when that Buick had been flying in her direction the only thought flashing through her mind was her mom would wake up to learn that Elaina had died. Never mind that there would always be another storm.

She'd never have another mother.

That was what mattered.

Elaina shuffled and sighed, her annoyance as obvious as the bright sun on a cloudless day. A quick glance at her watch revealed two p.m. had come and gone ten minutes ago. This was one of Dr. Pierce's mind tricks. Sweat them out, make them squirm while waiting for their punishment, then rush them through the sentencing phase before he escaped to class.

This wasn't her first rodeo. It wouldn't be her last, either.

Finally, as if he'd seen the sudden winning pattern in a game of Solitaire, Dr. Pierce clicked his mouse hard three times and shoved the keyboard tray into his desk. "You can come in now." His voice was as flat as the Oklahoma plains.

Unlike before, he gave them his full attention as they slinked into his office and took their seats like a couple of naughty school kids.

Heath sat with his chin nearly touching his chest and his hands cupped in his lap. Everything about his posture begged forgiveness.

Elaina, on the other hand, straightened her spine and squared her shoulders. She intentionally tilted her chin up, hoping the gesture added just a little bit of height.

With her thick hair long and wavy rather than its usual braided ponytail, she wanted to take up a little bit more space sitting in her advisor's office. If he was going to cut them down to the quick, she needed a little additional mental padding.

"Well," Dr. Pierce began. "I could say I'm disappointed, but that would be letting you off easy. I'm beyond that. I'm *embarrassed*. And I can honestly say no doctoral students have ever done that to me before, so…" He reclined and started clapping.

A hard sound that popped in her ears each time his palms collided.

"Congratulations."

Heath folded in on himself just a bit, as if hoping the professor would forget he was there.

Elaina glanced at her friend, and the frustration that'd been on a low simmer cranked up to a rolling boil. "I doubt we're the first students to miss collecting from a storm system." She pushed the words through her tight throat. Her brain told her to sit there and take it, but her mouth ignored the command.

Her partner sucked in air beside her, and his body lifted slightly, as if he fed off her strength.

"You're correct, Ms. Adams, if this were the first case of missing data, but you both were so far off the path, the only data you gathered was how much rain fell. If you're more interested in rainfall, might I suggest a change to landscape architecture."

"That's not true. We got some interesting stats on straight-line winds and barometric pressure and rear-flank downdraft." The words were sour in her mouth, as if fueled by the acid churning in her stomach. "The winds were strong enough to send a Buick flying in my direction."

That last sentence hung in the air between them. Dr. Pierce's steel-blue gaze dug into her eyes. He rubbed his palms on his useless legs. A shudder rocked his body as if shaking off her words. "Rookie. Mistake."

The sound of the gurgling fish tank drowned the thundering blood rushing through her ears. Ever since she'd stepped foot in his office the first week of her freshman year, she'd worked harder, longer, and smarter than her peers.

When she wasn't in class, Elaina was in the lab or in the field. When she thought she'd given everything she had to her studies, and to Dr. Pierce, she gave more.

She became drunk on the approval that a mentor gives a protégé.

That a father gives a daughter.

Only Pierce wasn't her father, and she wasn't his daughter. The minute she walked off campus for the last time as his student, someone else would be waiting to step forward and fill her shoes. Hopefully, that student wouldn't have to understand the soul-splitting agony of choosing between capturing data from one of the last spring storms for her dissertation and sitting vigil by her comatose mother's bedside.

Heath shifted beside her, inhaling and pulling his shoulders back, as if finally allowing himself to be seen in the office.

She could *feel* words about to escape his throat. "No, we did not disappoint you." Her own words were filled with angry energy as they exploded before her best friend could speak. "We did *not* make a rookie mistake. We did *not* embarrass you. We did what we do every day. Bust our asses *for* you."

Heath whipped his head in Elaina's direction.

Pierce crossed his arms over his chest and narrowed his eyes.

"What are you doing?" Her partner's face nearly contorted into a question mark.

"He's wrong, and he knows it." Her legs bounced, the extra energy needing another escape hatch. Or maybe her legs were trying to take her away before her mouth really got her in trouble. "How many dates have you cancelled with Chloe because of the weather?"

"This is not about me," Heath said through tight lips.

"Of course this is about you." She hopped up from her seat and leaned on the desk, answering her friend while staring down her professor. "This is about all of us and the ridiculous demands he places on us because he's locked in that damn chair and has to live vicariously through us."

Shit.

Her brain cursed as soon as the insult escaped her lips and her knees went wobbly, as if they wanted to be no part of her blasphemy. Elaina's hands turned white as they gripped the side of the desk, pulling double duty for her traitorous legs. "I-I'm sorry." Her apology gurgled with the water, bobbing like an air bubble waiting for a fish to come and suck it up.

Unfortunately, the fish weren't biting. Neither was her mentor.

Former mentor?

"Well," Dr. Pierce said, pausing to clear his throat. "A conversation about your future doesn't seem likely with your current state. Lucky for you, Ms. Adams, the radar is rather boring over the next few days, so you can take some of that time off you believe you deserve."

Her heart cantered with the fury of a hailstorm. Dr. Pierce had always been there to help her, to advise her, to show her what she'd missed in a way that was never patronizing. The raw edges of her nerves were quick to jerk at any comment. "I'm sorry," she said again, this time the sentiment melded with burgeoning tears.

"If you'll excuse me, I have to prepare to be insulted again with a class of brain-dead freshmen." He turned his attention away from Elaina and Heath, and the metal-on-metal sound of his keyboard tray scraped her ears.

Run. Leave. Go.

Her brain tried to command her to leave before she caused any more damage.

"Dr. Pierce." Her voice was weak and wet.

"Goodbye, Elaina."

"But, if you'll just let me—"

"Let you do what? Insult me more?" His words were wrapped in razor wire. "Go. You're done here."

She opened her mouth once more. She wasn't above begging. Wasn't above *anything* right now.

Even earthworms had a leg up on her. Before she could dig much further underground, Heath's chair scraped against the floor, and he pushed past her.

The anger rolling of him was strong enough to ignite a super cell.

He was nearly out of the building before she was able to catch up to him.

"I messed up in there, big time," Elaina said, grabbing his arm to slow him down.

Heath jerked out of her grasp, but he didn't walk away from her.

"I'm sorry. I'm not sleeping or really eating. My only excuse is my mom."

"Look, I'm really sorry about your mom," he said, not looking at her, but his shoulders caving in partial defeat. "You know I'd do anything for you, but—" he paused, shifting his weight on one leg and back to the other before facing her. "It's not just my future at risk; it's mine and Chloe's future. I've sacrificed so much for this. I can't fail now." Heath's eyes glistened for a moment before he cleared his throat and looked out over the quad.

He was right. Everything about the last few months had been through the murky haze of what she needed; the perfect positioning for a storm, the answers to the visions, the forgiveness of their mentor. Her friend had been on the field with her all along, but she'd been sacrificing him to the opponent.

And, for what?

"You're right." She swallowed against the stubborn lump in her throat. It'd been there so much lately she considered that it was an actual growth. "What can I do? How can I fix this?"

Heath continued to stare out over the quad.

Warm, dry air whipped up her hair, the long curls lashing across her face and stinging her eyes. It was only appropriate to get her ass kicked by her hair. Other parts of her body were likely lining up to go next.

When her friend couldn't find an answer looking over the campus, he shifted his gaze down to his feet, toeing a dandelion growing out of the sidewalk crack. Finally, he looked up. Multiple emotions danced across his eyes. Sympathy, contempt. Friendship, anger. Betrayal even flashed briefly. Heath shook his head. "You can't, Elaina. Just, leave me alone."

Elaina could barely see his retreating figure through the tears. They clung to her chin until the levee broke and she could feel them bouncing off the toe of her boots.

He was wrong.

She *could* fix this.

Even if it meant she'd have to resign from consideration as a doctoral candidate just to remove the stain from his research. She had no one else relying on her future. Nimbus wouldn't care as long as he spent every day with her. Her mom would prefer to learn she'd given up field work to wait tables if it meant she stayed safe. Seth would find another young storm chaser to flirt with.

The earth would keep turning. Storms would keep forming. The rain would fall, with or without her.

She rubbed the wetness from her face and sprinted back into the building. Her knees popped as she took the stairs two at a time, but she made it to Dr. Pierce's office faster than ever before. The only sound in the entire wing was the clopping of her boots against the linoleum. Elaina slowed to a fast walk before rounding the corner into his office. "Dr. Pierce, I know you said—" She stopped at the empty office. In her hurry back to right her wrongs, she'd forgotten he was in class.

She hovered in the doorway. She'd never been in his office without him there. She felt like she was snooping, like a kid taking a peak into mom's closet right before Christmas.

Well, I already made it this far.

Elaina glanced around his messy desk, scanning the mounds of periodicals, books, papers, maps, and charts for something as simple as a sticky note. The darkness of his office cast weird shadows, making something as innocent as a stapler look sinister. "Oh for Pete's sake, he's not a vampire." She sighed, banging her hand against the light switch on the wall.

The yellow florescent light cast a glowing beam down on a notepad, and she quickly penned her ninety-eighth apology of the afternoon along with her resignation from the program.

Behind his desk was a gaping abyss with the absence of his wheelchair. Elaina reached over to stick the note on one of his dark computer screens, but her shifting backpack banged into the keyboard tray, startling the mouse and waking the computer.

Her hand froze midair, inches away from words that were as familiar as a favorite song. Numbers and figures danced in the white space below, and her eyes followed them as far as the screen allowed.

Those were their words.

Her and Heath's data.

Elaina didn't remember dropping her hand to the mouse, to rolling the cursor up to the top of the document.

They might have been their words and data.

But, it was very definitely Dr. Tom Pierce's name at the top of the paper.

30

A bar on the outskirts of Oklahoma City was the only place Elaina felt safe enough to whisper her accusations.

After ten begging voicemail messages, Heath finally agreed to meet her. She could almost *hear* his eyes rolling on the other side of the line, but it didn't matter.

As long as she could see him. So he could look her in the eye and know she wasn't crazy when she told him Pierce was stealing their research. It was also easier to present her solution for finishing their research in person.

A smear of white clouds mottled the clear blue sky. The temperature stretched into the mid-nineties. If there was just a little more moisture in the air, this mid-May heat wave would spawn a round of thunderstorms.

Sweat rolled down her back as she shut off her truck. It was definitely going to be the last summer she could make it without air conditioning. Then again, perhaps the perspiration was more a product of the internal cauldron that'd been bubbling since the previous day.

The bronze ballerina swung in the dry wind. Now the good luck charm felt different. It felt more like a key into a secret room than a sentimental childhood memento.

Elaina's sense of self had been blown off the foundation. These past few weeks had been a futile attempt to clean up the debris in the midst of a raging storm. What she'd found was mangled, wet, dirty.

Ruined.

The roadside bar was as dusty on the inside as the near-empty parking lot. She traced circles on the table with the bottom of her sweating beer. She was early, mostly because if she didn't leave her house she feared losing her nerve. That was the one thing she couldn't afford to lose.

Heath's lanky frame was backlit when he pulled the door open. His shoulders were still hunched, head lowered, and hands stuck in his pockets.

She even imagined his eyes cast down, studying his feet as he shuffled toward her.

"You're early," he said, tossing his keys on the table.

Elaina wagged the nearly empty beer in the air. "I needed a little liquid courage."

He sighed and looked over her head toward the bar. "Yeah, me too. Another drink?"

"Might as well. I'm not feeling brave yet."

When Heath returned, his posture had loosened, and he sat across from her, his dark eyes staring directly into hers. This was one of the rare moments when she saw him as she imagined Chloe saw him. Handsome, self-assured, intelligent.

It wasn't that she had a crush on her research partner; it was like seeing a place after the storm had washed away all the dust that hung in the air. The light was always softer, the air fresher. Everything looked new after a storm. As if revitalized from a brush with nearly being blown away.

"So," her best friend said, popping the beer bottle from his lips. "It's a helluva long way to drive for you to buy me a drink to apologize."

Elaina took a deep breath. "It's more than that. I mean, yes, I'm sorry, but…"

The door pulled open and she jumped.

Pierce would never come to a place like this, but she couldn't help feeling like he could sense her mutiny.

The truck driver nodded as he passed their table.

She leaned forward, lowering her voice just in case the trucker was a spy for their advisor. "Yesterday afternoon, I went back to resign from the program."

"Elaina." Within her name, Heath managed to pack a whole monologue of chastisement.

She held up a hand before he could launch into it. "No, let me finish. I'm serious. I've got too much going on with my mom…" *And the crazy visions in my head.* "It was only fair, but never mind. It didn't happen. He wasn't there, so I was going to leave him a note. That's when I found this." Elaina pulled the printed copy of the paper Dr. Pierce had been working on out of her back pocket. The tightly rolled papers unfurled a little.

Her partner looked up at her and back down. His nose wrinkled as if the papers reeked.

Which they did.

She took a long sip of beer as his eyes traced down the pages.

Red rose up Heath's neck from just inside the collar of his T-shirt, and the papers shook as he went through them a second time. Finally, he tossed them back on the table. "It doesn't mean—surely he was going to. Maybe this is just the first draft." His voice climbed the octave with each word. If he added another thought, it would surely be as a soprano.

"Maybe." She shrugged, glad she'd had a day to process what Pierce was doing to them, and she could guide him through the hell of betrayal. "All he's missing is a final piece of storm data, a summary statement, and, oh yeah, our names."

Her friend cupped his chin in his palm, as if the burden of holding up his head was becoming too great. "Why would he? He doesn't have anything to prove."

"I thought the same thing, so I did some digging." Elaina pulled the last piece of paper from her back pocket. "He hasn't published in five years. He's co-authored, consulted, or has been referenced in some papers and journals, but nothing to call his own."

"He's tenured."

She shrugged again. "Even tenured professors have a boss. And an ego."

They sipped their beers in silence.

The bar remained empty aside from the grizzled bartender and somber truck driver. Disappointment draped over the bar, linking this band of wallowers together in a chain of grief and loss.

"What do we do?" he asked.

Was the question more for himself or her?

"Does he know we know? Do we go to him with this, or the department chair? University president? Do we just play the role of lowly doctoral students so we can shuffle across the stage?" He took a long pull from his beer, finishing the bottle and slamming it on the table with a *thud*. "Do we just quit? Walk away?"

"We don't quit, but to answer the rest of your questions. I don't know, but…" Elaina glanced at the time on her phone. Thirty minutes to convince him. "But I have a solution. You might need another beer for this."

Her friend raked his hands down his face and sighed. "When you say it like that, it makes me think I need to remain sober."

"How much more data do we need to complete the research?"

"I dunno." He shrugged. "One good outbreak with multiple touchdowns might get it, but likely we need at least two more." Heath sucked on the inside of his cheek and looked over her head. "Atmosphere is stabilizing though. Spring's almost over so to catch anything in the next few weeks we'll have to move fast. What're you thinking?"

The time ticked down on her phone. What would be the appropriate moment to mention her plan? How long would it take to convince Heath?

Elaina could run the risk of firing off the suggestion too soon and he'd leave. Maybe this concern was all for nothing and he'd readily agree.

There was only one way to find out.

"Pierce needs us more than we need him." Her voice was low and thick with contempt.

Heath huffed. "Not entirely true, we need him to sign off on taking the equipment out, and oh, he signs our paychecks. As meager as they are."

"What if I told you we can chase those last two storms without him?" She sucked in a deep, calming breath. "We might even be able to make more money than we do now."

He squinted at her through his thick glasses and pressed his lips together until they became a thin, white line. "I'd ask you who you sold your soul to."

She opened her mouth to answer, but the door to the bar opened, and the silhouetted figure of a man filled the entryway.

He stood there with it open, blinding everyone inside. It only took him a minute before he swaggered to their table.

Dammit. Of all people to be early.

Tuck flipped an empty chair around and straddled it, propping his elbows on the top as he smiled at Elaina, then at Heath.

"Well, hello kids." The older man reached over and grasped each by a shoulder. "This's going to be a blast."

"I should've known it was the devil," Heath murmured, standing. "I think I'll have that other beer now."

"Grab me one too, Heathcliff."

Elaina's friend wrinkled his nose down at Tuck. "It's just Heath."

"You promised to play nice," she said to Tuck when her partner was at the bar.

"I can play nice and have some fun at the same time, Moo-Moo." He shrugged. "You geeks need to learn to let loose out there."

"If this is just a game to you, we're out." She pushed herself to standing. This was a terrible idea. She'd grab Heath from the bar, and they'd just go home, back to Dr. Pierce and his data-stealing-commander-in-chief teaching methods.

"I could've just as easily let you set up in the path of the storm."

Tuck flicked open a pocketknife and began cleaning out his dirty fingernails. "Actually would've opened up the field some for me and my patrons. It might be a game on a sunny day, but I assure you, *Elaina*, when the barometric pressure starts dropping, I play no games."

She studied him, looking past his shaggy gray hair and scruff that sat between forgot-to-shave and growing-a-beard for a man who would uphold the promise he'd just laid out.

Faded mustard stains on the pocket of his Hawaiian shirt were one or two washings away from blending into the pattern. That was assuming this shirt got washed regularly. Underneath the open shirt, she could make out part of his company logo.

Uck Ours. Gawd, I hope we won't have to wear those shirts. Uck was right.

Tuck held her gaze, his chin dropping once in a firm nod.

She nodded back, sealing the silent pact.

Heath returned with a round for the entire table. He must've felt that even Elaina deserved a drink at the prospect of working with Tuck.

"Why?" her partner asked, not directing his question at anyone in particular.

Tuck and Elaina exchanged quick glances.

"You seem like a couple of nice kids," the old storm chaser said.

"He can get us into perfect position in the storms," Elaina chimed in on top of Tuck.

Heath took a long sip of his drink. "What's in it for you?"

It was a more than fair question, one she should've asked when Tuck had too-quickly agreed to her request. Elaina prayed that whatever answer tumbled out of his mouth would satisfy her friend.

"I'm a son of a bitch, Heath," he said after popping the top of his beer bottle out of his mouth. "I've been known to lie, swindle, steal, and—"

"You mean like the circuit board you stole from the lab?" Elaina stabbed the accusation at him.

The man shrugged. "Things get lost every day." He turned his palms up. "Let's just say, I'm sympathetic. I've had something very important taken from me. I know how betrayal stabs at the heart." Tuck took another long drink of beer. "Plus, it's going to be really active over the next few weeks, I've got some big tour groups lined up, and I need the help."

"The atmosphere's stabilizing," Heath said. "We're almost at the end of storm season."

"You need to spend a couple of weeks with Professor Tuck, kid. Get out from behind those computer screens. You'll see that it's not over until I say it's over."

Heath's jaw flexed, as if chewing on the man's surprising honesty.

Elaina had been hoping he'd be on board with the idea all morning, but seeing the skepticism cutting deep creases in her friend's face made her worry that this was just another bad, impulsive idea.

"How will this work?" Heath directed his question at her. One side of his mouth pulled up in an understanding smile.

Relief cooled her body, like a gentle misty rain washing over her. She could see it in his eyes; he trusted her.

With his research, with his career, and with his life.

Despite everything that'd happened over the past several weeks, their bond was still there.

"More importantly," he added. "Do we have to wear those ugly-ass shirts?"

31

The maroon T-shirt could have been a dress. It swallowed Elaina with a gulp, burping out her legs at the knees. It didn't matter if she forgot the shirt, soiled it, or burned it; Tuck had another triple extra-large ready for action.

She'd even considered trading shirts with Heath. He'd barely have to lift his arms before the shirt would ride up to show pale skin.

"Nimby, if I ever think about doing something as stupid as this again will you rip out my jugular?" she asked through a mouthful of toothpaste from the motel bathroom.

Her dog smiled from his perch by the A/C unit, the blast of dry cold air blowing his yellow fur.

She studied her reflection as she braided her long hair. How had she gotten here?

An almost-doctor of meteorological science holed up in a dank motel room in middle-of-nowhere Kansas, getting ready to greet a tour group of retirees with a smile—not how she'd imagined she'd spend her weekend.

Elaina had expected to be in a comfortable lab, with her advisor nearby while she and Heath put the final touches on their paper.

She'd expected to be speaking with Dr. Pierce about her role at the university.

She'd expected her mom to be there as she crossed the stage, but from her call with the doctor that morning, there'd been no change in Connie's condition.

Expectations were great when they became reality.

Nothing hurt as much as when an expectation spiraled out of control, plummeting to the earth until the only thing left was a charred hole in the ground.

"All right, Nim, stay here and enjoy the A/C." Elaina coated her eyelashes with mascara and rubbed some blush on her cheeks.

Tuck had given them the talk about how to maximize tips, but she wasn't trying to win them over with charm and a pretty face. The makeup was for the bright blue Forecast Channel trucks parked in the nicer motel across the street.

Not that she *wanted* to run into Seth, but just in case she did, Elaina didn't want to look like she'd spent the night in a room with walls so thin she could hear her neighbor binge-watching *Wheel of Fortune*.

"Should be a quiet day today. I'll be back soon."

Nimbus thumped his tail twice and gave her a quick glance over his shoulder before turning back to the blowing air, squeezing his eyes shut in doggie bliss.

The parking lot was filling up as more storm chasers descended on the bulls-eye of the next outbreak. TV weather vans, amateur ham radio operators, trucks lumbering with heavy equipment. This old motel hadn't seen this much action in a long time.

She walked to the eastern edge of the asphalt and looked out over the field of growing corn. Their bright green stalks were nearly as tall as she was. Her feet shuffled, as if eager to walk into the field, to lose herself to the crop.

How long would it take before someone realized she was missing? Would Nim follow her scent and lead her out of the labyrinth, or was he too content sitting in front of spewing cold air?

The sun cast a soft glow on the plants, nurturing them as a mother tends to her young. Elaina took a deep breath and lifted her arms up to the sky. She dove down to the next step in the Sun Salutation, her arms reaching behind her calves. If she could've seen around the billowing T-shirt, she'd try to see if Seth was watching her, but lightning wouldn't strike twice.

Unless she wanted it to.

Do I?

Obviously she had a rush of blood to the head. Why else would she hope to see the handsome TV reporter when she *should* be worrying about her failed career, her mother's declining health, and the fact that she was about to meet up with a group of tornado tourists for access to equipment and money?

"I'm such a loser," Elaina said as she kicked her legs out into a plank.

"Well, in my book I prefer losers over winners."

She jerked to look over her shoulder. Tuck leaned against the back of his van.

"Is that why you agreed to work with us?" She hopped her legs forward and joined him at the van. The thinnest layer of sweat dotted her forehead. "You needed fresh meat in your merry band of losers?"

He laughed and tossed the toothpick to the ground. "The thing about getting to the top is you're afraid to look around and admire the view. Winners are so worried about falling. But losers are fearless. Feral. They've survived the fall and aren't afraid to dust themselves off and claw their way back up."

Elaina studied the pot-bellied parking lot philosopher. He was right. Ever since Arkansas, ever since feeling the crushing pain of disappointment at herself for failing Heath, her mom, and Pierce, she'd felt a primal urge for success. It was a need as deep as breathing. She didn't have to think about it. She just needed it. *Win. Win. Win.* The mantra blew through her with each inhale.

"Plus," he continued. "You remind me of someone I used to know."

She propped against the van beside him, the dark maroon exterior warming her through her clothes. "Another chaser?"

"Nah." The man squinted into sun instead of looking at her.

"She was really afraid of storms. They'd send her into a panic." His voice sounded hollow, as if he was speaking to her from far away.

"Clearly not a loser like us." Elaina chuckled, but Tuck remained still.

He gazed out over the field. Was he looking into the past?

His face flushed red, then paled as the color washed away.

"I'm sorry," she added.

"She was definitely not a loser. She reminded me that all the time." His words were soft, barely loud enough to compete with the light wind blowing up from the south, but his words were hard and sharp. "Well, get your buddy rounded up, and let's go meet our tour group. Get them strapped in for the ride of a lifetime." He walked away, whistling an indeterminate tune.

She studied the sky. It was the deep blue of a newborn day, untainted by haze and moisture. While it was likely that clouds would start building, nothing more than a passing shower was in store for the group. "Yeah, like the merry-go-round."

Elaina found Heath at the motel vending machine, staring at the meager options of off-brand junk food. "Buy you breakfast?" she asked.

"You mean the sticky bun with an expiration date of 2022 or the stale-to-perfection donuts?"

She lightly kicked the vending machine. "Tough choice there, but something tells me the beef jerky might be the safest bet." She nibbled her bottom lip.

A silence heavy with anger, regret, and remorse settled between them, something that'd become more of a regular occurrence since they joined Tuck's Tours. "On a scale of one to ten, how mad are you at me?"

Money fell into the machine and her best friend stabbed at a couple of buttons. "Sometimes a negative two, sometimes a twelve." He bent to retrieve a candy bar. "But mostly, I appreciate that you're not giving up, no matter what gets thrown in our way."

"Even Buicks?"

"A Buick doesn't stand a chance against you. Know anything about the group today?"

They crossed the parking lot toward a cluster of several people at a Tuck's Tours van.

The older man's voice boomed as he told a fish tale of a storm story. He commanded the asphalt stage. A Shakespearean actor delivering a soliloquy. His sidekick, Biscuit, stood at the open passenger door, grumbling at a weather radar map.

"Nice days must be hell for business," she said out of the corner of her mouth.

"And there I was. It was pitch black, but I kept seeing the flares in front of me. I knew she was there. I knew she was big. And I knew she was coming after me." Tuck paused and glanced around the group until his gaze rested on Elaina. "There's my interns."

Interns?

"Please meet Elaina and Heathcliff. They're here to cater to your every need."

Cater? A white-hot chill crept up her spine. What had he meant by cater? Did he expect them to wipe noses and hand out peanuts?

Elaina had figured there'd be a certain amount of babysitting involved with working with Tuck, but not *catering*.

"All right folks, we'll be pushing off in fifteen minutes, so any last bathroom or coffee breaks need to happen now."

The crowd dispersed.

She stood still, arms crossed over her chest. Her gaze zeroed in on Tuck, sending him every dirty look she had in her arsenal. "We are *not* your hired help," she said once the customers were out of earshot.

"I hired you to help. So I guess that makes you hired help." He looked over Biscuit's shoulder at the radar.

"How're we going to gather data, if we're fetching sodas and taking people's pictures?"

"We'll tell you what you need to know." Tuck spoke to the computer screen. "Dammit, the frontal boundary stalled, so even if we drove clear into Nebraska, we'd still get nothing."

Her heart thumped so hard it threatened to break her breast bone from the inside out. "This was not the deal."

"Got anything in writing? I sure as hell don't."

"Come on Tuck, you agreed to give us access to your instruments."

"And I also told you I'd pay you. I like you Moo-Moo, but not enough to pay you for nothing."

"This is so unfair." Elaina cringed as soon as the words came out. She hated the teenage fallback argument. "I'm the top doctoral student in the program. I can see the slightest shift in the barometer and know what's coming. I can feel the wind change before it changes. I didn't join your rubberneckers' tour to put ice in the cooler and order box lunches. Don't you *dare* demote me to the role of waitress when I am so much better than that." Her words echoed around the parking lot, bouncing off cars and the stucco hotel across the highway before it floated away over the cornfields.

Tuck narrowed his eyes and studied her. He unwrapped a toothpick, tossing the wrapper on the ground. "Well, Top Doctoral Student in the Program, I'm sure you can see that there won't be anything to chase. Not today."

"I could've told you as soon as I stepped outside."

"So seeing that there's nothing to chase other than your runaway temper, then I'd say yes, your job today is waiting on these fine folks who paid their hard-earned money to get a glimpse into our lives. I'm doing something you weather geeks deem yourselves to be above." His voice rose and spittle clung to his beard. "I'm educating the everyday man, woman, and child about tornadoes. Giving them tools to stay safe and out of harm's way. So if you've got a problem with that, then you and Heath can take your asses back to Oklahoma and figure out how to finish your research on your own."

The air was still and quiet after the shouting stopped. Elaina tilted her chin up, trying to make herself taller, but she still only managed to come to the top of his chest.

"Don't try to out-stubborn me, girl," Tuck growled. "My don't-give-a-fuck will beat your I'm-the-top-of-my-class every day. You need me more than I need you." He brushed past her with Biscuit on his heels like an obedient dog.

Heath shook his head. "Really, Elaina?" Her partner trotted after Tuck, shouting at him to wait.

She closed her eyes and tried to focus on her breathing. *Inhale. Hold, two, three. Exhale.* Her heart still pounded, but the deep breathing forced her to calm down and not punch the side of the van.

A long, low whistle sliced through the wake of her tantrum.

Elaina opened her eyes and looked around the empty parking lot for the source. Then glanced at the nicer hotel.

Seth sat in the open passenger seat of the blue Forecast Channel vehicle. Even from across the highway, she could read the look in his eyes. *Appreciation. Curiosity. Attraction.*

Maybe just a little bit of fear too.

32

If it weren't for small town bars, the monotony of waiting for weather would've been insufferable. Seth parked the van at the back of the lot, not for advertising, but it was so much easier to maneuver the big vehicle when he was away from others.

He passed a brown truck. The parking lot light glinted off the small figure of a dancer hanging from a chain off the rearview mirror.

Elaina was a comparison of contrasts. Tough, but gentle. Her intensity sometimes gave way to a flirtatious laugh. Now this, a tomboy who could challenge any heavyweight in a boxing ring had held on to a childhood dream of being a ballerina.

Seth shook his head and kept walking. A woman with that many contradictions had to be one step away from going off the deep end. Roadside distractions were a great place to visit, but he'd never want to set up permanent residence.

Right?

Judging from the odd mix of people inside, the place was filled with storm chasers waiting for whatever Mother Nature would dole out to her patient children once that system fired up again.

It was easy to spot Tuck. Find a gathering of people and he was likely in the middle of it, telling some story that had a nugget of truth the size of a grain of salt.

Seth leaned against the bar, sipping his beer.

The crowd around the older man roared with laughter and broke up.

That was when he saw her.

Sitting in a corner on a barstool, scowling like a kid in timeout.

Tuck spoke in Elaina's ear.

Her scowl hardened, but she nodded and left the stool, heading in his direction.

"Three more beers, please," she said to the bartender.

"Triple fisting, I like it."

"Save it, Maddux. I'm not in the mood." She turned with the three cold ones and headed back to Tuck, handing him a bottle and passing the others to two men wearing matching leather motorcycle jackets.

Seth strained, trying to tell if the men were dentists who liked to dress up and pretend to be in a gang, or if they were actual members of a motorcycle gang.

Once the beers were delivered, she went back to her stool, as if awaiting her next orders.

"What the hell did you get yourself into?" he mumbled to himself. No matter how hard he stared in her direction, Elaina wouldn't allow her gaze to meet his.

He wandered from the bar, circling around the tables to put himself in her line of sight, but she turned her head. He shifted to the left, and she craned her neck further.

One more step and she'd rival Linda Blair in the head-twisting contest. Finally, she pulled her cellphone from her back pocket and studied it.

As much as Seth wanted to get closer to her, Tuck guarded her with the protective hostility of a Rottweiler.

A dart board opened up, and the men left her behind in the corner.

He swooped in from behind them, hoping Tuck hadn't erected an electric fence around Elaina. "Care for a twirl on the dance floor?" He held a hand out, but she ignored him. "Looks like your beer's empty. Buy you another?"

A heavy sigh escaped her lips. "I thought I told you I wasn't in the mood."

"You did, but why do I get the feeling you're a grounded teenager whose dad is punishing her by making her get his friends beer?"

"He's not my dad, and those are clients, not friends."

"But you *are* being punished."

Elaina didn't disagree with him. She chewed on the inside of her cheek and the dimple in her chin quivered just a little before her jaw muscle flexed.

There it was again.

The vulnerable little girl just got tucked inside a tough outer shell.

"Shots," she said, finally looking him square in the eyes. "Let's do shots."

Just one look in those forest green eyes made his stomach feel like he'd just gone over the first drop of a roller coaster.

Maybe he had.

"I'm pretty sure nothing good ever comes after those words." Seth pulled one side of his mouth up, hoping that his half-smile told her the whole truth.

"That's what I'm hoping for." She hopped down from the stool and strode across the dance floor to the farthest corner of the bar.

"Alrighty then," he said, easing into the chair next to her. "Pick your poison."

"Two tequila shots," Elaina said to the bartender.

Okay, so we're doing tequila. Great.

The bartender filled two shot glasses and before Seth could offer his glass in a toast, Elaina downed hers and slammed the glass on the bar.

Her face flushed green and her cheeks puffed out, as if the liquor threatened to come back out, but instead she croaked, "Another."

"I should tell you now, I'm not really the holding-your-hair-back-while-you-puke type. What're you trying to forget?"

"The last two months." This time she raised her glass to his.

His pointer finger twitched, as if it wanted to straighten and stroke the knuckles on her hand, but then the finger remembered she threw a hell of a punch and tightened its grip on the glass.

"Aren't there some things worth remembering? Some good storms, laughter, punching me on live TV?"

She laughed, a musical sound he wanted to hear more. "Okay, to forgetting things that should be forgotten."

"And remembering things ... ah, I'm a shitty poet when I'm drinking." They downed their shots. Seth watched her wall break down brick by brick. "So this is where you're supposed to tell me what you're doing with him." He gestured to Tuck.

Elaina paused with the bottle of beer just inches from her lips.

What would it taste like to kiss her? Salt, bitter, sweet?

Knock it off, Maddux.

"Who?"

"You know who. Was that a maroon shirt I saw you wearing this morning?"

She cringed and called the bartender over. "Can you just leave us the bottle?"

"What's going on?"

She threw back another shot and refilled her glass.

"Elaina." Seth pulled her glass toward him. "Slow down. Shots like this will make you sick. Trust me, talking about it is much better than trying to drink it away."

Elaina took a deep breath and glanced over his head.

He followed her gaze to the group Tuck was holding court over.

The man's back was to them, but he couldn't help but feel like the guy knew exactly where they were.

"You're right," she said, her voice was huskier, her words slower. The tequila must already be hitting her. "I need to run to the ladies' room, and then can we get out of here maybe? Somewhere to talk?"

"Sure, we can go wherever you'd like ... as long as *I'm* driving." Seth motioned for the bartender.

Her full lips stretched into a smile. It was a relaxed one, completely honest, filled with relief and tequila.

He wanted to make her smile like that again.

And again. And again.

Once Elaina was gone, the crowded bar felt empty.

How could a woman so small take up so much room?

A relationship was not part of his career-salvaging plan. Seth couldn't imagine a one-night stand with *her*. One night would leave him just wanting more.

His grandmother was right. Again.

"Get your head right, dude." He wrung the back of his neck.

"I'd say that sounds like a good idea." Tuck slapped a heavy hand on Seth's shoulder.

"You change your mind? Come begging for an interview?"

Where's that damn bartender?

The hand on Seth's shoulder tightened. He held his face steady, refusing to let the man see him flinch, no matter how deep Tuck's thumb dug into his muscles.

"What did I tell you?"

"That you didn't need it for your business." He reached for his empty beer bottle, just in case he needed something as a weapon. "But seeing that you took on two new employees, I bet your business expenses just went up."

The older guy leaned in. The smell of warm beer assaulted his nostrils and the ever-present toothpick twirled between his lips.

Was the man going to use it to poke his eye out?

"You have no business with her. You hear?"

"Not happy I stole your waitress away?"

"Watch yourself, boy." Tuck spat the words out like a shot of chewing tobacco.

"What're you doing with her? You have the hots for her? I'll be straight with you. Elaina doesn't strike me as the kind of girl who'd date someone old enough to be her dad."

The toothpick in his mouth froze on the tip of his tongue, dangling there as the man's face paled and his eyes hardened.

The facade of the good-time, yarn-spinning lovable-loser storm chaser fell away.

All the hair on Seth's body stood on end and every nerve ending tingled, begging his body to flee.

As if a storm was seconds away from erupting.

The bartender slammed the bill on the bar.

He jumped, putting two twenties in the folio without taking his eyes off Tuck.

"Hey," Elaina said. "What's going on?"

As quickly as Tuck shed his outer skin, he pulled it back on.

He dropped his hand from Seth's shoulder and shoved it back into his pocket. Even over the loud music, Seth heard jingling change.

"I was just coming to tell you to take the rest of the night off," he said to Elaina. "Get some rest, tomorrow's sure to be one hell of a ride."

Elaina narrowed her eyes, but then her face relaxed. "You sure you don't need me?"

"Nah, kid, I got this group covered. Get out of here."

She turned and Seth followed close behind, fighting the urge to put a protective hand on her lower back.

"Maddux," Tuck shouted, loud enough to be heard over the music, but stopping just at Seth's ears. "Watch your back out there."

33

Elaina made the decision to sleep with Seth between flushing the toilet and washing her hands. She'd never been that kind of girl, but somedays she wasn't sure what kind of girl she was. Maybe she *was* the kind of girl who'd jump into bed with any cute blonde with bright blue eyes.

There was only one way to find out.

Well, probably more than one, but the tequila gave her only one option.

Seeing Tuck at the bar with Seth had stirred something within her. Something that hid from monsters, was afraid of clowns, and screeched at the sight of a cockroach.

It shouldn't come as a surprise to see them talking. It was a small storm-chasing community after all. But the way Tuck had gripped Seth's shoulder sparked a flash of cold throughout her body, along with the desire to pull him out of her new boss's grip.

It must've had the same impact on Seth. The flirtatious sparkle in his eyes had dulled to the point that when their gazes met, she'd assumed he'd put her in a cab and send her on her way.

"Is it me, or is Tuck the biggest buzzkill?" Elaina added a chuckle, but it felt hollow.

"There's a convenience store on the way back to the hotel." He gripped her hand and pulled her past her truck to the waiting Forecast Channel van. "But take it easy, I'm serious about not holding your hair back. I don't do vomit."

The passing headlights illuminated Seth's tight face and his white knuckles glowed in the moonlight. He took the turn into the convenience store on two wheels.

"For the record, I don't hold hair back either." She tried to make her words light and teasing, but they'd sounded harsh and judgmental.

She sucked at seduction.

With a six-pack of beer nestled between them, they sat in the opened back of the SUV in the parking lot of his hotel.

Elaina scratched at the label on the beer bottle. The decision to sleep with Seth was an easy one; it was the execution that caused her to be aware of how his arm brushed against hers when he brought his bottle to his lips.

They sat in silence, watching silvery clouds drift across the moon.

As much as she wanted to make the first move, her muscles tightened as if her body was pulling in on itself.

He brought the bottle back to his mouth. If he squeezed the neck any tighter, it would break in his hands.

"So," Elaina said, popping the bottle from her lips.

"So," Seth answered. "The suspense is killing me. What did you do to end up working for him?"

She frowned as she took another sip. "You automatically assume I did something wrong? Nice."

"That's not what I—Look we were having fun back there. Can we go back to that? Maybe pretend the part from Tuck showing up until I just spoke didn't happen?"

She studied his profile. The handsomeness that'd earned him a spot on TV seemed translucent under the moonlight, as if it covered his true self. She leaned in, her face just inches from his cheek.

The faintest stubble of dark blonde hair covered his tanned face, but there was more. There was a man who hid behind a self-assured smile, but tucked beneath the surface was a scared boy. Elaina saw deep intelligence, the kind often dismissed if it came with strong cheekbones.

Seth turned toward her, his lips nearly touching hers. "What're you doing?"

"I'm seeing you."

"Considering how close we are, I can't imagine you're seeing anything other than me."

She shook her head and shifted her body toward his. "You're afraid."

His throat bobbed as he swallowed.

She could feel conflict swirling around inside him.

His muscles tensed, as if he wanted to move away from her, but his gaze drifted to her lips. "I'm afraid you'll hurt me."

"I won't, I promise."

A sad smile slipped across his lips. "An easy promise to make, a hard one to keep."

Seth's mask cracked a bit. Enough for her to peek inside and see how skittish he was.

It reminded her of the night she'd found Nimbus. A thunderstorm had raged overhead. Elaina had been outside the science building, watching the web of lightning trace across the sky when she'd heard a whimper.

A wet, shivering ball of yellow fur cowered behind the steps. Nim hid from her the first few days she brought him home. It was only after she'd given him some space that he'd come to her.

Guess men and dogs aren't really that different.

She scooted back, reclining against the side of the SUV. Her skin cooled the minute she moved away from Seth.

"I don't like that I'm working with Tuck, but it's the only way Heath and I can finish our research." The declaration was an offering. A treat.

Seth shifted and leaned against the opposite side. His outstretched legs brushed up against hers and a shiver blew through her body.

"What happened to Dr. Pierce?"

"Well, if my voodoo doll actually worked he'd be bleeding out of every orifice." Elaina drew in a deep breath. Was she really about to tell a guy who went on TV for a living about Pierce's betrayal? "He was stealing our research for his own paper."

"Weren't you listed as co-authors or contributors?"

"Nope."

"Did you guys quit the program?"

"Not officially. We're just not returning his emails or his texts. Or his calls, really."

"You're ghosting your professor?"

Elaina chewed on her lower lip. "Couples use it all the time for the non-confrontational, passive-aggressive form of breaking up. I thought I'd try it for quitting professors as well."

Seth shook his head and laughed. "You're even more badass than I thought."

She pumped an imaginary fist.

"But why Tuck?"

"We need a few more storms, and a little spare change wouldn't hurt since we're not performing our graduate student duties right now."

A cloud of worry crossed Seth's face.

"I can handle Tuck," she quickly added.

He studied her for several seconds before reaching over the backseat and pulling a laptop out of a backpack. He scooted next to her and pulled up a video file, fast-forwarding through people talking and tornado debris before pausing it. "A few weeks ago we ended up in Townsend." He paused and studied her face. "You know that town." It wasn't a question.

Elaina nodded. "EF1 from earlier this season. Heath and I drove through town after it passed."

Seth hit *play* on the video.

The little girl stood in the parking lot of the grocery store. Her eyes unblinking as she watched. "I'm waiting for the angel." The small voice was filled with assurance. She just knew an angel had saved her that day, even though most days Elaina felt closer to the other end of the spectrum.

"She was talking about you."

"The grocery store was hit. Shelves and food everywhere. She wouldn't leave her bear and got separated from her grandmother."

"I'm not worried you can't handle Tuck, or that you'd get hurt with him. I worry you'll lose your humanity with him."

She wanted to argue, but her throat closed up tighter than an interstate in a tornado warning. Was she already losing her humanity?

Leaving her mom alone in the hospital so she can finish her degree? Forcing Heath to follow her down an unknown path?

Her chin trembled and a hot tear slid down her cheek. If Seth didn't do vomit, he probably didn't do crying drunk girls either.

Dammit.

It was already lost.

Her humanity.

She'd left her mother back in Oklahoma City to chase after a past that was only an apparition.

"Hey, c'mere." Seth pulled her into a hug and the rest of her tears streamed silently down her face. "What else is it?"

She took a deep breath. "My mom. She had a stroke a couple of weeks ago. They have her in a coma, but—" Elaina hiccuped. "I shouldn't be out here, I should be there. I'm a monster. I left her all alone."

He pulled away from her, framing the sides of her face in his warm palms, and thumbing away the tears. "You're not a monster. A monster is someone who'd rather get high than raise her son." Pain drifted across his handsome features like a dark cloud.

"That's why your grandparents raised you." For so long, she'd thought her real mom was someone worth missing. What if she'd been saved from a horrible childhood of an addict mom?

Sitting there in the dark van with Seth, she could see his scars were still visible, barely healed. Easy to break open.

He nodded. "I see you too, Elaina." He twirled one of her long curls in his finger. "I see a smart, fearless woman with more compassion than she'd ever admit to. And truthfully, you scare the shit out of me."

Elaina blinked as her blood thundered in her ears. She could swear that her hair had nerve endings, because chills flashed through her when he touched it. "Is that good?" she asked, her body drawing to his like a gathering storm.

"Is what good?" His lips were just nearly touching hers.

"Scaring you." She closed her eyes, wanting every cell to feel the kiss.

"No. Yes." He paused. "Very definitely, yes."

When his lips finally met hers, lightning crackled across her vision. She cooled and warmed simultaneously, as if a warm and cold front were battling. She knew what happened when fronts collided, and if his kissing skills were any indication, it would be one hell of a storm.

They both wiggled, and their feet kicked the inside of the car as they slid down.

Seth covered her, but his weight wasn't crushing. Instead it was enveloping, comforting. A feeling she never wanted to end. He lifted only long enough to pull her T-shirt over her head before tugging his off. The cool night air only intensified the storm inside her.

Elaina's long hair dangled off the bumper, giving her a light, floaty feeling. Or, maybe the tequila was finally kicking in.

"Well, Seth, I guess this is why you're not returning my calls."

A woman's voice sliced through the silent parking lot.

Seth froze with his lips on her neck, a string of curses took over when the kisses ended.

Elaina opened her eyes. Standing before her, upside down, was a woman. Her strawberry blonde hair was blow-out perfect. Long, thin legs covered with leather pants so tight they might've been body paint grew out of a fitted sweater and ended in black patent heels.

"Here I thought I was the only girl you screwed in the back of the news van."

34

If Seth squeezed his eyes tight enough, he could will the scary monster standing in front of him away.

His ex stood before them like the self-satisfied succubus she was.

Her outfit was ridiculously out of place for rural Kansas. Hell, those leather pants and hooker heels would've been out of place in the newsroom. It wasn't her *'screw me'* outfit.

This was her *'screw you'* outfit.

"What the hell, Julia?" He scooted in front of Elaina, giving her a bit of privacy. "Why are you here?"

"I've been trying to call you for weeks." She intentionally deepened her voice and used a fake southern drawl to cover up her Long Island twang, but it still seeped out. Like using a Band-Aid to triage a nicked artery.

"I've been ignoring you for weeks."

Elaina shuffled behind him, pushing past to escape the back of the van. "I, uh, should leave you two alone." Her voice was so small, so broken, so unlike her.

Seth reached for her hand, but it slid out of his grasp.

Elaina slid out of his grasp.

He tried again, and this time caught her elbow. "Please, listen, it's—"

"What? It's not what I think?" Tears clung to her thick lashes. "Actually, it is what I think. You're exactly who I thought you were. I'm just furious for telling myself I was wrong." She jogged away.

The darkness wrapped a comforting arm around her shoulders and tucked her away.

As much as his brain told him to run after her, his heart said it wouldn't be a good idea. She needed space. *He* needed to have a good answer as to why his ex had showed up with her talons newly sharpened. Seth needed to be sure when he did talk to Elaina, he meant it.

"She's cute, spunky," Julia said, grinding the heel of one of her stilettos into the pavement. "And it seems like she has all her teeth. I'm sure that's a rare find out here. But she does look familiar…"

He took a deep breath and ran his hands through his hair. Hair that just minutes ago, *Elaina* was tugging. "Again," he said through gritted teeth. "*Why* are you here?"

Julia paced the parking lot. Her gaze darted up, her hand cupping her chin. A femme fatale version of The Thinker. Stone and all. "Oh wait, I do know her. She's that psycho fan." She dropped her arms and took several steps toward him. "Oh Seth, sweetie. You're so lucky I got here when I did. I probably saved you from a really uncomfortable situation, restraining orders, boiled pets. Maybe even crabs, too."

"Where were you when we started dating?" he grunted. Seth closed the back of the van, wishing his hotel room was more than fifty feet away. Fifty lightyears away would be a good starting place. He faced Julia. Somehow he'd avoided making eye contact over the past six months.

On the surface, she looked the same. Her long, reddish blonde hair had an effortless wave women paid lots of money for. Her light blue eyes sparkled under the parking lot lights, made up in her usual heavy-handed eyeliner and mascara, but the overhead illumination called attention to the feathering of lines radiating from the corners to her temples.

She'd tried to freeze herself at thirty, but her forties were thawing her out.

From where Seth stood, she was melting wrinkle by wrinkle.

"You didn't come all this way because you miss me." He softened his tone. Being combative when trying to have a conversation with her was like fighting fire with gasoline. "We both know the station wouldn't have sent you to say hi. And being in the field with an unstable frontal boundary moving in, sits just slightly above watching a hairy guy get his back waxed on your bucket list."

Julia laughed and ducked her head. That simple gesture chilled her enough to glaciate five years back on her. "Would you believe me if I told you I'd already knocked that one off my list?" She shook her head. "The stuff rookie reporters cover in tiny markets. But you're right, the suits sent me. They like what they're seeing."

"Me getting punched, you mean. Or was that just you?"

She laughed again, this time her sincere one. Unselfconscious and light.

What kind of woman would she have become if she'd chosen a different profession?

"Actually, that episode endeared you with viewers. This is a new Seth Maddux, someone who doesn't take himself too seriously." Julia pushed off the car and took two steps toward him.

Her perfume rode to his nose on a breeze.

"Someone who isn't afraid to throw himself into any situation to get the story." Her chest heaved and cheeks flushed.

Their gazes collided, but all Seth could see was a petite brunette with forest green eyes. Was Elaina still crying, or had she made a voodoo doll with blonde hair, throwing it up and down, causing Seth to feel like he was being tossed around in a twister?

"Someone who no longer gives a damn." Her nostrils flared and her gaze darted to his lips.

He crossed his arms. The classic Julia seduction move. In the past, she'd employ it to distract him when he started asking questions, spoke his mind, or otherwise asserted that he had a say in their relationship.

Luckily, he'd become immune to her moves.

"And…"

She snapped out of her temptress-trance and cleared her throat. "They want you to come home, back to the station. The evening desk." Julia smiled, a little bit sincere and a lot of forced. "Prime time, baby. It's yours."

"What about *Riders in the Storm*?"

"Oh it's a fun little piece of reality TV, but we can turn that over to someone else. New, dispensable."

Seth braced himself against the back of the van. This was it, the highest spot he could reach on-air at the Forecast Channel. A nice, cushy job in a safe, dry studio under the glare of fluorescent lights, reading someone else's words from a teleprompter. A human ventriloquist dummy.

If he took this promotion, he'd have Julia's hand firmly up his ass.

"When?"

She leaned next to him, her shoulder touching his.

Once upon a time, he'd felt a little spark; now it felt like an inanimate object.

"As soon as possible. We could probably get on the first flight out tomorrow, before the weather kicks up."

"And cancel this week's show?"

She looked him in the eye. "You're asking an awful lot of questions."

He squared his shoulders. "And you're pushing awfully hard to get me on a plane tomorrow. What gives?"

"Opportunities like this are like diamonds. You sit and stare at it too long without grabbing it, someone else will."

Feels like a blood diamond.

Seth shook his head. "What's in it for *you*?" She wouldn't invite him back into the spotlight where the glare from his rising star could risk blinding her.

"Why do you always think I'm out for something?"

"Because it's your MO."

Julia sighed and dropped her arms to her sides. "I was offered Vice President of Programming."

Even though she stopped with that statement, Seth could hear the ellipses that followed. He quirked an eyebrow.

"If I make amends with you," she said with an eye roll.

He snorted, but that turned into snickering which morphed into a full-fledge guffaw. "So you're telling me you *need* me?" He wiped amused tears from his eyes.

"The irony isn't lost on me." She blanched and looked away. "So you in or what?" Her Long Island accent sliced through like a bandsaw.

Taking that job would get him out of the field.

Away from the heart of the action. Away from the people who mattered most, those who lived in the paths of these destructive storms. Families who risked losing their homes, children who risked losing their parents. First responders who risked their own lives to save others.

Taking that job would also move him away from Elaina. He wasn't ready to run away from her.

Maybe Gram's right.

"No," Seth said. The word had never felt so right on his lips. "I'm happy where I am."

"Name your number. We'll pay it." Her voice had taken on that harsh tone, a step away from being a nasally whine.

"It's not the money."

"Okay, wardrobe allowance, car, someone to come over and floss your teeth for you." Julia paced and rubbed her temples.

"No." He was really enjoying saying that word. "There's nothing you could offer me. I like it out here."

She stopped abusing the pavement with her stilettos. Realization settled in her blue eyes, and she pursed her lips. "It's her, isn't it?" Julia hitched her thumb over her shoulder, in the direction of where Elaina had escaped.

Where Seth wanted to go.

"You're going to give up your career for someone you barely know?" His ex demanded.

"How is that different than giving up my career for someone I *supposedly* knew? Intimately." He spit out the words with more poison than he thought he had. Maybe he wasn't as over it after all.

Julia winced. "You can't punish me forever, Seth."

"Punishing you would indicate I think about you, which I don't. Tell the suits I appreciate their confidence in me, but my place is here." Rather than take off in the direction of Elaina's hotel, Seth went toward the stairs to his room. His gut told him he'd made the right decision. He just needed to spend some time convincing his brain.

"You're making a huge mistake," she called. "You think your on-air tantrum was bad, just wait until this gets back to the station."

"Go to hell, Julia." His voice echoed around the nearly empty parking lot.

35

The sunlight filtered through her hotel window too soon. Once Elaina had made it back to her room, she'd crawled into bed with Nim, crying into his soft, yellow fur until it was sopping wet.

Her dog had rested his large head on top of hers and sighed.

This was why she didn't do relationships.

The men she dated never seemed to live up to her dog. An unfair comparison for sure, but at this point, she preferred the strong, silent types who walked on four legs.

She'd drifted off to sleep at some point, but woke in the middle of the night flushed with sweat, and her mouth filled with cotton. The vise on her head had tightened as she stumbled into the bathroom to take an aspirin, washing it down with her mouth under the faucet.

Seth was right. Nothing good *did* come after doing shots. Despite her best, or worst, intentions.

Nothing good came *before* the shots either.

Her mom's stroke and coma, Pierce stealing their research, working for Tuck, the visions.

Like getting a glimpse of the wizard behind the curtain, were the visions telling her that everything she knew, the life she'd lived was nothing but smoke and cleverly positioned mirrors? Was it worth peeking behind it? What if she hated what she saw?

Or worse, what if she liked it?

What if the life she was meant to live was better than the one Connie had given her? It would be too easy, too convenient, if she came from a broken, abusive home. What if the little girl found in the rubble had come from a family who loved her and mourned her?

What if the scared little girl in the hospital room wasn't afraid of where she'd come from but was terrified of where she was going?

Her phone buzzed with a text message, the sound a hive of angry bees to her hungover brain.

A quick glance told her it was the last person she wanted to see.

Or was he the second to last? Maybe third?

Elaina needed to work on prioritizing the people she was pissed off at.

Buy you a cup of coffee if you promise not to throw it at me, Seth texted.

She tossed her phone back on the bed and covered her eyes. Somehow it didn't surprise her that *she* wasn't the first he'd seduced in the back of a news van. She probably wasn't even second. Or twentieth.

Fine. Coffee AND breakfast. He followed up to her non-response.

Her stomach rolled at the thought of food. Part nausea and part hunger. Despite her body's inclination, she wanted no part of Seth.

Sure, maybe the night before she wanted some part of Seth. Maybe all of him, but it was for her own benefit. Not his. It was to regain that last bit of control over her life that had slowly been slipping away from her.

Right?

How *in-control* was she?

She'd jumped his bones in the back of his company vehicle. Which was loaded down with cameras. And recording devices.

It had to be the tequila.

And Seth's blue eyes.

Ugh.

The siren of her ringing phone drilled into her skull.

"I don't want coffee, and I don't want food," Elaina barked into the phone, not even bothering to open her eyes to see who it was.

The person on the other end hesitated, but she could hear breathing. "Well, that's good, princess. What I do hope you want is to chase some storms." Tuck's words were laced with amusement and excitement. "Gonna be a good day. You and Heathcliff might even be able to finish your homework."

She exhaled. Was she really holding her breath, hoping it was someone else?

"It's not just homework." She stopped. It was *really* not worth arguing especially if this could be the last time she'd have to work with him. "So will we be able to get any actual data? Between taking pictures of people with a tornado behind them?"

"Yeah, Moo-Moo, there's gonna be none of that today." His voice took on a serious tone. "The atmosphere's wound up tight. So tight, all hell's gonna break loose. The clients are going to stay well out of harm's way."

Elaina sat up, holding her breath. "What about us?"

"I'll get y'all in a better position than you geeks have ever seen. No one else will be out there crowding the road. Storm will be yours for the taking."

She hopped out of bed, ignoring her brain bouncing around the inside of her skull. Elaina pulled back the yellowed, paper-thin shade. If she squinted, she could almost make out the frontal boundary line sitting on the northern horizon.

Waiting for her.

"You looking at it?" he asked, as if he was watching her.

"Yeah," she breathed. The sky was sliced in half. The part above her was blue with thick white clouds. The horizon was a roiling gray-green. A meteorological yin-yang.

"We're hitting the road in thirty minutes."

Elaina tossed her phone back on her bed. "All right Nim, this is it."

He thumped his tail twice.

She showered fast, not taking time to fully rinse the conditioner out of her hair. The reflection staring back at her through the fogged mirror looked like a ghost, even more so when she wiped the layer of steam away, exposing the dark circles under her eyes.

I bet that redhead looks nice and refreshed after romping all night with Seth.

She yanked a comb through her wet curls with one hand while brushing her teeth with the other. "What does it matter." She spit in the sink. "Finish the project. Get home to Mom." She switched the comb to the other hand and rolled deodorant on with her now free one. "Finish project. Home to Mom." She repeated it like a mantra.

Excited voices from the parking lot floated up through the thin motel room walls. The tour group was gathering, and if she didn't get a move-on, she'd make them late.

Elaina twirled her wet hair up into a bun and grabbed her jeans off the chair, hoping this was the clean clothes chair, not the dirty clothes chair.

She grabbed her oversized Tuck's Tours T-shirt when a fist pounded at her door.

She pulled the door open with her head still lost inside the cotton, expecting it to be Heath sent to fetch her.

The maroon fabric gave way to Seth's smirking face.

"Okay, coffee, breakfast, and dinner. That's my final offer." He was braced against the door frame. His smile didn't reach his eyes; instead they were the dull blue of a flat, cloudy sea.

Her treasonous dog hopped off the bed and slid between them, looking up with a big, panting smile.

Et tu, Nimbus?

"Didn't you get my response?" Elaina backed away from the door and searched the floor of her room for her sneakers.

Seth pulled his phone out of his pocket. "No…"

"Exactly." She popped up from the floor and balanced on one foot while pulling the shoes on. "What, the redhead doesn't eat?" Elaina grabbed her laptop and shoved in her backpack with other supplies, anything to keep her eyes off the man scratching her dog's ears in her doorway. "Then again, judging by those tight pants she probably subsists on air alone."

"She's not here anymore." His tone was tight. As if he was swallowing back heartburn. "I figured I could explain while you're chewing."

"That's not necessary." She glanced around her room. Camera. Check. Road maps. Check. Nim's helmet. "Come here, Nim, let's get you ready."

Her dog glanced up at Seth with big, sad, *sorry-my-mom-is-calling-me* eyes.

"Oh," he said, his voice climbing, as if it dropped a lead weight. "It's not?"

Elaina knelt down to fasten the bicycle helmet under her dog's chin. "Nope, she saved us—me—from making a huge, drunken mistake." She stood and pulled her backpack over her shoulders, taking the few steps to the door. "So, you have nothing to explain. You do you. Have a good chase."

Seth crossed his arms and filled the door. "Come on, Elaina. You know you don't mean that." He glanced down at her, his eyes warming, growing serious. "Sure, we were tipsy, but we both know it wouldn't have been a mistake. At least not for me."

Her heart somersaulted. She shouldn't have looked at him, because doing so told her the truth. That he'd wanted her last night. That if they hadn't been interrupted she would've still woken up hungover, but hungover *with* Seth. That if she'd woken up with Seth, there was a really good chance she'd skip storm chasing to stay in bed with him. Permanently.

There were already too many distractions in her life. Despite how he made her laugh, how she felt like she'd always known him, and even how much she wanted to hit him. There was simply no room in her life *for* him.

Elaina shook her head and closed her eyes.

When she opened them again, his face was pleading.

"I'm sorry, Seth. I was really drunk last night. She really did save us from making an uncomfortable situation out in the field." She pushed past him and locked her door.

Nimbus whined between them, as if apologizing for her callous behavior.

Seth looked at her, his mouth slightly open and his eyes blinking, absorbing her lie.

Absorbing it, but not believing it.

Elaina gulped and prayed she was wrong about that.

Tuck's clients were gathered around the vans. An excited murmur bounced around them.

She speed-walked across the lot, her dog in his silly pink helmet trotting beside her and the Forecast Channel reporter, in a bright-blue jacket, jogging behind her.

"Elaina, wait," he called. "Come on, talk to me."

The group looked up, but went back to their chatter.

Heath was hunched over his computer, and Tuck pointed at something on the screen.

Biscuit worked the crowd, offering an open box of donuts in one arm and pouring from a cardboard carafe of coffee from the other.

If the crowd wasn't hyped up with storm adrenalin, they'd be soaring on a sugar high.

"There's nothing to talk about." She skidded to a stop.

If Tuck caught wind of any confrontation between them, he'd swoop down on Seth like a vulture on prey.

Elaina glanced up at the sky. The humidity tangled with the cool wind, stirring the atmospheric cauldron. "Have you checked the models today?"

He cocked his head. "Yeah, should be a busy day."

She smiled weakly. "Be careful out there."

A giant hand crashed down on Seth's shoulder. "Hey there, Sethster. How's it hanging?" Tuck shook him, part good-natured jostling, part sinister putting-him-in-his-place. "You two kids okay? You sure were pounding the shots last night."

"We're great, just comparing puke stories." Elaina pulled her smile up higher so it would graze her eyes.

The toothpick in her boss's lips twitched and he stared into her, silently calling bullshit. "Well, Sethster, we gotta get on the road." He released her from his gaze and shifted it to Seth. "Remember what I said. Watch your back out there."

The reporter whitened and stilled, as if forcing his body to hold back a shudder.

It was the same feeling *she* sometimes got around Tuck. As if there were two men hiding deep inside there. The good-natured, semi-scam artist would quickly slip into a dangerous, watch-your-back filcher.

Which was the real Tuck? Both? Neither?

"I need to get moving, too." Seth's Adam's apple bobbed. "Promise me you'll be careful, Elaina."

An inner voice whispered his warning was less about the impending storms and more about the man standing next to her.

36

Elaina watched Seth and his cameraman ready their vans from the corner of her eye.

The redhead was nowhere to be seen. Maybe he'd been telling the truth. It wasn't what she'd thought—assumed. Had she been wrong about him too?

Regardless, those notions had no place in her mind, in her life. The woman really had saved her from crossing a threshold she couldn't walk back across again.

"What's he doing here?" Tuck nodded to her dog.

Nim sat by her truck, patiently waiting for her to open the door. He'd been smile-panting, but with Tuck's question, he closed his mouth and side-eyed him.

Even Nim didn't trust Tuck.

"He's coming with me." She didn't wait for his response before opening the door.

"No, he's not."

They were a team.

He told her what to expect, where to go. With her dog beside her, she could face anything. Even what terrified her the most.

"Yes, he is. He's always with me on the chase."

"As long as you're working for me, he's not coming." The older man jingled the change in his pocket. "Elaina, he's an animal. He's going to react like an animal and that's to get the hell away from danger. You can't focus on the storm if you're worried about your dog." He softened his expression. "It's for the best for both of you. The motel's well on the backside of the frontal boundary."

Elaina glanced at Heath.

He looked up over the top of his glasses. "This is going to be a really active day. We need to be focused. He'll be fine here."

Nim whined next to her, pleading his case.

What would she do without him? Not just on the chase, but if something *did* happen.

An argument bubbled from her gut, but it was quickly snuffed out by the reminder that she'd been wrong about Seth and that woman. Maybe she was wrong about needing Nim? Maybe having him out in the field was only good for her?

She sighed. "Just this one, Nim. Okay?"

He chuffed and fidgeted, but finally thumped his tail. His brown Lab eyes said he understood.

With her dog back in the room, Elaina rejoined the group.

The temperature seemed to have jumped several degrees with sun's climb to mid-morning.

The Forecast Channel vehicles were gone. Many of the other cars with the tell-tale ham radio antennas and storm chasing bumper stickers were also missing.

Only a few stragglers and Tuck's Tours remained.

"Biscuit and I will drive the vans; you kids follow in your own. I'll pull over when I've got these guys in good position, but I'll show you guys where you should go."

Heath hopped behind the wheel and Elaina balanced the computer on her lap, toggling the screen between computer models and GPS.

The radio crackled between them, picking up chatter from several chaser groups. A collective excitement mixed with apprehension of what was sure to be a busy day.

He pulled out, following the two maroon vans north on the interstate.

The number of cars heading toward the boundary outnumbered those heading away from it. This was definitely *the* breakout of the season.

"You and Seth disappeared pretty early last night," her friend said, not taking his eyes off the road.

Rather than look at him, she watched the fields flash by her window. Corn gave way to wheat, which gave way to something low to the ground, vivid green smearing across her vision.

When the plants turned to cows, she finally answered him. "Tequila makes bad decisions look like good ideas."

Heath laughed. "I saw him walk up to your room this morning, not *out* of it, so you didn't make *that* bad of a decision."

Elaina went back to studying the models, constantly refreshing the screen in hopes that, with the click of a button, the storms would fire up. They could get their final data points so she could get back to her dog.

Maybe run into Seth along the way, although she hated that idea.

Didn't she?

"Moment of weakness," she said, flipping over to check the barometric pressure. It was sinking but not fast enough.

Tuck's vans veered to the right, taking a rutted out dirt road on two wheels.

"What's he doing?" Heath mumbled under his breath. "In all fairness, Seth seems like a good guy."

"Yeah, and porcupines seem all nice and cuddly until they get their panties in a wad."

"Are you talking about him or you?" Her partner ducked as she tossed a week-old, dehydrated French fry in his direction.

Heath was right. Seth was a good guy. Her partner managed his relationship while always being at the beck and call of the storms. She could as well. It wouldn't necessarily mean that she and Seth wouldn't see each other. They'd chase the same storms.

Unless having him in the field was the same distraction as Nimbus.

Her heart sank where the barometric pressure refused to go. Was her dog worried about her? Was he as uncomfortable with her being in the field without him as she was leaving him behind?

She shook her head and went back to watching the radar, willing her mind to push out thoughts of the reporter and her dog with each update.

After another forty-five minutes, the vans ahead of them slowed, pulling off onto an intersecting dirt road.

Heath pulled up next to the lead van and Elaina rolled down the window.

Tuck leaned one elbow on her window, his eyes looking out on the open, flat landscape in front of them. The toothpick in his mouth flickered back and forth. "Well, this is as far as we go, but if you kids drive east for another ten miles, then hang a left, go north a bit, that should put you right where the hook will form. From there, the chase is on." He took his eyes off the horizon and looked into their van, glancing at Heath, but anchoring his gaze on Elaina. His forehead creased. "But stay in constant radio contact. This storm's a brute. I'm expecting multiple touchdowns."

If she'd been driving, she would've floored the gas pedal, leaving a cloud of dust in their wake. She'd never been more ready for a storm system to fire up. "Got it." Her words came out in breathless excitement. "See you on the other side."

Elaina started to roll up the window, but Tuck covered the button with his fingers. "I mean it, kiddo. Focus. Stay aware and keep an eye on each other." The icy honesty in his voice cooled her fiery anticipation.

She nodded. "Always."

Heath followed the older man's instructions. The clouds thickened and sagged toward the ground. Thick raindrops thudded against the windshield. Not a consistent rainfall, but random, as if the clouds held tight to their moisture, but a few drops escaped.

The world around them darkened.

Nightfall in the middle of the daytime.

"We finally set a date," Heath said, navigating around ruts in the road. His already pale knuckles were alabaster against the black steering wheel. "July first."

Lightning fractured across the sky in front of them.

"Something small at Chloe's parents' house. You should bring Seth," he added.

Elaina only half-listened to her friend. She watched the radar on the screen. The patches of red and purple swirled on the computer to match what churned ahead of them.

The clouds ripened to a gray-green hue. At the next pass of the computer radar, a dimple formed in the boundary, the first sign of the hook.

"Ha," she said, as if catching a naughty rabbit. "Hook forming. If we can get another mile or so up the road we should be in perfect position."

The wind was already kicking up, whipping the van left and then right.

She looked behind them in her side mirror. No other cars followed. As Tuck had promised, they were in prime position, and it was all theirs.

"You kids seeing the wall lowering?" Tuck asked through the radio.

Her face cracked into a wide smile, and she ducked her head down, trying to get a look at the circulating clouds above them. "This is fantastic. We should have ground truth in just a few minutes," she said into the radio.

The radio crackled with static at a shot of lightning. "Remember what I said. Y'all take care out there. Have fun."

Heath pulled the van off the road near a windmill back-bending to the ground. The only other structure was an old house being consumed by a thick vine.

They set to work, in tandem, dropping probes and checking their computers.

The air shifted. Elaina's eardrums popped. A flash of pain made her pause and look over her shoulder.

The tail of this tornado slammed into the ground with self-assured force. Even at a couple of miles away, it was a monstrous size, possibly emerging as an EF3 before picking up steam from the ground.

She stood, enchanted by the twister.

It wasn't a dancer. It wasn't lithe and couldn't skip around the empty fields in front of them. This one was stout, a sumo wrestler of a storm. Staking its claim on the land with one thudding stomp.

The air around her darkened more, as if the funnel cloud had sucked up even the daylight.

She walked toward it.

Shouts of her name competed with the roar of the storm, but the tornado lured her. *Come closer*, it said. *I have secrets that no one else can tell you. I know where you came from. I can tell you where you're going.*

Elaina closed her eyes against the stinging wind. When she opened them, it was night. She was running down a rain-soaked street. The streetlights overhead sparked with electrical bursts, but still stood upright.

Fear flooded her small body, but was she afraid of the storm, or —no, it was something else, she had to get help.

Her mommy was sick.

She gasped. Not Connie.

Mommy. A raven-haired woman.

Her lungs seized, and Elaina doubled over.

The tornado in front of her tugged at her. Yanked her back into present day. Threatening to suck her into oblivion. This was the first time she'd remembered her mother.

Her real mom. Maybe if she got a little closer...

She stood again, but Heath's shouts sliced into her flashback.

"Elaina, it's turning! We have to go."

She could barely see his face as thick sheets of debris-filled rain swept across the plain between them.

The driver's side door of the van was open. The windshield wipers worked overtime, but rain still enveloped the vehicle.

The tornado tugged at her.

Elaina looked back over her shoulder. The vortex of the giant swelled even more as it sped toward her. Getting out of its clutches was going to be tough.

She glanced back at Heath. Her gaze caught a thin, rope tornado slinking down from the sky behind him. Like a snake, it slithered up, down, left and right before finally settling on touching down. When it did, it hesitated, getting its land legs before racing toward the old windmill.

Toward her friend.

"Heath!" Elaina shouted, but the pressure stole her breath. She was barely able to hear herself over the roar of the dueling storms. "Get down!" She gestured with her arms, hoping he'd see instead of hear her, but his attention was absorbed by the beast behind her, not the villain sneaking up on him.

The rope twister hit the windmill at its base, and the dilapidated structure exploded. Thin rods of wood shot out in every direction.

Something hit between her shoulder blades. What little air she had in her lungs fled, and she fell face first on the ground. Elaina tried to get up, but an unseen force pinned her to soggy earth.

She must've passed out.

What felt like seconds later, she was able to lift her head, to push upright.

The rope tornado was gone, the monster lumbered off to the south.

Above her blue sky shoved aside the gray and the sun warmed her soaking wet body.

Elaina winced as she stood, reaching one arm back to see if she was bleeding on the back of her head.

The old farmhouse was gone. The vine, boards and foundation whisked away somewhere else. The windmill looked like matchsticks scattered across the ground. Except one...

"Heath!" She sprinted to her friend. "Heath, oh my God."

He was pitched forward, his hands gripping a bloody beam that'd impaled him through his stomach, like a javelin stuck in the ground.

His whole body shook.

Her partner's face wasn't just pale, it was a grayish-yellow and blood dribbled from one corner of his mouth.

Elaina skidded to a stop, wanting to reach out to him, but afraid to touch him, afraid to cause him more pain. "I'm so sorry, I'm so sorry. Sweetie, stop, don't move."

Heath was trying to get his feet under him, tugging at the wood. "I've gotta pull it out, once I pull it out I'll be fine." His pupils were dilated, his words slurred together.

"No, stay still." She wanted to put pressure on his wound, but blood flowed out of him like a river bursting through a dam. "You're losing a lot of blood. Let me radio Tuck."

It was then he stopped moving. As if her acknowledgement of blood awakened in him the direness of his situation.

He let go of the wood and looked at his hands. A wet cough rattled his lungs, flinging bloody spittle on Elaina. "Shit. This is bad."

"Yeah, it is, don't move. I'll get help."

He grabbed her wrist. The blood on his palm was warm, but his hand was icy beneath. "No, too late." His words came in gasps. "Stay. With me."

A sob burst from her lungs, but she held it back, not letting it out. Elaina nodded, but Heath couldn't see her, his gaze was now fixed on some spot in front of him.

Something only he could see.

"She's going to be beautiful." Peace coated his words. Acceptance. "The most beautiful bride."

The shaking stopped first.

Then his back stopped lifting with each pained inhale. Finally, his body went slack, draping over the stick.

As if in solidarity with her dead friend, Elaina's lungs refused to work, resisting air until her vision grew fuzzy and she had no choice but to take a deep, painful breath.

Her hands were numb. Her legs weak. Her brain unable to think. Her heart...shattered.

"Elaina, Heath, check in. Over... Elaina, Heath, check in... Where are you kids? Over." At first, Tuck's voice over the radio sounded like white noise. It was only when he was shouting that she jolted back to reality.

"Tuck," her words came out hoarse. Hollow. "Tuck, there's been an accident. Heath's—" She couldn't say it. He'd know soon enough.

"Are you okay?" His panic was palpable.

"Yeah, I think—"

What did it matter? Her best friend was dead. Heath'd never see the beautiful bride he'd saw in his dying breath.

"Elaina, I'm so sorry."

"I-uh, I don't know what—"

Tuck cut her off again. "Kiddo, the motel was hit."

37

Tuck had never seen someone so torn in half. Not just Heath, although that poor kid was skewered like a shish kebab.

When he'd finally made it to Elaina, she clutched her stomach while pacing in front of her friend's dead body. Her small fist tugged at her T-shirt, as if she were trying to rip herself in two. Half of her would stay with Heath until the authorities arrived. The other wanted to race to the motel to find her dog.

He'd had no clue this storm would turn out to be such a son of a bitch.

From his vantage point, the giant wedge had touched down roughly where Tuck had told them to set up. It'd touched down as a fiend and grew into a devil.

It was when he'd seen the rope tornado touching down around them that he'd nearly swallowed his toothpick. If they'd listened to him, if they were where he'd told them to be, they'd be boxed in.

When Tuck parked his van behind their ruined vehicle, he could hear the wailing sirens growing louder.

"Heath. Nim." Elaina's words came out in breathless gasps. Her face was wet, eyes bloodshot and unfocused. "Heath's...I can't lose

Nim, too." She covered her mouth with the back of her hand and doubled over.

Tuck shuddered. Her pain radiated from every pore of her body. Threatened to infect him. To infiltrate his body like a virus, spreading in his blood, settling in his heart. The result would be disastrous.

He hadn't given a shit about anyone in decades.

Starting now would send his body into shock.

"Listen, kiddo." He gripped her shoulders hard to get her attention, but still gently enough to not leave any marks. Mostly on *him*. "Heathcliff knew the risks. We all do. Stuff's flying from all directions and sadly, shit happens."

She shook her head and backed out of his grip. "That's not—" Elaina looked out over the now empty field. Her forest green eyes focused on something out of his reach.

The ambulance emerged on the horizon, the sheriff's car followed. Both had their lights going, but had cuts their sirens once they'd turned off the main road. They knew this was no emergency.

Tuck pulled away from Elaina. He'd let her talk to the authorities. Even if he was doing nothing wrong, cops seemed to sniff guilt on him. Like he wore *eau de low-life* or something.

The stick that'd impaled Heath had to be about seven feet long. The end stuck into the ground was splintered, sharp. It was probably better for the kid to have been pierced with the sharp end than the blunt side. He'd been struck mid-back, and it emerged from his stomach in the O of his Tuck's Tours T-shirt. Bull's eye.

Blood dripped down the spike in thick, dark dribbles. His glasses were askew, but it didn't matter, his unseeing eyes were focused on something on the ground in front of him. The young man's usually pale skin was even whiter, except for his chin which was covered in rivulets of blood.

He'd had seen a lot of messed up stuff in the field, but this was the most messed up of them all.

The mechanical chattering of the radio broke the silence. No one was in a hurry to get out of their vehicles. There'd be no unseeing what'd happened to Heath.

Tuck separated himself from the authorities. He stared at the spot where the EF3 touched down. The twister burned into his vision like staring at the sun. His hands found the change in his pocket. Three quarters and a dime in the right pocket. Four nickels, two pennies, and a rusty old pocketknife in his left. The feel of the metal soothed him. Cool to the touch, some smooth on the edges, others ridged. Same but different.

Like Elaina. Same, but…

Every time he saw her, he had to urge to run away and pull her to him. Like a junkie trying to get clean. He'd swear her off, tell himself she was just some nerdy scientist out to get in his way, but then he'd see her and feel that tug. Not sexual, not even close.

He was old enough to be her…

"They're all done with me." Her voice was quiet, flat. "The van is totaled. I really need to find Nimbus. Can you drive me?"

The change in his pocket had grown warm. Not just warm, it seared his palm. "Sure, kiddo."

Elaina was so quiet on the drive, he'd nearly forgotten she was there. The road out from the touchdown point was perfectly intact. Like two separate worlds from the one he'd just left. Twisters did that.

They *picked* their prey.

Tuck passed Biscuit with the other van and the full tour group. Flicking his pointer finger in recognition as they flew past them. The chasers were all gone. No doubt following the beast. In their place was the electric company, first responders, and volunteer groups.

The motel was mostly still standing, but the marquee sign had a hole in it. Several cars in the parking lot were huddled together, as if comforting each other. The U-shaped, two-story building was lopsided now. The office on the far side was flattened, but the motel seemed to grow from that pancake as it went around.

Elaina's room, on the first floor in the middle of the structure, wasn't crushed all the way, but the room above hers sagged heavily on top. If her dog was still in there, still alive, they had to get him out before the building collapsed.

He hadn't put the van into park before she was already out the door and sprinting toward her room.

"Nim!" Her panicked shouts were contagious. He almost felt the fear himself.

People crawled from the rubble. Their faces slack, dazed by the new reality facing them. Electricity sparked from the broken lines.

Water poured from burst pipes. A woman tugged at a hastily packed suitcase with clothes caught in the clasp. The echo of sirens bounced around the destroyed motel, barely audible over the cries and screams for help.

Elaina hesitated at her closed door, giving Tuck a chance to catch up.

Her chest heaved. The pause at the door, it was all denial.

He'd been there. Hell, he was there himself.

Stepping through that threshold changed everything.

"Why don't you let me go first?" Tuck asked.

She nodded and handed him the room key.

The lock turned easily, but the door wouldn't budge.

He pushed again, but it was like trying to move a freight train. Tuck took a step back and looked up. Part of the concrete walkway from the second floor slanted down. Chances were, the other side of the door also had that same slant. "Elaina, wait back by the van." He didn't turn around to speak. Instead he kept his gaze on the precipitously balanced concrete above his head.

"No, I have to be here—"

"As soon as I get your dog, you'll have him, but you're not going to do him any good if you get yourself killed." He glanced over his shoulder. "Now, git."

Elaina pressed her lips together and furrowed her brow. After a few seconds, she sighed and backed up. Not all the way to the van, but far enough back, if the roof caved she'd be clear.

Tuck turned back to the door and gave it one more half-hearted push. Why the devil was he risking his life for some mongrel?

Because there was more sorrow in those green eyes than he'd care to see for the rest of his life. Or any lifetimes that came after that.

"Hey pooch, you in here boy?" He put his ear against the door. There were so many sounds of despair it was hard to tell if Nimbus whined on the other side or not. He cupped his eyes and looked through the dirty window. The aluminum blinds clung to one side of the window, having given up on the other.

The room was dark. Pink puffs of insulation hung down from the ceiling at the front of the room, confirming his suspicion that part of the ceiling caved in.

Tuck moved, trying to get a better view of the room. The bed was still in the middle of the room, but the dresser that held the TV had scooted to the back of the room. Her clothes were strewn around; the bed, the floor, the lampshade. Somehow he thought that was more from Hurricane Elaina than the twister.

He held his breath, waiting for any sign of canine life. Then he saw it. At first, he'd assumed it was the strap to a yellow bag sticking out from under the bed, but then it shook, twitched, a nervous, irregular wag.

Of course, the dog would go straight under the bed to escape the storm.

Damn, he's alive.

He pushed on the pane of glass and felt it wobble. Kicking down the door was out of the question. Tuck would have to go in through the window.

A torn shower curtain hung out of the window a few doors down. He wrapped his fist in it, and pretending the glass was every bookie, loan shark and casino he owed money to, shattered it with one furious punch.

His boots crunched on the broken glass when he stepped into her room. Water poured down in the far corner and the room hummed with electricity. It wouldn't take a rocket surgeon to deduce this was a stupid idea.

Tuck whistled. "Nimbus, come on you mangy mutt before you get us both killed."

The dog's tail stopped its erratic movement and then started wagging a more regular beat.

"Come on boy, Elaina's waiting on you."

The dog whined his response but didn't move.

He bent down, bracing his hand on the sopping wet carpet and looked under the bed. From what he could tell, the dog didn't appear trapped. Tuck pulled his cellphone out and lit up the flashlight app.

A coil from the mattress punctured the flesh above the dog's shoulder. The only way to get him out would be to crawl under and free his caught coat.

"Dammit dog, you got us both in a fine pickle."

He only needed to get his shoulders under the bed, so his belly wouldn't have to worry about getting squished. Either by patience or shock, Nimbus sat perfectly still while pulled free.

A quick check showed he wasn't caught on anything else, but the dog still cried out when he pulled him from under the bed.

"I know, buddy, sucks for me too." Tuck heaved the big yellow Lab up into his arms and carried him to the window, bending over sharp shards of glass to set him on the other side while he climbed over.

The dog looked up at him. His brown eyes full of appreciation and fear. He picked him up again and carried him free of the destroyed motel.

Elaina stood by her truck, chewing on her fingernails. Relief loosened her face when she saw them coming. "Oh, Nimby." Her voice was filled with a sob. "I'm so sorry." She clutched his face, checking him for wounds and gasped when she saw the tear in his back.

"I don't think it's deep, but you'll want to get him to a vet," Tuck said, still holding the dog. "Your truck drivable?"

"Yeah, I think."

He gestured with his chin. "I'll put him in there for you. Take him to the nearest vet. I gotta get back to my group." Tuck gently laid the dog on the passenger seat.

Nimbus looked up at him again. His mouth opened in a slight canine smile.

"You're welcome," Tuck mumbled, one side of his mouth flinched into a grin.

A glint of light caught his eye. A tarnished gold chain hung from her rearview mirror. At the end of it, a tiny ballerina twirled in midair. Like the tiny dancer he used to lift up, swing around in circles, her chubby legs kicking as if she could make him go faster. The only song they danced to was the music of her childish giggles.

A cool hand on his forearm sucked him back to the present.

"Thank you. For saving him. For saving me. I've lost so much, I couldn't—" Elaina covered her mouth with her fist.

Tuck grimaced, hoping she'd think it was sympathetic toward her instead of a side effect of the acid rising in his gut. "You take care of Nim. I'll find out where they're taking Heath and give you a call."

She took a deep, shaky breath and nodded.

He watched her drive off. Her old pickup truck moved slow as it circumvented debris.

When it was well out of sight, Tuck exhaled.

Mother.

Fucker.

38

She was never going to forget the smell. It hung thick in the over-air-conditioned building, assaulted her nose, clung to her clothes. A sickening chemical odor to mask decay that was not-so-successfully covered up with a floral air freshener.

Death reeked in a way that if she had food in her stomach, she would've puked it up all over the white tile floor.

The sheriff saved her from having to deliver the news to Chloe, but Elaina couldn't hide from her forever.

She dropped off Nimbus to a kind, older vet who promised her dog would be fine. All he needed was some stitches and a good once-over to make sure there were no internal injuries. The vet wanted to keep him for a couple of days to administer some strong antibiotics, and monitor him.

Elaina had numbly agreed. She walked out of a vet clinic empty handed only to head to the morgue, to meet her dead best friend's fiancée.

A cup of coffee appeared in front of her, attached to Tuck. The man followed through with everything he'd promised. He'd saved Nim, texted her with the address to the morgue and showed up as soon as his tour group had dispersed, safe and with a healthy dose of fear.

"Thanks." She pushed her elbows off her thighs, trying to get as vertical as possible.

The older guy eased himself into the chair beside her. "The coroner said it's likely he didn't feel any pain. It severed his spine. He probably didn't even know what happened."

She sighed. Heath might not have felt physical pain, but her friend very definitely knew what'd happened. What had caused it.

Who had caused it.

Her phone buzzed in her hands. Seth. She sent it to voicemail. With all the other missed calls from him. He was just calling to check in on her. She'd been relieved when she'd gotten his first message. To hear his voice and know that he'd made it through the outbreak in one piece. Alive.

This time he didn't leave a voicemail, but a text message popped up instead.

Really worried. Rumors a chaser was killed. Please respond.

Elaina closed her eyes and banged her head on the wall behind her. The last thing she needed was Seth holding up a mirror, showing her how awful she already knew she was.

Her phone buzzed again.

Before I make an ass out of myself at the hospitals.

She felt the sides of her mouth spasm, as if they wanted to pull into a smile, but the rest of her body shut them down.

Later she'd respond. After Chloe.

When her self-worth was so low that cheap tequila was too good for it.

Then again, when he hears she'd caused Heath's death, he'd want nothing to do with her. She'd rank right up there with that redhead.

Been in worse company.

"You know, I never asked where you grew up," Tuck said, crossing an ankle over the other knee and resting his coffee on his belly.

"Small town, Oklahoma panhandle." Her words felt robotic exiting her mouth. "You've never heard of it."

"You'd be surprised." He took a sip of coffee. "How did you end up in this field? Your momma or daddy storm chasers?"

Her mom. Her moms.

The one who'd raised her. Who, because of her prodding, was lying in a hospital in another state. The other mom, the one who'd given birth to her. Lost somewhere in Elaina's mind.

"My mom was a nurse, but now she just farms and ranches."

"What about your daddy?"

Elaina shrugged one shoulder. "Sure I've got one, but I was adopted. Single mom."

Tuck *ahhed* next to her. Slurping at his coffee.

She glanced at him. His shoulder length hair hung in stringy curls, and the hair on his cheeks was almost as filled in as his goatee. She rested a hand on his arm, halting the sip he was about to take.

"I'm sorry, I don't meant to sound short. I owe you so much right now."

His steel-blue eyes froze, his mouth slightly agape. Tuck almost looked scared of her. Maybe she *was* as awful as she thought.

"Think nothing of it, kiddo. I'm just trying to take your mind off—"

The opening automatic doors cut him off. Heath's bereaved fiancée jogged in. Harry following close behind her. From the way Chloe was dressed, she'd left straight from the clinic. Even still wearing her white doctor's coat.

Elaina stood, dropping her arms, ready to give her friend a hug or block a punch. Whichever was coming.

"Where is he?" The woman's blonde updo hung mostly down. Her nose was rubbed red, her skin pale. Chloe's eyes roamed around the empty hallway, narrowing when they settled on Elaina. "You did this." Her voice was low, tight with anger. "You put him in this situation. You convinced him to abandon Dr. Pierce. You manipulated him into working with someone he didn't trust." Her gaze flashed above her head. "You can bet there's a wrongful death suit coming."

"Chloe, I'm, I'm—" Elaina stammered. *Sorry* was such a weak word.

"Save it, Elaina. This has always been about *you*. About your career. About whatever's going on in your fucked up brain. Yeah, Harry told me. What were you *thinking*? You're more than unfit for field work." Heath's fiancée broke down crying, her arms wrapped around her waist.

Was she imagining Heath holding her? Wanting him to tell her it would all be okay?

She stepped forward, reaching out to the woman, but Chloe drew back, as if afraid of the Elaina's leprosy.

"Don't. You. Touch me!"

Harry stepped between them. "Right. Elaina, I think it's best you leave."

"Chloe, please listen," she pleaded. Listen to what? She had no justifications. Her friend—former friend—was right on every accusation.

A big hand gripped her elbow, tugging her gently. "Come on. You've done all you can. Let's go."

She turned, her mouth opening to argue, but a quick shake of Tuck's head told her it wasn't worth it.

Elaina glanced back over her shoulder, but Chloe had turned her back away. Just like how she'd turned her back on Heath and didn't see the second tornado touching down.

Until it was too late.

Tuck led her out of the building. It was dark. The front moved through taking with it all the clouds, leaving only a canopy of brilliant stars. "Let's get you some food."

She let him lead her to his van. "Not hungry."

"Fine, you can watch me eat."

They stayed silent until they were snuggled into a booth at a chain restaurant one could count on to be at every interstate exit.

When the waitress asked for their drink order, Elaina's brain wanted whatever was the strongest liquor the bar stocked, but her mouth said iced tea. That was fine; her brain had made enough mistakes lately. It was time to let some other body part be in charge.

She didn't remember ordering food. Maybe she had, or maybe Tuck had taken the liberty to get her a burger and fries.

Time skipped ahead and suddenly the waitress placed a piping hot plate in front of her. It repelled her. Enticed her. Her stomach begged for it, but it also warned her she might be seeing it again.

"She spoke out of grief," Tuck said through a mouthful of food. "Give her a few days."

"Chloe couldn't be more right." Elaina dipped a fry into ketchup, but it looked like the bloody wooden stake through her best friend. She tossed it aside. She'd never look at ketchup and fries the same way again.

"Sure, you're a bit ambitious…"

"It's more than that."

He chewed another huge bite, studying her as his jowls worked over his burger. "That part about your head? Well, that's just…that's just pain."

She threw her napkin over her food and pushed it aside. "That's the part she's most right about."

The man reached for his tea, sipping through the straw, his gaze never leaving her face.

Elaina twisted the paper from her straw around her finger, pulling so tight the tip turned white. She couldn't bear another person looking at her as if she was crazy, but with Heath gone, Nim being cared for and Seth…she could talk to him, but he wouldn't be able to relate to what she was going through. Everything in his life was perfect. Perfect career, perfect purpose, perfect hair.

Tuck, *he* could understand. It was written all over him. Life had knocked him around, sucker punched him, pushed him down, and yet he kept standing up, coming back for more when he probably should've stayed down.

That was who Elaina was. Someone stubborn enough to ignore every sign of defeat until the sign was sticking through her research partner.

Her gaze flitted from her cold, untouched dinner to the man sitting across from her. She took a deep breath, holding it in until she was sure she could speak. "Have you ever heard of a drug called Rententamine?"

Tuck pressed his lips together and shook his head. "Is that what kids are doing these days?"

"No, it's what doctors give to people suffering extreme PTSD to help them re-write memories. It's not perfect, and I don't know this for a fact, but I'm pretty sure I was given it as a child."

He tossed his own napkin over his empty plate and leaned forward on his elbows. "What do you mean?"

"A few months ago, at the start of the season, I got too close to a tornado. Except I didn't see the storm. I was inside rubble and saw the face of a man rescuing me." Her mouth went dry, and she sipped on her nearly empty tea. "When I asked my mom about it, the woman who raised me…" Elaina took a deep breath. "She had a stroke before she could answer, and she's been in a coma since." A rogue tear slipped down her cheek. She sniffed, wiped it away, and looked out over the mostly empty restaurant.

How many fellow diners had caused one person's death, another person to have a stroke, and nearly got her dog killed? Elaina no doubt took the gold medal in the death and destruction category.

When she turned back to Tuck, his face was unreadable. His eyes were narrowed, hard; his mouth moved, like he chewed on his tongue or an imaginary toothpick. "What did you see today?" His words were laced with a seriousness she'd never heard before.

"My mom. My real mom. She looked like me. I was running, down a street in the rain. To get help." She wasn't looking at him when she spoke. Elaina went back to that place in her head, the field with the tornado-fueled vision.

Tuck stared at her for several seconds before whistling for the waitress to bring their check. He pulled his wallet from his back pocket. "You know, Elaina, not all of us have what it takes to be out in the field." He peeled off bills as he spoke. "Not everyone has the temperament, the nerves to handle the storms. Maybe it's best you stay indoors, behind a computer." He stood and started for the door. "Come on. I'll take you back to your truck."

Elaina sat there, silently cursing herself for sharing her darkest secret with the last person who didn't think she was crazy.

39

It was a gorgeous day for a funeral. Which felt wrong. Sunny days with low humidity and perfect seventy degree temperature weren't made for saying goodbye to her best friend.

They were made for playing in the park with her dog. They were made for sitting at an outdoor cafe sipping lattes and going over data with Heath. They were made for planting seeds and pulling up weeds with her mom.

None of which Elaina could do.

Her black dress absorbed the heat of the sun. She could've joined the rest of the procession under the tent, but she wasn't welcome there. No one called with details about the arrangements. Not Chloe, or Harry, or even Dr. Pierce.

She'd only discovered where the graveside service was to be held by stalking the obituaries in the paper. The side-eye glances told her they knew she was there, even if she hid behind a dress and over-sized sunglasses.

Dr. Pierce sat at the end of the front row. Even with his back to her, she could feel him watching her, scowling at her.

Her legs twitched, eager to carry her over to the tent, into the heart of the service, interrupting a prayer about how Heath was no longer in pain, to confront their former advisor.

This was *his* fault. He'd driven them to it. Pushed them beyond their limits. Propelled them into the path of a deadly storm.

Tom Pierce deserved to be in that grave, not her best friend.

If she had any emotional energy, she'd tell him that. For now, all she could do was stare at a closed casket hovering over a hole in the ground and pray she'd wake up.

"Well, I guess it's not your body in there."

Elaina jumped at Seth's voice. "That's a hell of an opening line." She grimaced. The words came out much harsher than she'd expected. "Sorry, I meant to text you back."

"Nah, think nothing of it. I'm sure you've been busy."

She glanced at him from the side of her shades. He was dressed in a black suit with a pewter gray shirt underneath, tieless with the collar open, aviator sunglasses hiding his eyes. A bead of sweat escaped his temple and slipped down the side of his face.

"You doing okay?" he whispered during a prayer.

"Nope," she said to her feet. As much as she craved human interaction, she also wanted to cloister herself away. Away from anyone she could hurt, anyone she could love, anyone who would leave her.

"That was a dumb question. Of course you're not okay." He looked away as he spoke. "You're far from okay. I mean you're alive, so you're better than Heath, I guess."

Elaina used his aimless mumbling as a chance to slip away. The service was coming to a close. The last thing she wanted to see was her friend's casket being lowered into the ground, to have to face his family, their friends, Dr. Pierce.

She'd almost made it to her truck when she heard gravel crunching behind her.

"Hey," Seth said a bit breathless as he jogged. "Sorry, I don't know what to say. There's no manual for this." His face was pinched in sadness. For Heath, but most likely for her.

She should've texted him to let him know what'd happened, but somehow, not saying the words, not breathing life into the fracture in her heart, in her spirit, would prevent it from being true. That the fewer people who knew Heath had died, the less real it was.

"I know. Trust me, I looked for one."

A shuffling of bodies drew her attention back to the ending service. People would start filing up the road, going back to whatever was left of their lives.

What was going to be her new normal? Her studies and career, gone. Her dog, would most likely become terrified of storms. Her mom. That was her next stop, to meet with the doctors to see how Connie was doing.

"Want to grab lunch?"

"I've got to go." Elaina spoke over him and instantly felt guilty. "Maybe a raincheck." She backed the final few steps and pulled open her truck door. "Get it. Storm chasers. Raincheck?"

Seth gave her a soggy smile. Not his usual bright one, but a smile doused in rejection. "Yeah, I get it." He shoved his hands in his pockets and walked away, his usually squared shoulders hunched forward.

"Jokes at a funeral. Crappy idea, Elaina," she mumbled as she started her truck. "I bet you got it." She glanced up, hoping wherever Heath was, he found her corny attempt at humor endearing.

She arrived at the hospital an hour before the doctor was scheduled to stop by her mom's room.

Even though it'd only been a couple of days since she'd seen her mom last, the woman seemed different. Deflated. Her color was better, not quite her normal rosy tint, but a faded peach was a step up from the ashen gray from when she was first taken in.

Elaina stroked her mom's straight, white hair. It'd gotten longer, drier. "I'll bring some leave-in conditioner next time." She reached for the lotion on the tray and lathered on her own hands before reaching for Connie's arm, rubbing the excess on her dry skin. "Heath's funeral was today." The lump in her throat threatened to strangle her. "There were a lot of people. Hanging out way in the back gave me the perfect view." She paused, watching her mom's face for any reaction. "Nim's still at the vet. He had some internal bruising so they wanted to keep an eye on him. The doctor said he'll be fine."

She moved to the other side of the bed, rubbing lotion on Connie's left arm. "I saw her. My, um, mother. The woman who birthed me. It felt like I was looking in a mirror. Maybe I was. Maybe it wasn't real. Maybe none of this is. Maybe I created one giant mess because I'm messed up, like Chloe said." Elaina cleared her throat and looked up at the white tile ceiling. "I don't know if I should go out again, to see what else I can pull from my memories, or if I should just hide from it all before I lose someone else." She sniffed and placed her mom's hand gently back on the bed. "You'd know what to do. I just wish you could tell me."

A trio of voices filled the hallway. Their low level murmurs not making words, just sounds.

Dr. Parker entered the room, followed by a doctor who looked like his mom drove him to work every day, and the harried nurse who was there so often Elaina suspected she lived at the hospital.

"Ms. Adams, it's good to see you."

She wiped her clammy palm on her dress before shaking his outstretched hand. "When is she going to wake up?" No sense wasting time on mundane topics, like *how she's doing*, or *it's going to be another hot one*, or explain why she looked like she just came from a funeral.

The doctor exhaled a heavy sigh and motioned for her to sit while he perched on the foot of the bed. It was the classic one leg up, one leg anchored to the floor. A casual, we're-in-this-together gesture.

Elaina had seen that posture so many times, it must be taught in med school.

"That's actually what I want to talk about." He frowned and furrowed his brow.

She glanced down at her mom, not wanting to see whatever bad news the doctor wore on his face.

"Connie's out from under the meds keeping her in the coma." Dr. Parker let the words hang there several seconds before adding, "We stopped giving them to her three days ago."

Hope cleared the clouds over her heart. "So she'll be waking any minute now, right?"

The doctor flashed her a weak smile, and the nurse made a sad grunt, but no one answered her.

"Actually," said the younger doctor. "If she's going to wake up, she would've done it within hours of us stopping the drugs."

If.

Two letters put together to form a word that pierced Elaina's heart with the same blunt force of the stake through her friend's body.

"What do you mean?" Her voice sounded small in her own ears.

Dr. Parker cut a hard look to his colleague before adjusting his face back to a look of confident compassion. "Everyone's different, Elaina. So just because something should've happened, doesn't mean it won't. But really, we've done all we can for your mom." He shifted his gaze down to her the woman who raised her. "It's up to Connie to wake up."

Whatever the doctor said next floated by her ears without sinking in. Something about watching her carefully, brain scans, for Elaina to talk to her. The nurse checked her vitals, chirped that her mother was a strong woman, she had a good heart, steady blood pressure.

Outside her room, she heard Dr. Parker bark at the young resident about his lack of bedside manner.

Really, Elaina didn't mind. As much as she needed coddling, she also wanted the truth, no matter how painful it was.

She chewed on her fingernails. Chewed on an idea. Maybe the doctors were right. The drugs were stopped a long time ago. Everyone was different.

Elaina pulled up the national models on her phone. Searched across the country for any sign of atmospheric instability. A high and low pressure system looked to be on a collision course over northeastern Nebraska.

If Elaina was going to wake up to the truth of who she was, where she'd come from, and the meaning of the memories, it *was* up to her.

40

Getting ready for the chase was both the easiest and the hardest.

Elaina itched to text Heath, to remind him what to bring.

He wouldn't answer. Wouldn't bring anything.

Her eyes fell to the empty food and water bowl on her kitchen floor. Her house felt lifeless without Nim. Her bed was cold without his warm Lab body nestled next to hers. Her days were empty without taking him for walks or scratching his ears as she walked from one room to the next.

She'd already planned to stop in Kansas to pick him up on her way home, but that felt so far away. In time and distance.

Elaina stood in her living room. Even though nothing had changed in her house, enough had changed in her life to make the space feel foreign. Could a person change to a point where she outgrew her own place? Her life?

Whether she never got the answers she craved, never finished her dissertation, or if her mom never woke up, she was telling her old life goodbye.

One way or another, when she came back to her little house, she'd be a different person.

She locked her front door, sealing away the past. But not throwing away the key. She might have to come back and visit it at some point.

It was late afternoon when she hit the road driving north. If she drove straight through she'd pull into Lincoln, Nebraska before midnight. The storm chaser channels on the radio were alive with chatter about this next outbreak. Some even thought it would be bigger than the storms that hit Kansas. That'd taken Heath.

Elaina thought she heard Tuck on the radio a couple of times, but she didn't dare call out to him. Not after dinner, after he'd told her she was unfit for the field.

She pulled off the interstate, needing to refill her truck and hit a bathroom, but a bright blue SUV sitting next to its companion satellite truck forced her back onto the road, hoping both her gas tank and bladder would hold out a little bit longer.

The motel she'd picked had no hail-beaten cars, no SUVs with radio antenna reaching toward the heavens, no Forecast Channel vehicles, and no maroon Tuck's Tornado Tours vans. As far as the old man at the front desk knew, she was simply a young woman in need of a room for the night.

Morning came before she was ready to face it. Tornado warnings already lit up the map on her laptop. The barometric pressure had dropped substantially and the humidity was shooting way up. Thunderheads bloomed around her like a field of spring flowers.

Tuck leaned against the driver's side door of her truck, wearing his uniform cargo shorts and Tuck's Tours T-shirt. He cleaned his fingernails with the point of his pocketknife. His mouth worked over a toothpick. "Thought I told you to stay indoors," he said without looking up at her.

She ignored him and tossed her backpack in the passenger seat.

"How's Nimbus?" Tuck asked.

Elaina paused at his question. For the months she'd known him, she'd seen about every side of him.

The teller of tall tales. The demanding boss. The slacker who couldn't beg his way out of a paper bag.

She'd never seen this side of him. A man who showed genuine concern.

"He's going to be fine. Had some bruising on his spleen so the vet kept him to make sure it didn't rupture. I'm picking him up on my way home."

Tuck nodded and put away his knife. "Look, Moo-Moo, I can't say I understand what you're going through, but you have no business being out here by yourself."

"Well, I'm not getting anyone else hurt." She stood in front of him. "Do you mind? I want to go ahead and get on the road."

He looked over her head and squinted up at the sky. His hands found his pockets and jiggled the change. "Could be the last outbreak of the spring."

"Yeah, I know, that's why I don't want to miss it."

His gaze found hers. Unreadable eyes studied her, causing her to shiver under the warm morning sun. "I've got a pretty big group today. Could use an extra set of hands."

Elaina sighed and shook her head. "I appreciate all you did for me, for Heath and Nimbus, but I'm not working for you, Tuck. Not today. This storm is about me. About what I need to find about myself."

"You need someone watching your back." The man pushed off her truck and brushed past her. "Let me do that for you."

She watched him cross the parking lot to the motel next door.

A large group was gathered around his vans. From what she could tell, the people were a mishmash of all the tornado tourists she'd met over the spring.

A few retirees chatted with Cub Scout dads, keeping an eye on their small wards. A cluster of people nervously took pictures of the sky and each other, flashing peace signs with wary smiles.

Tuck was unlike anyone she'd met in the field. Brash, careless, and indisputably the best at reading the sky.

"Here's the deal," she shouted after him.

He paused, but didn't turn around.

"I'll follow in my truck. I'm not taking anyone's picture or getting anyone a drink. I'm not on the clock. I'll watch the models and the sky and help with that. But this is *my* chase. Okay?"

"Anything else, princess?" he said over his shoulder.

"Yeah." A bead of sweat tickled her temple, and her heart pumped with the ferocity of a hailstorm. "Stay the hell out of my way."

41

Seth never wanted to see another cornfield. Or another dirt road. He marveled at how a country so big and vast could end up looking the same. Interstate after interstate. Roadside diner after roadside diner. Motel room after motel room.

Why couldn't tornados pick a more picturesque part of the country to touch down? Would it kill a storm to break near the Rockies?

They could happen anywhere, after all. It felt like they kept picking the most mundane locales to annoy him.

He and Rick positioned their vans at the edge of a field. Pancake flat landscape welcomed them, taunted with its sameness from the last outbreak.

Is this how rock stars felt? Same concert, different arena, but really every arena looked the same.

The sky ahead of them was bruised an ugly yellowish-black. Clouds churned like in a pressure cooker, but they refused to pick up any real rotation.

Cars rushed by. Many of them fellow chasers, moving closer to the epicenter of the frontal boundary. Two maroon vans flew past him, followed by a beat-up, rusty brown truck.

Seth grabbed his driver from the back seat, twirling the golf club in his fingers while he rummaged for a bag of cheap balls. He hoped the farmer wouldn't mind a few golf balls in his crop.

He dropped a ball and took a couple of practice swings before stepping up to the tee, launching the ball into the thick black storm clouds with a satisfying *plink*.

No matter how hard he tried to focus on the storm and golf balls, his mind kept shifting back to Elaina.

How alone she'd looked at her friend's funeral. Discarded to the side, no one inviting her to share her grief. The fact she was able to stand upright proved she had more strength in her body than he had in his big toe.

But why was she out there? And, most importantly, what was she doing back with Tuck?

He pulled his phone from his back pocket and shot her a text. *Have a good chase.*

Now *she* knew that he knew she was out there.

Seth watched their procession of cars turn left and park closer to the wall cloud. The flat land made it seem like she was right around the corner, but she was most likely a few miles away.

His phone buzzed.

Thanks. You too. Be careful, she texted back.

He smiled, telling himself not to read too much into those five words, especially after her multiple brush-offs. The girl went from hot to cold faster than the weather changing in Texas.

Seth hit another five balls, but his attention kept getting pulled to the three cars off by themselves.

Everyone else lined the road they were on. Sure, Tuck was a lone wolf known for getting in better position than any other chaser. The man had no problem taunting the devil, sticking his tongue at all him, blowing raspberries, daring the demon to catch him if he can.

Seth didn't care if the devil gripped Tuck by the throat and squeezed the life out of him.

He wasn't letting the man drag Elaina to hell with him.

Seth folded his arms across his chest and watched a crowd

gather around the maroon vans. A solitary figure stood to the side. If he squinted, he could almost make out her clinched fists held at her sides, her hair braided down her back.

"Hey, radar's showing rotation." His cameraman broke his contemplation. "Really tight, too. This one's going to be awesome. Wanna go live?"

"Sure." He shoved the golf club in the SUV and pulled on his Forecast Channel rain slicker.

Rick set up the camera while Seth pulled out the microphone and stuck the earpiece in his ear. A talk back with the station would be an exercise in futility with the roar of the twister behind him.

He checked the radar one more time. The hook was much more defined. It'd only be a few seconds before the twister would emerge.

Seth looked out over the field.

Tuck's group was closer to where it would touch down, but they were positioned behind it. The people on his tour would get a good adrenalin rush, but with as much danger as walking through a haunted house filled with actors, a scary soundtrack, and rattling chains.

Rick counted down from behind the camera and pointed at Seth.

Showtime.

42

E laina could feel it as soon as she stepped out of her truck. The air crinkled with electricity. The smell of ozone so strong her nose twitched. The air on her arms stood on edge. Maybe because of her nerves, or maybe from the raw power of Mother Nature.

The Forecast Channel vehicles sat across the field, at a respectable distance. Seth whacked his golf club against little white balls. Was he hoping to poke holes in the storm clouds?

Tuck's group milled about. Some of them pointing at the rotating clouds, pulling out phones to record it. Others glanced around nervously, obviously wishing they'd spent their hard-earned vacation at an amusement park or staring at a giant hole in the ground.

Elaina distanced herself from the group, hoping they'd forget about her. If she needed to walk right into the storm to get answers, no one would stop her.

At the center, at the point of the most pressure, would be the truth of her past. Her ground truth. She was already in the vortex. Just needed to open her eyes and see.

The tail of the twister touched down. Narrow, sleek, almost

white, it stood out against the dark gray backdrop of clouds. It dropped a few miles from where they stood, but the pull of air tugged her toward it.

When it dropped, it hovered in one place. It seemed to study her as much as she studied it. Was it checking to see if she was worthy? Contemplating if she could handle the truth of her past?

Elaina closed her eyes and tilted her face up. Her mind thumbed through the memories so far. Being trapped, afraid, but the face of the kind man who found her. The hospital, strangers, and the blinding light. Dancing with a woman who looked so much like her. Running. She had to get help.

She wiped her cheeks with the back of her hand, rubbing the dirty tears from her face. The memories weren't just pictures, they were emotions. Emotions that stole her breath.

Emotions that made her want to crawl into her mother's lap and have her tell her it would all be okay.

Emotions that reminded her she was loved.

Both before *and* after the storm.

"Come on, come on," she mumbled, squeezing her eyes shut and begging the final piece to come forward, to tell her what happened to the woman who'd birthed her. To tell her who she was and where she'd come from.

The roar of the storm dropped off to the sound of a mewling kitten. She opened her eyes. The twister had backed away from her, its tail lifting off the ground.

"No," she whispered. "Come back."

The storm retreated more.

The clouds overhead slurped the tornado, *her* tornado, back into its lair.

She ran after it, her boots slipping in the soggy field. "Don't do this to me. Come back!" Rain pelted her, stinging her eyes. Elaina tripped, she caught herself before landing face down. She reached around, grabbed the rock at her feet and threw it at the place where the tornado had touched down. "You owe me," she screamed at the storm. "You took everything from me. You owe me this."

Elaina knelt in the mud, wrapping her rain jacket even tighter around her. No memories. Nothing to tell her anything else about who she was, except a soaked failure who managed to get her best friend killed, her dog injured, and caused her mom to have a stroke.

She scanned the sky, searching for any sign if that was curtains for the storm, or if the outbreak was just getting started.

That was when she saw it. A few miles north of her. Like water running down the drain, the clouds circled and churned, picking up speed. The tiniest hint of a tail peaked at her from the base of the clouds.

Elaina hopped up from the ground and sprinted to her truck. The backend spun in the mud, but managed to find enough solid ground to shoot her onto the dirt road. Her foot pressed the accelerator to the floor and the old truck's engine growled over the sound of the wind.

She kept an eye on the clouds, watching the tightening rotation. She slammed on the brakes, not bothering to pull the truck off the road.

With confident even steps, she strode onto the field, stopping just below the rotating clouds.

If the tornado wasn't going to answer her questions, it might as well suck her into oblivion.

43

S eth watched the reflection of the tornado on the camera lens. He'd seen more twisters in this storm season than he had his entire life, and yet each touchdown sparked an icy explosion of fear through his veins.

This season had taught him a lot about those storms, but most importantly, it'd taught him they couldn't be trusted. As soon as he got comfortable with the knowledge they'd always move from the southwest to the northeast, a sneaky bastard came up behind him.

This storm season had also taught him a lot about people. Sometimes tornados and people weren't that different. What lay in the center was usually a swirling mess of earth and emotions, regret and debris.

"And we're clear." Rick dropped the camera from his shoulder and wiped sweat from his brow with his free arm. "The folks back at the studio are going to wet themselves over this footage. I'm going to head back to the truck, and check the models to see where the next hook is forming."

Seth threw him a nod and turned to the now-empty field. This had been a quick one. A thin, ropy twister that'd looked more like a water spout he might've seen over the Gulf than some of its larger cousins he'd seen over the plains. It was simply the scout. Something larger would soon be striking from this system.

Movement across the field stole his attention from the swirling clouds.

Elaina sprinted to her truck, her long braid whipping in the wind behind her. She was headed further down the dirt road before she even got her door shut.

"Hey, Rick," he called out, not taking his eyes off her speeding truck. "You see that other hook yet?"

"Yeah, man, about two, three miles northeast of us. We should be good if we stay here."

Elaina seemed to be headed in the direction of the hook. Deeper into the heart of the storm.

He narrowed his eyes, straining his vision to watch her even closer as her truck disappeared behind a plume of dust. Seth whipped his head back to Tuck's group.

The man had broken from his guests and jogged to one of the vans. The massive maroon vehicle fish-tailed as it shot onto the road following the petite storm chaser.

He trusted that man less than a fickle EF5, especially with the ferocity in how he took off after Elaina.

"Looks like the next one might be rain-wrapped."

Seth jumped at Rick's voice. His cameraman stood next to him, and he'd not heard his approach.

"Not sure if we'll be able to see anything or not."

Those words squeezed his heart with the pressure of a dropping barometer.

The sky churned and rolled in on itself. Gray so dark it might as well have been black. Lightning shot out from the top of the cloud, crackling and shattering against the clouds with thunder like breaking glass.

Elaina wasn't heading into a storm. She was heading into hell.

He had it wrong. Tuck hadn't made a deal with the devil.

He was the devil.

Seth swooped down and grabbed his club, turning his back on Elaina's truck and Tuck's pursuit long enough to jog to the SUV.

"Hey, where're you going?" Rick called.

"Stay here, I'll be back," he growled.

His cameraman looked behind him, his gaze following where Seth had been staring.

Elaina's truck took a hard left, and Tuck's van followed on two wheels.

"I take it you don't want the camera," Rick said. "Watch your back, man."

Seth looked over his colleague's head and nodded. "You might want to go ahead and dial 9-1-1."

44

Her ears popped at the tightening pressure, sending a cold wave of pain down her neck. The braid lost its hold and tendrils of hair slapped her face.

The developing tornado was greedy, stealing the young crops from the ground, branches from trees, the air from Elaina's lungs.

Even though the storm had the energy for a twister, it was hesitant. Drop down, pull back up. Like a shy child hiding behind its mother's skirt.

The sound of an engine roared behind her and headlights lit the darkening field. She glanced over her shoulder long enough to see a maroon hood.

Elaina turned back and took several steps forward, ignoring shouts and whistles behind her. "Come on, come on," she mumbled, closing her eyes once more.

"Kiddo, what the hell are you doing?" Tuck shouted behind her.

"Stay back, Tuck." She stuck an arm out behind her. "This is my life, my memories. Don't stop me." She emptied her mind, focusing on the raw power of the storm. Dirt pelted her, stinging as if it were being shot from a gun.

A strong hand tugged her elbow, pulling her back. "You're too close. Back up, Lainey."

The nickname hit her in the gut, pushing all of her air from her lungs.

Lainey.

A word she hadn't heard since...

The dark-haired woman was crying, her pretty face twisted in anger. She argued with a man.

Their words didn't make sense, but the intensity behind them scared Elaina.

The woman, her mother, frantically tossed their clothes in garbage bags. Not to throw them away. To go.

The man pulled their possessions from the woman's hands, but the woman wouldn't let go.

They tugged with the ferocity of a dog with a bone. With a mother trying to save her life.

The man let go of the bag, and the woman flew back, stumbling until she tripped.

Her head hit the edge of a table with a thunderous pop, and she fell to the floor. Everything stilled.

A dark red circle grew from under her mother's head.

Thunder boomed overhead. Elaina stood frozen. Both in her memory and her real life.

The man turned, facing his crying daughter.

His hair was darker, cheeks smoother, no graying goatee covered his face, hiding the dimple in his chin he shared with...*her.*

His flat, blue eyes chilled her.

Even at her young age, instinct told her to hide. She dove under the bed, pushing herself as far back as possible.

Tornado sirens wailed outside. Lightning lit up her father's hand, grappling to reach her from under the bed.

Then he stopped. A door slammed shut.

She crawled out, toward her mother. Mommy was hurt. Needed help.

Elaina ran out the door. Her footie pajamas got soaked. It was dark. She didn't know where they were. It wasn't home.

Doors stared back at her, but none of them opened when she banged on them. She had to get help.

She had to run.

Elaina opened her eyes.

The rotation scooted back, but still churned overhead, not yet birthing a tornado, but definitely in labor.

"You," she breathed.

Tuck stilled beside her. His face morphed from confident arrogance to recognition, then white with fear.

"You killed her."

His Adam's apple bobbed. "It was an accident. She was going to take you from me. You have to believe me." He reached for her, but she swatted his hand away.

Headlights bounced down the road toward them, a bright blue SUV swaying in the rising wind.

"You left me there! I was a child. You killed my mother and left me." Anger spun in her gut, heating her despite the wet chill washing over her body.

"I was going for help." His voice was pitched higher, and he grabbed her shoulders, his fingers digging in, hurting her. "I swear. When I came back, the motel had been hit. You both were gone."

"Hey." Seth's words sliced through the howling wind. He walked toward them, golf club in one clinched fist. "Let her go, Tuck."

Her *father* turned toward the reporter.

Elaina slipped out of her raincoat, out of his grip.

He was faster than she'd expected, and he grabbed one wrist.

"This doesn't concern you, Maddux. It's between Lainey and me."

Every time he said that word, the name he'd called her as a child, her stomach twisted.

Seth narrowed his eyes and took three more stalking steps.

She looked back up at the cloud.

The twister snaked down, getting closer to the earth.

Something flew past her, heading straight for the reporter. She opened her mouth to warn him, but it'd already struck him, knocking him flat on his back.

"Seth!"

She tried to pull free of Tuck, but he held even tighter. "What're you doing? Let me check on him."

"It's too late for him." The man's eyes were wild, desperate. "I messed up, Lainey, you have to believe me. I was scared. I was just a kid when we had you."

The tornado thudded onto the ground behind them. Ever the storm chaser, Tuck shifted his attention from her to the storm, his jaw dropping slightly to take in the twister.

Elaina used the distraction to get away. She slid on the ground next to Seth.

Blood streamed from his temple.

She pushed up his sleeve, pressing his wrist to feel his pulse, but she was tackled from behind before she could find one.

Tuck pulled her back.

She fought and kicked at him, but he dragged her by her feet.

Elaina tried to anchor herself to Seth, but only succeeded in grabbing hold of his golf club.

"Leave him, he's not like us." Her father spoke as he tugged her toward the tornado. "He doesn't understand. No one does. We can go. The two of us. Father-daughter chasers."

She twirled around. Her backend bumped over the rough, wet ground as Tuck pulled her away from Seth. She dug her nails into the earth, but Elaina was no match to both his strength and the suction of the storm.

Finally, one of her flailing feet struck its mark, colliding with his gut.

Tuck dropped her and doubled over, his face paling before turning red. "You're just like her," he growled through gritted teeth. "You look just like her, and, princess, you're stuck up, just like her. Thinking your degree is better than my street smarts. She thought she was better than me, but who won, huh?" Like an animal leaping on its prey, he squatted back and sprung on her.

She rolled over and swung the golf club in one motion. The shaft caught him in the throat.

Tuck dropped forward onto his hands, coughing and gagging.

Elaina jumped to her feet and held the club up high, like a base-ball bat.

The twister crawled closer to them, creeping up on her father from behind.

"I won then, I'll win again," he rasped, pushing himself back to standing.

"You won nothing." She swung the club, but only hit air. "You lost your family, your daughter. You killed my mother. You're going to jail, Tuck." She shuffled forward and swung again, but he jumped back. "It's over! You ruined everything." The swing got him, the head of the club striking his shoulder.

He ducked, throwing his arms over his head, but Elaina swung again, hitting his ribcage, sending him to his knees.

Debris scurried around them, burning her eyes.

The tail of the tornado was getting closer.

Closer than she's ever been to one.

Dangerously close.

She raised the club overhead, ready to strike once more.

He shot a bloody wad of spit from his mouth. Tuck's face soft-ened. His gray eyes warmed.

"Those were Beth's final words." His voice was full of remorse. Her father shifted his gaze behind him and lifted his arms. "Get out of here, kiddo." He closed his eyes, a beatific smile spread across his face.

Elaina dropped her arm, the club hanging loosely in her grip. "Not without you. You have to pay for what you did."

He squinted against the driving rain. "Lainey, you were the only thing I ever did right, until I did you wrong. I paid every day thinking I killed you that night. All these years…" Tuck stood and started walking backwards, away from her, toward the waiting storm. "I'm too old for jail." He glanced behind him once more. "I loved you more than anything. More than life—I've always wanted to see what lies in the heart of the vortex."

She chewed her lower lip, the approaching wind tugged her in and pushed her back, as if threatening to take her, but deciding it didn't want her.

Not yet.

Elaina sprinted back to Seth's prone body, pulling him upright. They had to get to the ditch, get low.

He groaned and winced, opening his eyes a sliver, before they widened at what stalked them. Seth stumbled as they ran. He practically threw her into the ditch, covering her body with his.

The tornado howled and wailed over them.

Metal screamed. Or maybe it was Elaina.

She tried to breathe, but there was no air, only muddy water. It felt all consuming, as if the entire world was made up of this single tornado.

When it was gone, when the air was still. When her ears rang from the silence, when her heart questioned everything that'd happened, and when she looked up to find Tuck vanished, everything felt hollow.

45

Elaina rubbed her thumb across the top of her mother's hand, smiling at the lively pink flesh, the blue veins strumming with life.

The hand jerked, tried to close, but the muscles were weak from the stroke and underuse.

"I should've told you about your history. But you didn't remember it. You'd blocked it." Connie's words were slow and slightly slurred. But from what the doctors told them, nothing that couldn't be overcome with physical therapy. "I thought it was for the better to not reopen old wounds." Her lower lip trembled. "As time went on, I thought you'd hate me for keeping it from you."

She wanted to argue with her mom, tell her she could never hate her, but Elaina called herself a liar. Sometimes growing up didn't happen gradually; sometimes it happened in a flash.

Like standing too close to an Impressionist painting. It was only when she'd backed up that her life came into focus.

A few more memories had flooded in after the storm. Little bits like ephemera. Dancing on her mother's feet. Playing in clothes drying on a line. Her father spinning her around until she was drunk with dizziness.

They weren't all happy glimpses. She had one terrifying memory of Tuck that had brought on a panic attack.

He'd been angry, stumbling, his words not making sense.

Her mother had sent her away to her room, hiding her from her father's drunken rampage.

What would've happened if she'd had these memories her whole life? Would she have grown used to them? Numb?

"I understand," Elaina said. "And, yeah, I can be kinda bratty."

Connie laughed. A beautiful sound like chimes blowing in a gentle, loving breeze. "Have you thought about hiring an investigator?"

She shrugged. There were no missing person reports for a Beth Tucker, but that was assuming Tuck's real name was Robert Tucker, something she'd questioned due to a lack of history on the man.

There was a Jane Doe recovered from a collapsed motel at the time Elaina was found, but no one claimed the woman's body, and the old proprietor of the motel told police he only remembered a man renting the room.

When Tuck's battered body was found, his fingerprints provided no clue into her family history. There was no doubt he was a criminal; he just happened to have been one of the kind who was never caught.

The best Elaina could tell, her parents had lived a nomadic life, moving from state to state, chasing storm after storm.

"I think I have everything I need."

Her mom's eyes filled with tears, causing a lump to ride up her throat. It had been in her throat so much over the past week, she'd threatened to charge it rent.

It had first emerged when her phone dinged with a voicemail, as soon as she'd gotten back to an area with cell towers still standing after the storm.

Her mom had woken up, and aside from some slurred speech and a little weakness on her right side, she was mostly okay.

"You sure you'll be okay without me?" Elaina asked. "I can stay with you while you do your therapy."

Connie smiled, one side of her mouth a little higher than the other. "We'll be at each other's throats by the end of the day." She squeezed her hand tighter. "You deserve some time off. Go get your dog and enjoy life."

She kissed her mom's forehead and promised to check on her every day.

Elaina looked for her old truck in the hospital parking lot, temporarily forgetting that the screaming metal sound she'd heard during the tornado had been her truck getting tossed upside down. She'd quickly picked out a used Jeep, choosing it because Nimbus would love the ragtop.

Nim. She ached for her companion like a missing limb. The vet had been kind and understanding when she'd called after the storm, explaining why she needed to leave her dog with him for a few more days. Now it was time to bring him home, back to her.

She burst through the door at the clinic, doing all she could to not shout his name. Elaina tried to listen as the vet talked through medicine, what she needed to look for, but she kept her ears peeled for the jingle of his collar, his happy panting, or sniffling nose.

Finally, when she was no longer able to nod in agreement any harder, the technician retrieved her dog.

Nimbus burst through the door, tearing the leash from the young woman's hand. His coat was shaved from his collar to his mid-back. A straight line of puckered skin glistened under the fluorescent lights.

Elaina knelt on the floor, but her happy, bouncing dog quickly knocked her down, his big, pink tongue covering her face in kisses, and his high-pitched yelps echoed around the room. "Nimby, I missed you." She inhaled his warm, corn-chip scent that now mingled with antiseptic gel on his back.

"This goes without saying," the vet said. "But dogs that've been in storms like him aren't the same after that."

She rubbed his ears.

Nim squinted his eyes and groaned.

She understood.

The same was true for people.

Nimbus trotted beside her as they walked out of the clinic. He paused, looking around the small parking lot, then pulled toward the blond man standing by her Jeep.

"Nice ride," Seth said. "Nimbus, buddy. What d'ya think? We'll have matching scars."

Elaina peered at the stitches at the reporter's temple. "Too bad you don't have as much fur to cover it."

He laughed and ducked his head. "You've been avoiding me again."

She opened her mouth, but he cut her off.

"It's okay. How's your mom doing?"

"Good, getting discharged today."

An awkward silence settled over them. Seth looked away and squinted, his jaw tight. "What about you?" he finally asked.

"I'm good." Elaina exhaled and nodded, hoping to convince herself that she really was, but the lie fell flat. "Okay, I don't know. Right now, I'm great, but who knows what tomorrow will bring. What about you?"

He flashed her a smile that stole her breath.

"I think viewers will find my scar sexy," he said, but then his face grew serious. "So, what're you going to do?"

It was a question she'd asked herself a million times. Go back to the university, finish her research so Heath could get his degree posthumously? Spend more time searching for her birth mother's family? Or maybe just get a job teaching yoga somewhere far from tornado alley?

She simply shrugged her answer. "Are you going back to Atlanta?"

Seth shuffled and looked at his feet. "Pensacola, actually, hurricane season is about to start."

Elaina chewed on the inside of her cheek before letting a slow smile spread across her face. "I've never seen the ocean."

He reached out and twirled one of her curls around his finger. "Well, let me be the one to show you why hurricanes are better than torn—"

She cut his words off by slamming her mouth on his. "I could use a few boring, sunny days,"she whispered into his lips, and Seth took over the lip-lock, making her hard kiss into something softer; something that mattered.

~

The End

NOTE TO MY READERS

Thank you for reading Vortex! Elaina is my spirit animal, and I hope you enjoyed spending time with her and Seth … and Tuck as well.

If this is your first book of mine to read, thank you and welcome! If you liked Vortex you might enjoy my Phoenix series, a story of a woman's journey to clear her name of her ex-boyfriend's crimes. You can check out the first chapter of Phoenix in the next section.

If you've enjoyed Vortex, I would greatly appreciate if you'd take the time to leave a review on the store where you purchased it, on BookBub or on Goodreads. (Writing a review in sea shells on a beach works for me as well)

If you want to find out about my next novel, sign up for my newsletter. Don't worry. I won't spam you. I forget it exists half the time (plus, spam is gross!).

Until next time!

K

PHOENIX PREVIEW

Amanda Martin didn't believe in casual Fridays.

Sloppy dress, sloppy work, she thought as matching golf-shirt-clad tellers ignored the growing line.

Amanda paused at the door as she weighed her options. How long would it take her to deposit eighty hundred dollar bills into the ATM? Why didn't Josh have HR cut her a check? Should she just wait it out for a teller? Why did Josh clean out his office? What is in El Paso? Or, who? And, what's her bra size? The thumping headache from polishing off a bottle of wine alone jumbled her usually decisive thoughts.

"Dammit, Josh," she murmured.

The line curved back on itself twice and each of the three tellers had four customers before it would be her turn at the window. The envelope of money poked at her collarbone from its haven in the interior pocket of her coat. No matter how she tried to maneuver it to a more comfortable position, the corner of the envelope continued to jab her.

She sighed, *it's probably a sign.* Quarterly bonuses were standard for her at the mid-sized investment firm where she worked. But, this was different. It felt like a payoff.

After days of being avoided by Josh in every sense of the word—text messages unanswered, emails neglected, voicemails unreturned and his assistant running interference for him—Amanda strode into his office the previous evening ready to end their relationship. As CFO, Josh kept their office relationship professional, but Amanda found it difficult keeping his behavior at the office from bleeding into the bedroom.

"Who is she?" Amanda didn't bother knocking; she wanted the element of surprise to catch him with his pants down, literally or figuratively. Instead of finding Josh, either with or without a junior trader, Amanda found his office devoid of the stacks of files that reminded her of a childhood fort. She often teased that he used the piling system, with his desk stacked with an endless amount of paper. It looked naked now. The top of the heavy wood desk sat empty except for a single manila folder that looked out of place without its brethren, like a lost sheep left for the wolves.

Amanda was just able to read that the top sheet was a boarding pass for a flight to El Paso before she heard Josh's voice outside his door. She snapped the folder shut and marched to the door just as he hurried into his office. No matter how mad she felt, the first sight of his wavy blond hair and light green eyes made her feet go cold.

"Eh, Amanda, what are you doing here? How long have you been waiting?" He pushed past her to his desk and put the folder in his briefcase.

"I just got here. So, what's in–" Her question about El Paso was smothered by a sudden kiss.

"I owe you an apology," he said. Amanda glanced behind her shoulder to check his open door for snooping colleagues, but he gently turned her face back to him. "Don't you think everyone here already knows about us? Anyway, I've been distracted with a problem client and haven't been attentive. Why don't you pick up some wine and take-out? I'll be over in a couple of hours."

Amanda nodded. *I'm just being paranoid. He wasn't avoiding me, he was just dealing with work.*

"One more thing," Josh said, going back to his briefcase. "I almost forgot to give you this. Go buy some shoes and lose the receipts." He handed her a bulky envelope. She knew without looking that it was filled with cash, lots of it.

"What?" She couldn't get her question out before his phone rang.

"I'll explain later. Oh Amanda, please close the door behind you. Thanks, babe."

After midnight and a bottle of wine, Amanda went to bed with no word from Josh despite the numerous calls to his cell and office. She woke up hung-over and ready to give him her iciest treatment.

Amanda stepped towards the ATM, the line for the tellers having grown in her moment of indecision. Her BlackBerry buzzed as she reached into her purse for her debit card. With her throat cleared, she put on her best professional voice.

"Amanda Martin," she answered.

"Hello, love, Roland Burrows here with *Financial News*."

The smooth British accent of her favorite reporter put her at ease. Her shoulders drooped as she dropped her act. The envelope jabbed into her collarbone.

"How are you darling?" Her animated voice echoed in the cavernous bank lobby. "We need to meet up for martinis soon."

"Listen, Amanda," he started, but she was distracted. She loved the way he pronounced her name ending in an 'er' rather than an 'a' and launched into a catnap of a daydream imagining herself with a British boyfriend after Josh. Her trance soon ended, catching only his last sentence. "So that's why I was calling, to see if you had any comment."

Her heart thumped against the envelope when she realized this was a serious business call and not their usual banter.

"I'm sorry Roland, can you say that again? I'm getting horrible reception in here."

"Right. I just got a tip from someone inside the SEC that they're pursuing indictments against several executives at Jefferson Williams Investments: chief legal counsel Keith Cooper, CFO Josh Williams and you, Amanda." He paused. "I'm breaking this story in a few minutes and wanted to see if I could get a comment."

Amanda tried to breathe, but her throat closed as tight as her French twisted hair. "Roland, I'm going to have to call you back."

Amanda didn't wait for a response. She ended the call and dashed out the front door.

The late March freeze accosted her with a burst of cold air as she pushed through the door. BlackBerry still in hand she dialed Josh's number while navigating the busy sidewalk. The line didn't ring—it went straight to voicemail. She tried it again. Same result. Third time was no different. Amanda didn't leave a message. *I'm not giving him any opportunity to come up with excuses. I want to hear his reaction.* She dialed her office number.

"Diane, it's Amanda. Transfer me to Josh," Amanda said, cutting off the receptionist during her greeting.

As soon as the receptionist transferred the call, Josh's voicemail picked up. Amanda looked at her watch. It was past nine in the morning; Josh was always in early to get a start on the day.

"Dammit," Amanda screamed at her phone, punching the end button with such force it lodged in the down position for a few seconds before popping back into place.

She moved out of the flowing traffic of pedestrians and leaned against the side of an office building. The smooth granite chilled her through her cashmere coat, the cold reassuring and frightening.

"Think, think," she whispered. "Ten ... nine ... eight ..." she counted backwards, a trick her anesthesiologist father taught her as a child when thunderstorms scared her in the middle of the night. The raw power from above and the inability to control her surroundings terrified her as a young girl, and even now as an adult, a particularly booming shock of thunder caused a pulse of fear down her spine.

When Amanda got to one, she still faced a catastrophic news story and indictment, but she could breathe. Her BlackBerry buzzed with her office number flashing on the display.

"Josh?"

"No, it's Liz. What is going on? Roland Burrows just called me, something about indictments. Where are you?"

Liz was going to be her next call, but it would also be her toughest. Friends since college, Amanda recommended Liz for a job in the legal department. "I'm on my way in. Can we talk? I'm going to need some help."

"*You're* going to need some help? What the hell is going on Mandy?" Amanda winced at her nickname. "I'm sorry. You're on your own with this one. I have to comply with investigators. I can't risk going to jail, especially now that I have Jackson to think about." Amanda couldn't fault Liz; the woman threw herself into mother-hood the same way Amanda did her career. "I'll give you the names of good attorneys. I can do that for you, but nothing more. I can't risk getting dragged into this," Liz added, softening her voice as if sensing her friend's defeat through the phone. Amanda heard someone speak rapidly to Liz in the background. "Crap. The story posted."

"Dammit," Amanda said, letting her body fall back against the side of the building once again. She wished the building wasn't there, that instead it was just a gaping abyss that allowed her to fall into nothingness. "What is it I'm being accused of?"

"You manipulated the market through media announcements with false information. A lighter offense than Keith and Josh, but nonetheless, you're in trouble." Amanda heard the phone shuffle in Liz's hand. Her voice was a whisper when she spoke again. "I shouldn't ask you this, but I need to know. Did you know what you were doing?"

If bad judgment was a crime, I would be guilty as charged. Amanda knew better than to get involved with her boss, but they were a classic power couple; attractive, blond, wealthy and successful. Three years earlier, when her former boss abruptly quit and Josh asked her to dinner to offer the vice president job, she thought her life was on the fast-track she longed for. There she was, at the tender age of twenty-four, given the responsibility heading communications for the company. Initially, she thought Josh's dinner request was simply a professional courtesy, but after his second invitation she realized it was much more.

Only recently did Amanda suspect something was amiss with the investment firm's business practices. She remembered innocently asking, "How is it the firm and our clients continue to turn a profit when our competitors are losing money?" She shuddered at the memory of his enraged reaction, "You should never question me, as my girlfriend or my employee. You got that?" he yelled. By the end of his outburst, she feared he would fire her or break up with her, or both.

"I trusted Josh."

For the remaining ten minutes of her walk, Amanda tried to reach Josh on his cell phone, but each call went straight to voice-mail. She left no message, but composed one in her head. *What the hell did you drag me into? Is it true? Why did you do it? Where the hell are you? When I find you, I am going to kill you.*

Rather than board the elevator to her office, she sank into one of the fashionably uncomfortable, contemporary armchairs in the building's spacious lobby and stared out the soaring glass wall. The weather outside was clear and bright, completely wrong for the way she felt.

Her ringing cell phone alternated between displaying her office number and various media outlets. After sending the twelfth call to voicemail, she shut her phone off. *What did I do?* Amanda went over her press releases and statements in her head. All the information came from Josh. Keith had the final approval before she sent out anything over the wire. The long hours she put in to get everything right, the dinners with friends and family she canceled to answer to the media's beck and call, and the lies she inadvertently told—they only lined the pockets of Josh and Keith. *And, mine. That's the reason for the bonuses, to keep me happy.* No amount of blinking could stop the fresh tears from springing.

Unable to sit there any longer, she boarded the elevator for her solitary ride to the forty-second floor. When the door opened, she saw a flurry of activity, but Amanda couldn't become part of that. Her colleagues were accustomed to the unflappable Amanda Martin, the one who could handle the toughest question from the harshest reporter. Not the woman standing outside the office with mascara running down her face.

Inside the ladies room, Amanda stared at her reflection. Her normally porcelain skin was gray, her hazel eyes were bloodshot and her carefully applied makeup was gone. Before Roland's call, she was an average ambitious businesswoman who was dating, or maybe just sleeping with, her CFO. She felt untouchable as one of the highest-ranked executives at the firm. Now, she just saw a haggard-looking criminal. Her eyes fell to the brown roots fading into her straight blond hair flawlessly twisted back. No need to keep her hair appointment for that afternoon. Chances were there would be no salon services in the federal penitentiary.

Leaning against the bathroom wall, she heard the elevators on the other side whooshing past her. The mechanical whir of the motors and the hum of the cables put her in a trance only inter-rupted when a ding sounded on her floor. "Josh. Finally," she whis-pered as she hurried to catch him.

Amanda stepped through the heavy glass door of her office lobby just as she heard a man ask for her. Instead of Josh, she saw the back of an older gentleman, clad in khaki pants and a wind-breaker standing in front of the receptionist. With a backpack slung over one shoulder and a baseball cap covering his white hair, he looked as though he should be heading to college instead of a retire-ment home. The woman motioned to Amanda's office as she tried to answer the constantly ringing phones.

He thanked the receptionist, pulled a pistol from inside his back-pack and shot her in the head. The phones continued ringing as though nothing happened. Some of the traders in the cubicle area stood up at the sound of the gunshot, and he emptied his magazine on them as though they were ducks in a video game.

Amanda's office door swung open and Liz froze in the threshold.

"Amanda Martin?" the man asked, casually reloading his gun.

Amanda could see the fear in Liz's eyes ten feet away. Liz shook her head, "I have a son." Her voice was soft and weak.

The man was unflinching. "I have a wife who is very sick. My retirement fund was going to make her better, until some greedy bastards stole it all. She's going to die and so are you."

"I'm Amanda Martin," Amanda shouted at the man's back, but her voice vanished in the thunder of his gunshot. She watched Liz crumple to the floor. Amanda felt her own body go numb as she released the death grip on her purse and phone. She covered her mouth to stifle her scream.

The man reached into his backpack and pulled out a grenade.

"A few weeks ago, I called Williams about cashing out my retirement fund to pay for my wife's cancer treatment. He gave me the runaround: forms, taxes, bullshit. I knew something was fishy, and I was on my way down here to have a little chat with Mr. Williams when, guess what, my wife called to tell me he's been indicted for stealing people's money," his commanding voice presided over the screams. "I'm not here to hurt everyone. I want Josh Williams and Keith Cooper. If you can point me in their direction, I'll finish what I came to do and leave." While he said this, he tossed the grenade up and down in his hand, toying with it like a tennis ball.

Liz's outstretched hand beckoned Amanda, but she would be shot if she moved in plain sight. She edged over to the receptionist desk and sought cover under the heavy brown wood.

The man quizzed her colleagues as to the whereabouts of her co-conspirators, but she couldn't register what he said. With each blast from his gun, her ears rang louder, muffling his voice. She didn't see him pace the office; instead she focused solely on the body of her friend.

Please be alive, please be alive ... Amanda mouthed silently.

"It's clear you are all in this together and therefore, all guilty. You have until the count of five to tell me where they are, or we're all going up together. I've got a bag full of grenades, and I'm not afraid to use them all. Got that?" the man bellowed over the startled silence of the office.

Amanda got up on her haunches to make her way to Liz, but a rush of blood to her head made her dizzy. No matter how much Amanda commanded her body to take deeper, slower breaths, it wouldn't comply. She steadied herself.

"Ten...nine...eight...," her quivering lips barely moved.

The man began his count much louder. "One," he boomed, the pin of the grenade clicked out of place. "Two... three..."

They reached "five" at the same time. When the grenade went

off, it knocked her backwards against the swinging glass door. A second blast forced her against the door again and this time pushed her all the way through. When she opened her eyes, fire blazed through what used to be her office, and a heavy breeze blew through the blown-out windows of the forty-second floor. Papers floated like soft snowflakes. The piercing screech of the fire alarm joined the ringing in her ears. Her hand automatically felt her body, acting purely on instinct to make sure she was still in one piece. When her right hand moved over the breast of her coat, the envelope inside gave a little jab signaling it was okay. Amanda decided to move.

ACKNOWLEDGMENTS

Thank you to my husband, Colby, for not thinking I needed a straitjacket when I'd start giggling over something Elaina or Seth "said." To my wonderful critique partners, Christine Brodersen, Chris Crawford, Vanessa Foster, Sarah Hamilton, Susan Sheehey and C.A. Szarek, thank you for always pushing me to be better (and for helping me deal with my pronoun allergy. I'm starting shots soon…promise!).

To my parents, sister and brother-in-law, there's no way I could ever adequately thank you for your love and support.

To Carol Barreyre, for being my wing-woman and sharing laughs and tables at book signings.

To Lisa Van Gemert and Veronica Garza, for helping me brainstorm on that drive back from Austin.

To Alexandra Sokoloff and my awesome classmates at West Texas Writers' Academy - Jolene Navarro, Linda Fry, Linda Trout (Trout-Fry!), Carol Kjar, Melody Robinette, Vaun Murphrey…and gosh I hope I didn't forget anyone. You guys were there in the very beginning and helped me shape this idea into a story.

And, finally, to my grandfather, Dennis Dodson, for showing me my very first tornado.

ABOUT THE AUTHOR

Kimberly Packard is an award-winning author of edgy women's fiction. She began visiting her spot on the shelves at libraries and bookstores at a young age, gazing between the Os and the Qs.

When she isn't writing, she can be found running, doing a poor imitation of yoga or curled up with a book. She resides in Texas with her husband Colby, a clever cat named Oliver and a yellow lab named Charlie.

Her debut novel, *Phoenix*, was awarded as Best General Fiction of 2013 by the Texas Association of Authors. She is also the author of a Christmas novella, *The Crazy Yates*, and the sequels to *Phoenix*, *Pardon Falls* and *Prospera Pass*. Her latest novel, *Vortex*, was released in early 2019.

ALSO BY KIMBERLY PACKARD

The Phoenix Series

Phoenix (Phoenix Series Book 1)

Pardon Falls (Phoenix Series Book 2)

Prospera Pass (Phoenix Series Book 3)

Standalone Titles

This Time Around

Dire's Club

The Crazy Yates | A Christmas Novella